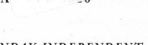

'Written with a keen insight into female friendships and dripping with wit and charm, *You Have to Make Your Own Fun Around Here* is a truly immersive story. Macken has a visual eye, bringing simple scenes to life with a carefully chosen word or perceptive detail, and her ear for dialogue is pitch-perfect. The ways in which she captures the pull of the places we call home and the people from our childhoods who shape our lives is also impressive… Reminded me of the best of Maeve Binchy's work, albeit set in a more modern era.'

Reading Matters

'Few writers have articulated the intricacies of friendship – the dependency, the uncertainty, the fragility of the pecking order – with as much authority… A debut bursting with heart.'

Irish Independent

'Frances Macken's *You Have To Make Your Own Fun Around Here* charts the friendship of three small-town girls from their childhoods through to their early careers, exploring envy and self-belief with consistent, natural humour and spot-on observations.'

Caoilinn Hughes, author of *Orchid & the Wasp*

'This exploration of the seething hinterland of growing up, with its often unspoken passions, unrequited longings and intense jealousies, is melancholy, funny, dark and affecting.'

Deborah Kay Davies, author of *Reasons She Goes to the Woods*

'*You Have to Make Your Own Fun Around Here* vividly captures life in a close-knit community, while examining the intricacies and anxieties of female friendship… Katie is a vibrant creation, whose insights are often fresh and startling… The ups-and-downs of going places is ultimately what makes the narrative come to life.'

Irish Times

'Hugely enjoyable, profound and humorous.'

Mayo News

you have to make your own fun around here

frances macken

ONEWORLD

A Oneworld Book

First published in Great Britain, United States of America,
Ireland & Australia by Oneworld Publications, 2020

This paperback edition published 2021

ISBN 978-1-78607-860-5 (UK paperback)
ISBN 978-0-86154-150-8 (US paperback)
ISBN 978-1-78607-767-7 (eBook)

Typeset by Tetragon, London
Printed and bound in Great Britain by Clays Ltd, Elcograf S.p.A.

Oneworld Publications
10 Bloomsbury Street, London, WC1B 3SR, England

Stay up to date with the latest books,
special offers, and exclusive content from
Oneworld with our newsletter

Sign up on our website
oneworld-publications.com

MIX
Paper from
responsible sources
FSC
www.fsc.org FSC® C018072

*This book is dedicated to those precious people
who help us to see who we can be.*

1
Glenbruff

Glenbruff is alive: there are fields and meadows, a valley with swaying grasses, gates to swing upon and hollows to hide in, and arched canopies of billowing trees set over narrow boreens.

Myself and Evelyn and Maeve trek the overgrown railway track set deep in an incline, play at being tied to the sleepers and rescue each other in the nick of time. We go into the graveyard and visit the lichen-blotched graves of long-dead relatives, and ride bikes we've long outgrown over steep hills, swooping into the air before thudding onto the tar with a jaw-rattling jolt. We play in the disused quarry and sit in the old machinery left to rust, attempting to force the dusty gear stick and turn the gigantic steering wheel, its rubber coating bubbled with age and heat.

The door of the church is always open, and we go in and gaze at holy statues, willing them to wink at us. We're never chosen for apparitions, but it's for the best; we might get too much of a fright, or we might be given a big job by God to carry out when all we want to do is play. Saint Jude is the saint of hopeless cases, and he stands inside the vestibule in a big maroon cloak with plaster folds, his forefinger pressed to a gold medallion. Maeve leaves flowers from the roadside at his chipped feet.

We watch a group of older boys walking to school, spread out across the road, long legs striding. Black trousers made of cheap fabric flap in the wind, white socks garish beneath. The boys give chase, kicking plastic bottles that tipple into thick hedges.

We girls hang back and knot ourselves together.

3

I adore Evelyn. I endure Maeve. I don't like them being too close, or doing things without my being involved. Unfortunately for me, Evelyn and Maeve are cousins, and when you're cousins it's a given that you're friends; it's a bad sign if you can't be friends with your own cousin, and even if the cousin is in the wrong, you stand by them. That's the rule of being cousins.

For Maeve, it's a mixed blessing having Evelyn for a cousin. Evelyn is bold, and I know it, and the children at school know it, but the grown-ups don't know it at all. Evelyn has a small, round face. She has hazel eyes that dart about, with violet shadows beneath. Her skin is sallow and her hair is long and dark, worn with a middle parting. She is thin and angular, with a curious sort of frame, the hips leading and the spine tilting backwards, her body appearing crooked from the side like a straw distorted in a clear glass of water. She gets away with things and that's why I find her so interesting.

Maeve has wispy hair that catches in the breeze, a small and compact barrelish body and a protruding tummy. She has large slate-grey eyes that droop at the outer corners, like a sad dog. Her teeth resemble little pegs, and she can carry a masterful whistle. She has wet bubbles in her nose in the winter that bring about weeping scabs, and a mysterious bald patch behind her left ear, and we whack anyone who asks her about it, but even me and Evelyn don't know why it's there.

4

I can't say for certain why the three of us are friends. Sure, who can answer a question like that. I suppose there aren't many children along our road, so there isn't much choice, and I don't give it a lot of thought. We carry on as we are, and there's plenty of fun to be had. That's not to say that I couldn't make nicer or better friends in another place, but how would I ever know the difference.

I hold my fingers in a frame, place them in front of my eyes and peer through to see what the photographs would look like. I even make a *tsch!* out of the corner of my mouth to mimic the mechanical sound of a shutter.

The quarry fills up with water in the wintertime, but in the summer it's abundant with unusual ferns, caterpillars pulsing along the fronds, miniature frogs and lizards blinking and bulging, and purple flowers sprouting from bristles. No one knows that we play in the quarry, and our parents would be disturbed if they were to find out. Evelyn's brother, Mickey, is in the habit of following us, so we have to ensure that the coast is clear if we intend to play there.

The council have put up a wire-mesh fence around the edge, but it's easy for us to peel it from one side and clamber down onto the quarry's floor. We are girl explorers, out in the unknown: the outback, the jungle, the desert, distant planets and kingdoms. I take a rope from the shed at home and we practise at bullwhip-flexing for a long afternoon, thwapping the rope off the ground until we can hardly see for dust.

I might announce that I've discovered a dried clod of dinosaur dung, and we stand around and prod at the ground with twigs. 'A herbivore. See the fibres. That's a sign that this dinosaur feeds off grass and leaves.'

'We'll have to build a trap so we can catch him,' Evelyn says, her chest puffed out and hands on her hips.

'What'll we use for a trap?' says Maeve.

'We'll set out some bait. Then we can hide over there, and when the dinosaur comes, we'll take pictures,' I say, patting the invisible camera slung around my neck.

We place our imaginary bait on the ground and huddle behind a set of skinny saplings, and then Evelyn exclaims, 'Here he comes. Look at him!'

Maeve and I gasp, and we gaze up high as though the creature has suddenly manifested from a prehistoric age, plodding before us as pterodactyls spin in the sky. *Tsch. Tsch. Tsch.* We stay in the quarry all day long until the hunger weakens us, and then we bolt home, leaving our imaginings behind to be picked up again the following day.

Evelyn likes to play a game she calls 'Cleopatra'. She sits on a boulder and commands that she be cooled by the wafting of ferns. Myself and Maeve stand either side of the boulder and do the wafting. We are commanded to set out on a quest to find diamonds, and we scuttle about, searching for a chunk of sparkling quartz before presenting it to her. Evelyn says that the largest diamond of all is hidden in the old rock crusher, and we are ordered to fetch it. 'Bring it to me.' I look to Maeve, and she looks to me, and we both look at the crusher. The old crushing machine is orange with rust and wrapped round with glossy green ivy. It resembles a tall chimney stack, close to twenty metres in height, with a great metal chamber at the bottom. A fierce wind has pushed the chute of the crusher into a slanted position so that the opening of the chute rests against the quarry's edge. I don't know the mechanism on the inside, but I imagine gargantuan teeth within the crushing chamber, and cogs and plates that spin around, whittling rocks into rubble.

Hesitantly, myself and Maeve approach the crusher, and we slowly amble around it, looking to see if there's a way of getting inside without going down the chute, but there isn't. We glance back to Evelyn and her gaze is authoritative. Maeve steps onto the metal chamber and begins shunting herself up the outside of the chute, deftly clutching onto the ivy. She hauls herself to the lip of the chute and punches the air with her small fist. 'You did it!' I exclaim. I hadn't thought she had it in her.

'Don't forget the diiiamonnnd,' calls Evelyn, and Maeve promptly swings herself inside the chute. There's an alarming scream, followed by a metallic clanking and an almighty bang, as Maeve tumbles down the chute and into the crushing chamber.

I knock hard on the side. 'Are you dead, Maeve?' I press my ear to the chamber, and I can hear heaving and gasping, and then a long, anguished wailing sound carries out of the chute and across the fields.

Evelyn leaps off the boulder. 'Fuck,' she says. You don't use words like that, words that pierce the heart of God, unless the situation is very grave. She takes a stick and raps it off the side of the chamber. Maeve howls again, louder than before, like a sonic boom reverberating around the thickness of the quarry.

'You'll make her deaf. Stop it.' I hope there aren't teeth in the chamber, and I imagine Maeve impaled in the darkness. The wind rises up and the chute shudders, and a ghostly howl pitches into the air, the likes of which you might hear all over the county. Maeve is like Alice, falling down, down, down the rabbit hole. Maeve is like the Little Match Girl, delirious and dying in the dark.

Myself and Evelyn scramble up the side of the quarry to the grassy landing and close to the top of the chute. 'You'll have to push your back against one side and your feet flat against the other side, and try and get out that way.'

Evelyn cups her hands around her mouth and sings, '*I'm the ghost of the quarry, and you'll never escape.*' She can be a terror, but we're well used to her.

'Come on, Maeve. You can't stay down there. We've to go home soon. Put your back against one side and your feet against the other side and wriggle up towards us. You can do it.'

'Don't worry. You won't starve. We'll come back tomorrow with slug sandwiches and throw them down at you,' Evelyn jibes. She lays back against the grass, places her palms behind her neck and sighs impatiently.

The wind picks up once more, and Maeve's howling rolls out from deep within the chute and across the land beyond the quarry. I persist with the coaxing. We begin to hear small grunts interspersed with snivelling, and make out the sound of Maeve's rubber plimsolls scuffing within the chute, and the *prang* and *pop!* of metal panels as her back shimmies upward. 'Good girl, Maeve. I see you coming. Not long to go now.'

'I'm going to fall. My legs hurt.'

'I can see your head. You're nearly there.' Maeve is close enough now that myself and Evelyn can catch her under the arms and haul her out onto the grass. Maeve is like a feeble newborn foal, coated in a thick grey dust. Her small legs are trembling, her yellow shorts barely visible beneath the crud.

'You look like someone sucked you up into a hoover,' says Evelyn, offering Maeve an apple. Evelyn can give us strength, but she can steal it away from us too when she feels like it. Maeve takes the apple and tears her teeth into it. I'm hungry myself. It's time for home.

We often meet Aidan Morley and his brother, Peadar, in the summer-time, and we stop on the road and talk with them about what they're up to, and more often than not we'll all hit off together, the five of us, for the full day. 'We were going to go up to the bridge and make wishes,' I might say.

'We were going to go up to the bog for a look,' Aidan might say, and it's something we wouldn't have thought to do, to go up to the bog for a look. Aidan is ten, the same age as ourselves. He looks like a smiling boy on the side of a box of cheese, with sandy hair and a snub nose and hard white teeth. I think I might be in love with him, but it's only when I'm anywhere near him. I saw him skipping happily along the road once, and it didn't surprise me, knowing Aidan, though I later learned that skipping in such a way is a popular exercise for footballers. His brother Peadar is older than us by one year. He has a tan all year round, and straight black hair worn long at the front and clipped close at the back. His eyes are narrow and framed with dark eyelashes, and he has a sulky-looking mouth.

It's a hot day and the horizon shimmers before us. We come off the road and begin walking across the bog, and the peat is spongy with a crumbly surface, like a burned cake. Maeve shields her eyes from the sun with her hand. She refuses to take her cardigan off because she loses her things if she doesn't keep them on her, and she's been well warned at home not to do it again. 'Do ye see there's a man across the bog,' she says. We turn and look but we don't see a man. We see a line of black trees, and beyond the trees is more bog for miles and miles.

'There's no man there, Maeve,' I say, disturbed.

'There is. He's waving at us.' There isn't a man at all. I think Maeve has had too much sun.

'What'd happen if the bog went on fire?' enquires Evelyn.

I have a good imagination, and Evelyn and Maeve and Peadar and Aidan turn to me, awaiting my answer. 'I suppose the fire engine would come from Adragule, and we'd have no turf for when the weather gets cold. We'd all have to stay in the community centre for the whole winter, the whole lot of us under a gigantic blanket. All the blankets in Glenbruff would be sewn together, and Father Christopher would have us praying morning, noon and night.' We have a good laugh at the thoughts of it. Evelyn gives me a warm look, like she's pleased with me for concocting the amusing story, and then she says she wants to look for bog bodies, so we all hold hands and walk across a good stretch of the bog.

'This is how they find clues when people go missing,' Evelyn says, and we creep along with half-steps, scanning the peat. At school we learned that bodies could be preserved in peat for thousands of years, and we've seen one ourselves in a glass case in a museum up in Dublin: a crinkled, small man with mahogany skin whose throat was slit as a sacrifice. I suspect that if we were to come across a bog man, we'd end up in the paper, or even on the news.

'What are we looking for?' Maeve scrunches her eyes together. It seems to me that her frispy hair is crackling in the sun.

'Anything that looks like a sack or a piece of string. Or we might see a bit of a face looking up at us,' Peadar says.

I don't want to see a leather face peeping out of the ground. It's fine to look at one in a glass case in a museum, but I don't want to trip over a bog man in my new Velcro sandals. There's no sign of anything, thank God, and I quickly become bored, in addition to being overheated. I think of the cool kitchen at home and I feel like going there without further ado.

'It's too hot. I'm off home.' I make to move, but Evelyn clutches me in the thin fat at the back of my arm.

'Don't.'

'Let me go.'

She watches me for a moment and draws back her hand. 'Only babies run home in the middle of things, Katie.'

'I'm not a baby. I can go if I want.' There's nothing worse than being compared to a baby, especially in front of the Morley brothers.

I make my way back to the road. I'm walking along then, happy enough, until I think of the man Maeve claimed to have seen in the bog. I try to put him out of my mind, but it doesn't work. I have a bad feeling that there's someone following me along the lonely road. I imagine a bog body staggering in the rippled air, the deflated mahogany man with a sack over his shoulder and a dirty rope swinging from his neck. I pick up the pace until I'm scrambling down the road, slapping along, and the Velcro sandals are half falling off me. I'm frightened out of my wits, and projectile tears shoot out of my eyes.

'You're home early. Did something happen?' Mammy asks, turning to me as I burst in the back door. Mammy makes us eat salad in the summer: hacked-up lettuce and a boiled egg and cubes of cheese. She is 'taking a holiday from preparing dinners', so we have to eat cold things and we've no choice.

'I just got lonesome for you,' I admit, but that's only the half of it.

'You're a little dote.' Mammy hands me a mandarin orange from a bowl. I'm high with relief. It's only when I'm next to Mammy that I can think sensibly.

At six o'clock, my small brother, Robert, careens into the backyard on his BMX bike, casting little stones in a shower. He lets out a roar. 'The bog is on fire!' Mammy rushes out the back door and I'm quick on her heels. We can hear the siren of the fire engine blaring, and see a grey blanket of smoke encroaching the sky. Daddy arrives home not long after that, and we all pile into the car to go and look at the bog on fire. Great whapping flames have ripped along the centre of the bog and are spreading fast. The churning smoke is thick and black. Four heavyset firemen trudge across the bog with two big hoses as thick as pythons, and all of the neighbours – the Morleys, the Lynches, the Cassidys and ourselves, the Devanes – are standing around and taking in the spectacle of it. The fire is put out in fifteen minutes, and the grown-ups say it's not unlikely for a fire to catch with the dry heat and the peat being so flammable.

The remainder of undamaged bog is harvested at the end of the summer, and Aidan and Peadar sit up on the high stack of turf on the back of their father's tractor. That's one of the most dangerous things you can do. If the tractor was to take a sharp turn, you could be flung off the turf and break your neck in a ditch. Still, I want to sit up on the turf and wave at everyone. I haven't the courage, but Evelyn does. The tractor rolls away and Evelyn is cocked on top of it, waving like a queen at all of her subjects on the ground below. Maeve and myself watch enviously as they take off into the distance.

I've an awful fear of Johnny Grealish, who sits with his back against the obelisk monument in Glenbruff. He's a horrible thing: a mound of crumpled brown clothing, and only the one ear and the one arm. He roars at everyone, no matter their age or circumstance, and furiously thrashes his stump in the air. He has a turkey's neck and a swollen face with a maze of violet veins across the midst of it. His teeth are bonded with plaque. You have the sense that he has a sort of a wizened monkey's body beneath his coat, all downy skin and bone. Evelyn says he shares a bed with his mother, and that he baits badgers and eats them, but there are a hundred and one rumours about him, and we don't really know which of them is true. He's often carted off in the evenings into the box at the back of a tractor. Daddy says he is a 'dipsomaniac', and I look it up in the dictionary and find out that 'dipsomaniac' is another word for 'alcoholic'. Mammy says to pay no heed to Johnny Grealish, and to pray for him when I see him. She says he's had a tragic life, and has every good reason for being a crackpot.

The way I understand it, ladies die in secret, in a hush, and men die making a big fuss. Louise Morley has died from cancer. She's Mammy's friend and she's the mammy of Aidan and Peadar. I'm not allowed to go to funerals because I'm only ten, but Evelyn goes wherever she wants. Evelyn is allowed to go up to the Morleys' house with her father for the wake, and she says there was Battenberg cake, and the coffin was open and she was able to reach in and touch Louise Morley's hand, and she said it was warm. She said it looked as though she was only just gone asleep. She said Aidan was bawling and he'd put a handful of primroses from the back garden in beside his mammy, and Peadar was sitting beyond in a corner and wouldn't budge, and then he went walking around in the fields on his own with Sheba the dog until eleven o'clock at night. There were neighbours out looking for him but he didn't get in trouble. Evelyn says Peadar is to be kept back a year in school, and himself and Aidan will be in the same class from now on.

The day after the wake, I'm lying on my tummy on the carpet in my bedroom with Evelyn, and we're cutting ladies out of the slippery pages of magazines. We're going to Sellotape them onto the bedroom wall. As I trim the ladies, I'm thinking about Louise Morley. I'm thinking she must be queuing up for a gauzy white gown and a halo and a pair of wings. 'Mrs Morley must be up in heaven now. God will be meeting her at the gate and she'll be let straight in.'

Evelyn sits up on her heels. 'There's no such thing as God,' she says nonchalantly.

'How do you make that out?' I ask, annoyed with her for saying such a mad, strange thing. You'd have to be soft to think there's no God. Sure, who else made all the people and the animals and the sun and rain – only God.

'You can't see him, you can't talk to him, you can't even send him a letter. Sure, anyone with a spark of sense knows there's no God. There's no scientific proof.'

'You don't need to send God a letter. He can see into your head with his holy powers. It's not like he's a person like the rest of us.'

'All the adults tell us he's real because they want us to be good,' she says. 'But the truth is there's no one watching. God is only made-up. So you can do whatever you want.' She's so casual about it, not forceful at all, that I'm struck with a magnificent terror, the likes of which I've never experienced before. If there's no God, then there's no heaven, and there's no pattern to anything, and nothing makes sense.

'I don't think all the adults would gang up and tell us such a big lie.' Who's to say that Evelyn has all the answers, even if she does watch Sky Television.

'Adults tell big lies all the time. Why do you think the newspapers are so heavy? They're full of stories about adults telling lies.' In my mind's eye I see Peadar running through the fields, lit up by the moon. What if there's no one out there minding us and keeping an eye on things? My eyeballs burn hot, and the tears rise up behind them, slipping down my cheeks and steaming my glasses. Evelyn quietens down after that and we busy ourselves with taping up the cut-out ladies. Every time we open or close the bedroom door, they rustle and dance on the wall.

In the evening time, after Evelyn's gone home, I ask Mammy if there's any God. A God who made us all and looks after us. She has a long think about it – 'Mmm, let me think about that now' – and that alone makes me feel very anxious, and then she says God is *inside* a person, inside in a person's heart, and that we all have a bit of God in us. It's not a real answer. It's not a lie, I don't think, because Mammy wouldn't tell me a lie, but it doesn't answer the question, and after she's said it she gives me a closed smile with no teeth.

~

When you talk to Maeve, it feels as though your words are falling into an infinite black hole. No matter what's said to her, Maeve laughs, and she's the sort of a girl who reminds the teacher when she forgets to give us homework. Maeve is an only child, and her adoptive parents, Tom and Mary Lynch, are bordering on elderly. Tom Lynch has a jaundiced-looking face and smells of wood smoke. His cows are miserable and hungry-looking. Mary Lynch is a biddy and wears a headscarf to Mass. She keeps spider plants in stained woollen crochet holders on all the window sills, and there's a sticky fly catcher suspended above the dinner table, studded with fizzing black flies and long-legged creatures jerking towards a slow death.

Evelyn's parents have a holiday home in Lanzarote, and she goes there regularly with no warning to myself. In her absence, myself and Maeve are playing in Tom Lynch's dilapidated timber shed. Tom Lynch's shed is a scary place, full of milky animal medicines kept in old cough bottles, massive pills for cows and sheep, and glass ampoules strewn loose on the dirt. There's even a metal bucket with stinking chicken feet sticking out of it. The crows *ark-ark-ark* in the pine trees beyond.

Maeve's toys are pure rubbish. Her jigsaw puzzle is soft with damp. Her xylophone has two of the bars missing from it, and her doll has a glued-on wig that rolls away from its forehead. Maeve hasn't much to say, just whistles away by herself and rocks the doll in her arms. It's a doll with blinking eyes, but one of the eyes is stuck closed. Maeve's too old for rocking dolls. I can't bear Maeve's presence for too long without having Evelyn to balance things out. Evelyn says it's fine to pal around with Maeve for now, but she can't see her ever leaving Glenbruff. Maeve isn't cut out for the kinds of lives we're going to lead. She won't be coming with us in the long run.

'I've to go home, Maeve.'

'I'll give you a go of the doll,' she says, holding it out to me.

'No, thanks. We've visitors at home. I was told not to be gone for long.' If she knows it's a lie, she doesn't let on.

It's a long stretch until Evelyn returns, as brown as a berry and with coloured embroidery thread wound around a slip of her hair. It's awfully difficult not to envy her. The furthest I've been away is to a caravan park in Cork, where Robert contracted ringworm of the leg.

Evelyn has a television combined with a VHS player in her bedroom, and she can watch television all night if she feels like it. There's a SodaStream in the kitchen, and we make popcorn without supervision, and no one gives out if we burn the pot. Evelyn's mother, Alma Cassidy, buys heaps of groceries sometimes, and at other times there's nothing in the press at all. Alma is forever having a nap upstairs, or listening to her Enya tapes, or walking around with the cordless phone. Herself and Dan have a bad marriage. They married young and used second-hand wedding rings because they hadn't any money, but they've plenty of money now. We always hear the *beeep-beeep-beeep* from the Cassidy Haulage lorries doing three-point turns in the yard before driving over to France. I often wonder what'd happen if I crept into one of the lorries and fell asleep. Would I end up awakening in an exotic, faraway place? I suppose I'd walk around for an hour and take it all in, and then go searching for a grown-up. I wouldn't like to have Mammy and Daddy worried sick over my whereabouts.

Evelyn's younger brother Mickey didn't talk until he was four, and from thereon out he never again shut his gob. He has a small gaunt face with a big red mouth, white-blond hair and eyes the colour of Connemara marble. He often follows us up and around Glenbruff, and he's always looking for attention. He has no one to play with, and Alma is always tired, and Dan is always in the Portakabin office or in the courthouse in Adragule.

'Let me come with ye,' Mickey cries out of his big red mouth.

'Go home, Mickey. We don't want you. You're haunting us,' Evelyn shouts, but he's undeterred. We often see his little white face and big red mouth peeping out of bushes at us. You'd want him around like a hole in the head. It's fair to say that Mickey and Maeve have myself and Evelyn plagued with their presence.

Mammy works as an aide in Saint Fintan's Psychiatric Hospital, and she cleans the church for twenty pounds a week. She has a bouncy blow dry and wears silk blouses with shoulder pads and Peter Pan collars and a pair of clip-on earrings resembling anchors. Mammy loves us all, but we are the runner-up prize. We represent the broken dream. The dream that has been broken is the pursuit of acting. Mammy had been up in Dublin when she was in her twenties and she'd been in several amateur stage productions: *Playboy of the Western World*, *Dancing at Lughnasa* and *Juno and the Paycock*. She met Daddy at a dance at Christmas time and got engaged to him, and then she had to come down to Glenbruff and close the door on the whole lot.

It's easy to know what life is like for Daddy. Daddy is happiest when he is fixing up a place and putting it in order. Daddy smells like turpentine and he has black and white hair like a sheepdog and when he's at home he wears white sneakers stained green from mowing the lawn. He's the maintenance man at Amperloc, an American pharmaceuticals company on the outskirts of the town, and he goes about planting deciduous shrubs, replacing the filters in air-conditioning units and patching the car park. As well as that, Daddy is the chairman of the Community Improvement Committee, and regularly telephones the county council enquiring about pothole repair, the faulty water scheme and the removal of lead pipes. Daddy believes he can revive Glenbruff, but it seems that each time he turns his back, there's a stone wall falling down in one place or another. 'There hasn't been a house built in Glenbruff in over a year,' he says, 'but the graveyard is nearly full. What does that tell you.' Daddy's always speculating about Amperloc, fearing they'll move to a cheaper manufacturing base in the likes of Eastern Europe or Asia. The maintenance budget has taken a hit of fifteen per cent, and according to Daddy, the first sign of a company in difficulty is a cut to the maintenance budget.

Robert thinks he knows better than anyone. He has black hair and big black pupils in his brown eyes and a cleft chin. He has a creaking accordion, and a big book called *Bridges of the World*, and he uses parchment paper to trace the outlines of well-known bridges. The middle of the book has a pop-up bridge in it. When he's grown-up, Robert says, he'll design a special bridge carrying road and rail, and within its structure there'll be residential and commercial units. This style of bridge, according to himself, will make him a millionaire many times over.

'The real world isn't as generous as Desmond Duignan is making out. The real world has hurdles and setbacks and all sorts of interference,' Mammy tells him, but her words have little effect.

'That's what's known as a "limiting belief",' Robert says, cracking his knuckles.

'You've an answer for everything, is that it.' Mammy worries that the liveliness has been leached out of Robert entirely. His rigid personality has been forged in Principal Duignan's classroom. When Robert was due to enrol in primary school, the school in Glenbruff was at risk of closure due to insufficient numbers, and so my parents enrolled him at the primary school in Saint Malachy's Parish, two miles beyond Glenbruff in the direction of Adragule. As Mammy and Daddy signed the enrolment forms, the principal of Saint Malachy's National School, Mr Desmond Duignan, told them he had all his money made on the stock market. He said he was only teaching so he could give back, and pass on the secrets of success to subsequent generations.

It's said that Principal Duignan attends a summer-long conference in California every year without fail, the contents of which are a closely guarded secret. Robert says he keeps a chin-up bar in his classroom and raises himself up and down thousands of times a day as the children pore over their workbooks. He plays self-improvement cassette tapes, which they listen to intently, their foreheads pressed to the table. He assures the children that they can have anything they want and be anything they want to be, and advises them never to take no for an answer.

Principal Duignan's approach has divided parental opinion. Some of the children have been removed from the school, overwhelmed by the vigorous campaign of aspiration and industry. The remaining pupils, however, revere him completely, absorbing his every platitude with absolute willingness. These children get themselves ready for school, prepare their own lunch boxes, complete their homework without supervision and promptly put themselves to bed. Their parents speak of their approval, and remark on the significant maturity of their children in comparison to others of the same age. After a time, these parents come to a disturbing realisation: their offspring have little need for them at all.

It often feels as though myself and Evelyn were born friends. We're always on the edge of things and looking on. It's as though we're the only people who're truly alive, and the people around us aren't real at all, existing merely for our own amusement.

Evelyn has squeaky hair. She rubs her hair with her fingers and you can hear a faint squeak out of it. She says hair isn't clean unless it's squeaking. It was hard to get the knack of getting the squeak out of my own hair, but I manage it in the end. I'm very careful to keep my hair clean, as it's the sort of thing Evelyn would notice as soon as she'd lay eyes on you.

Maeve can't get a squeak out of her hair. 'Come here and I'll give it a go,' Evelyn says impatiently, and she rubs her index finger and thumb together over Maeve's hair, but there's no sound from it. 'It doesn't work if your hair is dirty.'

'It isn't dirty. I only washed it last night.'

'Well, there's no squeak out of it.' Maeve hasn't the same kind of hair as Evelyn or myself. She has coarse, dull hair.

'I had a bath and washed my hair after.'

'Did you dunk your head in the dirty bathwater?' Evelyn says, laughing, and I clasp my sides with laughing too. I haven't always the confidence to be kind to Maeve in Evelyn's presence. 'And did Tom and Mary have the bath before you as well? I'd say they did.'

'They did not. I had a fresh bath,' says Maeve with a shaking voice.

We sit there hooting at her for several minutes, watching her grasp pieces of hair and rub at them furiously. I know that the squeaking hair is only a trick to make ourselves feel superior, but there's fun to be had in getting a rise out of Maeve. There's a pecking order, and we know our place in it. It's Evelyn, then me, and after that it's Maeve the Mope.

When myself and Evelyn and Maeve happen to meet Aidan and Peadar out on the road, I slip my glasses into my pocket as quick as a wink. I don't think I'm ready for being seen and admired. I'm thirteen, and I haven't yet decided if I'm ugly or otherwise, but slipping off the glasses makes me feel like a happy ghost in a hazy world.

When we're all together, the world revolves around Evelyn, and why wouldn't it. Her long hair shimmers in the glare of high summer, sun-bleached at the temples. She has new things to wear: a peach sundress and sandals with leather butterflies sewn on the ankle straps. She's full of herself in the lovely outfit, gaining great pleasure out of her own appearance. I see her glancing down at her sandals, fondling the hem of her dress and repositioning the thin straps over her tanned shoulders. I can almost feel the straps brushing my own shoulders. It must be great being Evelyn. 'Any of ye see my dad in the paper?' She's walking backwards along the bog road, her arms thrust out for balance. 'He's in the courthouse in Adragule. They'll never get him. The judge is my mother's second cousin.' I don't like Dan Cassidy. He's only an average-sized man but he seems far bigger than he is. He takes up a whole room when he's in it, and he changes the feeling of it. Daddy says he sits up at the counter in Donovan's Bar with his friends and he looks at people sideways when they're coming in the door. Daddy says there's always whispering between himself and his friends and you know they're saying something cruel about the people coming and going.

'Your father has the roads destroyed,' Peadar taunts. 'If he'd any decency at all he'd be going around filling in potholes after himself.' There's a bit of resentment for the Cassidy family locally because of the bad roads.

'I could have your father fired if I wanted,' she says, slanting her eyes. 'I could just say the word.' Peadar and Aidan's father, Terence Morley, is a trucker. He works for Cassidy Haulage and drives around France, Germany and Spain delivering butter and cheeses.

'You could in your arse have him fired,' Peadar says gleefully. 'How about I'll bring you a shovel and you can get the job started yourself. We've a boiler suit up at the house you can put on. You'd be a fine girl going up and down the road filling up craters.' Aidan and myself guffaw, while Maeve appears fearful, unsure of how Evelyn will react to the goading. Evelyn comes to a standstill on the road and gives Peadar a hard shove, and he's only laughing harder at her.

Aidan spins round to me. I am suddenly ashamed of my faded dungaree dress and striped T-shirt from two summers gone, the puffy lettering crumbling off the front of it from the washing machine. 'Come on and I'll race you to the bridge,' he says before bolting ahead, his long legs beating off the tarmac. I run after him, though I haven't a hope of winning the race. When I reach the humpback bridge, he's already perched on top of it with his arms folded, and making a big show of looking at his Casio watch. I slow down to a patter and bend over, trying to catch my breath. My ribcage presses up and down and my heart pumps forcefully underneath. My brain tingles from the exertion, and pins and needles bloom in my fingers.

'Why did you want a race?'

'I didn't really want a race. I only wanted peace and quiet.' His face is bright and flushed, his tousled thick hair soaked with sweat. 'I'd prefer it being just the two of us.' The air around us is changing colour. There are forces at play beneath the surface. There are invisible filaments reaching out from me and sparking with the invisible filaments emanating from Aidan. I can feel the energy rolling off the trees and fields, and see prisms of light dancing on the river. I imagine myself hovering above my body and seeing the two of us, not even a metre from the other. And then we hear the shouts from far away, snapping us back into staidness, back to the old humpback bridge, the dull brown water, the oppressive warmth, the odour of hot tarmacadam. We peer over the road and Evelyn and Peadar are running towards us, and along comes Maeve, lagging behind, huffing and sucking her cheeks, and wearing the wrong shoes entirely for summer weather. I feel the interference as they make their way towards the bridge. Evelyn is marching now, the peach sundress twisted about her torso. I feel the biting twinge of inadequacy, the rise of frustration, because Evelyn has a hand in all I do.

'What're ye at here?' she demands.

'Nothing. We only had a race.'

'We got bored of ye shitin' on,' musters Aidan.

'Where are your glasses, Katie? Why aren't you wearing them?' Evelyn enquires, tilting her head and pursing her lips.

'I have them in my pocket.'

'What good are they doing you in your pocket?'

'I don't know.'

'I bet you're not wearing them because they're for boys.'

'What do you mean?'

'They've a bar across the top of them. That means they're for boys.' You'd think she would have told me before now. I've been wearing boys' glasses and didn't know it.

'It doesn't bother me. I don't care,' I say, humiliated. I haven't the right clothes, I'm no good at running, and to top it off, I've been wearing glasses for boys. Aidan won't think much of me now, if he ever did at all, and as for Evelyn, I think she said what she said on purpose. I'm sure she was storing it up.

The following summer, and Mammy and Daddy have the idea to send me to the Gaeltacht for the full month of July. I suppose they're hoping I'll make a few new friends out of it.

The Irish school is a spartan set-up in Connemara, accommodating two hundred boys and girls from twelve up to sixteen. Eight girls including myself sleep under faded bedspreads in a dormitory room in a local house, and we're served cheap sausages and chips out of a deep fat fryer at teatime. The girls in the dormitory are only alright. There's a girl from the Midlands whose accent is incomprehensible. The other girls are aloof towards me. I feel it keenly. They're a different sort of creature to myself, and down from Dublin. Evelyn has told me two things about girls from Dublin: they think they're better than girls from the country, and they're thick.

On the first night, a girl called Gwen cries over missing the qualifiers for the Dublin Horse Show. How could her parents do this to her. Isobel commiserates. She says parents are evil. Gwen keeps me up all night with the crying, and Isobel wets the bed, and the girl from the Midlands whistles through her nose in her sleep.

There are Irish classes in the morning, and then we're all herded out to play Gaelic sports in the afternoon. There are céilís in the evening time, and we're taught how to *hup-two-three* and *hup-two-three* in parallel lines. You prance towards the person opposite you, and then you prance backwards, and forwards again, and then you clasp hands and spin each other around until all the colours whip together.

I slip away from the céilí and go and sit on a stone wall, and I suck on sweets, longing for the time to pass. I spend long hours thinking about all that I'm missing out on at home. I imagine Evelyn and Peadar and Aidan and Maeve traipsing over the roads under the humming telephone wires, rambling along the railway track and finding things to do at their leisure.

The girl from the Midlands sits up next to me on the stone wall. 'I'm fed up. Are you?'

'I am,' I admit. The girl from the Midlands, Oona, is worn out having to speak slowly to the other girls in the dormitory, not to mind speaking in Irish the rest of the time. I allow her to pluck my eyebrows, and she makes a dog's dinner of them. It's a misadventure in the strongest sense of the word.

I post a letter to Evelyn every week, and send my regards to Maeve. I make out that I'm having a whale of a time. I tell them there's all sorts of carry-on happening at the Gaeltacht, and I'm meeting people from all over Ireland, and I'll have to buy a big wad of stamps when I get home because I've an eager new set of pen pals.

All the girls and boys cry on the last day. The crying is infectious. Even the older boys are crying. I'm not sure what I'm crying for. I'm only crying because everyone else is crying, but I feel hollow on the inside. I hug people I haven't even spoken to, and sign their shirts, and scribble my address into people's notebooks. Gwen writes '*Don't cry because it's over, smile because it happened*' into my notebook with a neon biro. I haven't had one letter from Evelyn in all the time I've been away.

Upon my return to Glenbruff, Evelyn informs me that herself and Maeve have been practising telepathy. Maeve sits under the humpback bridge, and Evelyn uses chalk to draw symbols and shapes on the tarmac above. Maeve shouts up a guess of what the drawing is, and she's often right, or so they let on. 'She guessed my initials, and a smiley face, and she guessed yin and yang,' says Evelyn, searching my face.

'I don't believe you.'

'Suit yourself,' she says.

The next stunt is the pair of them claiming to have had the same dream the night before. I pretend not to care, but it bothers me that I'm the outsider and not having the dreams. I suspect that Evelyn isn't wholly pleased with me for going off to the Gaeltacht without her, and this show between herself and Maeve is a punishment. I'm not to go off without her again.

A letter arrives from the girl from the Midlands. It's badly written, in loopy, exaggerated handwriting slanting downward along the page, and it's the sort of letter a person sends when they want to get a good one off someone in return, but only send a poor excuse of a letter themselves.

> *Well Girl,*
>
> *How's things? How are you since? Do you miss me? Not got much news. Write back soon with all your news and gosip.*
>
> *Keep in tutch.*
>
> *Oona.*
>
>
> *PS. I haven't spoke a word of Irish since I came home!*

There's no use wasting time on a person who sends tedious letters. A friendship with Oona would do more for her than it would for me. I can't see the use in having boring friends, and in any case, I'm still bearing a grudge over the eyebrows. It goes without saying that the letter remains unanswered.

It takes a while for things to return to normal between myself and Evelyn and Maeve. At the school sports day in September, we sign up for the three-legged race. When Evelyn and Maeve's legs are tied together, the whole lot goes arseways and they tumble down in the grass. When myself and Evelyn have our legs tied together, we run in time with one another, and come in in first place and get a medal apiece.

Evelyn has the ability to slip in and out of boldness. She takes cosmetics from Crotty's Chemist without paying for them, sliding tubes of make-up and lipstick up the sleeves of her school jumper. She doles out the stolen things to myself and Maeve. I know stealing isn't right, but I've no money for buying cosmetics, and it's important to have a few bits and pieces to smarten myself up. 'You're unreal. Thanks Evelyn,' I say, feeling the objects heat up in my hand. Maeve yanks the lid off an orange lipstick and applies it haphazardly. The instinct burns within me to rise to Evelyn's rank of daring, and to slip into boldness myself.

'It's your go next,' she says abruptly. 'I'm always doing the hard work.' That takes the goodness out of it.

Cora Crotty catches me heading out the door with two scrunchies and a comb. 'Come back here, you bold girl. I see you. I know your father,' she bellows, curling her finger at me. There's something hypnotic about the curling finger. Cora instructs me to stay put in her back kitchen, and she phones Daddy from the black plastic telephone on the counter by the cash register. 'She's inside in the kitchen, Mossy. She's as sorry as a caught thief.' I sob quietly in Cora's drab kitchen, roiling with rage and humiliation. I haven't even the need for scrunchies and combs.

Daddy lands down like a shot and he even keeps the car engine running out on the street. He hands Cora ten pounds to cover the stolen items. It takes a while for him to say anything on the journey home. 'Who put you up to it?'

'No one.'

'Was it Evelyn Cassidy?'

'No. It was my own idea.'

'Myself and your mother want you to keep your distance. You're too attached to her.'

'I am not. That's strange talk.'

'The likes of Evelyn Cassidy will never have to work for anything. It's people like us who have to buckle down and get serious. You must start thinking about your own future, and less about what Evelyn Cassidy is doing.' In the days to follow, Daddy goes about the town asking if there are any part-time jobs going for a sixteen-year-old. I suppose he wants to fill up any free hours I have, and keep me out of trouble. I get a job working in Angelo's Chip Shop on Friday nights. The chip shop is operated by a man by the name of Pascal Hamrogue, a middle-aged bachelor from over in Kiltane. He has a greased-up Teddy Boy hairstyle, and holds his arms in such a way that reminds me of a trussed-up chicken: elbows stuck out either side, the fronts of his hands flat against the small of his back.

I like the job. It's good to have money of my own, and I'm excited to ring up the items on the cash register. I've never had power like it. Evelyn and Maeve and Peadar and Aidan call up to Angelo's from time to time on the Friday nights. 'What are ye up to?' I have to project my voice over the sound of hot, crackling oil. I can see Aidan outside the window in his school uniform, skilfully rolling a football under his feet. Maeve stands under the lamp post, her eyes fixed upon him, a camogie stick resting against her shoulder.

'Arrah, this and that,' Evelyn says, yawning, her forearms resting on the glass counter. She's wearing a fashionable tracksuit with popper buttons along the sides of the trouser legs. 'Will you be coming out with us after?'

'I won't be out until one o'clock. I've to clean up.'

'You're always stuck in here. You're missing out.' I think she's the one missing out. I have a great sense of eminence out of minding a chip shop on my own. Peadar lights a cigarette outside, and the four of them amble away up the street.

As the last of the sun's rays come down, the countertop and the tables gleam golden. I get to thinking about Evelyn and the way our lives are intertwined. We're not completely certain as to where we're going, but we're going to go together, bolstered by the other. It's what we've always said to one another.

After the chip shop is shut for the night, I cycle home in the dark. The hushed air wills me along. I can hear the gentle spin of the wheels, the subtle rhythmic catch of the pedals. Cycling is as close to flying as you can get. You'd forget there was a bike beneath you at all. I bear down on the handlebars. One day I'll show them all who I am and what I'm made of. One day we'll show them all. I have a big ball of white fire beneath my ribs just thinking about it.

Myself and Evelyn and Maeve are out walking in Glenbruff of a Saturday afternoon when we hear the scratch and whomp of hip hop music emanating from the community centre. We stick our heads round the door to see Pamela Cooney dancing alone on the varnished floor next to an enormous ghetto blaster. Her copper ponytail whips the air as she flicks her long arms and kicks her long legs. She even drops into the splits without a flinch. What does it take to be her? I wonder. What does it involve? Do I have it in me?

When Pamela's out dancing in front of the monument, the adults clap heartily and fling coins and even a five-pound note onto the chipboard. Peadar remarks that Pamela is a fine filly, and Evelyn is badly rankled by it, withdrawn for the whole rest of the day. Thereafter, Pamela dances at the vintage rally, the fundraiser for the levelling of the surface of the football pitch, and the blessing of the humpback bridge.

Pamela came down from Dublin with her mother and brothers as part of a rural resettlement scheme. She attended the primary school in Saint Malachy's Parish for a time, and then the family relocated back to Dublin for one reason or another, but they're after coming down again, and she's in my English, history and home economics classes. I'm not a lesbian, like Geraldine Dobson's auntie who was asked to leave the nuns, but there's something about Pamela that makes my heart race. She's like a doll fresh out of a box: upturned nose, bright brown eyes and shiny copper hair in a ponytail over her shoulder. She has straight, even teeth, like perfect gleaming baby shells, and pale skin with a lilac hue.

Evelyn says she's fed up to high heaven of seeing Pamela Cooney doing the hip hop dancing. She's fed up of Pamela continually being paraded around. Even Mammy makes a fuss over Pamela Cooney. 'That girl is a real bobby dazzler. She has real class. The same as her mother Maureen.'

'She's alright.'

'She's better than alright, Katie. She's gifted. Who does the dance lessons with her?'

'She only has an aul videotape with the dances on it.'

'She learned all that off a tape. I might get a tape myself and surprise ye all.' Mammy laughs long and hard at her own joke, revealing her milky grey fillings and bright pink tongue, and the clip-on earrings wobble on her earlobes.

When Dan Cassidy comes into Angelo's, himself and his pals hang over the counter and have a good eyeball at me and talk about me as if I'm not there. There's Eugene Gormley sucking his gut up into his chest, Paddy Brannigan with his bristly bottom on display above the workman's trousers, and Jarlath Quinlan, the sergeant in Adragule whose tight white curls resemble a head of cauliflower. How is it they think they're attractive, or that any woman would look at them twice, not to mind a young girl like myself.

While I'm counting out the change for Dan, I drop the coins on the ground and have to kneel down and pick them all up. My face is flaming with embarrassment. 'Would you say she'd be often down on the knees?' Dan remarks.

'Oh, I'd say she does be.' All four of them are laughing like slobbering hyenas.

'I'd say she does be praying for you, Eugene. I'd say she's praying for your withered soul,' says Jarlath.

'That's not all that's withered,' Dan quips.

Dan lets on that I gave him the wrong change, and I know that I haven't. I gave him the exact right amount. 'You'll have to come here now and give me a kiss to make up for it.' I only wish I had the smart answers ready, but I never do.

Pascal is coming in the door with the cash box and the men filter out. 'Did they give you any trouble?' he asks me, popping open the register and rifling through the notes.

'N-no,' I stammer. 'They were fine.'
'I'll drop you out home.'
'There's no need. I've the bike.'

'It's called synaesthesia. It's like a crossover between the senses. When I listen to classical music, I can see things floating in front of me in the air,' says Evelyn. We're lying against the hillside behind Maeve's house, propped up on our elbows with the breeze ruffling our school skirts. We can see the steeple of the church, yellow ragwort catching over the hills and the white nubs of old houses built too close to the road. We can see all the way as far as the quarry, five fields over.

'Like what?'

'Streams of colour. Patterns.'

'Ah here.'

'Lots of the classical composers had it.'

'That sounds lovely,' says Maeve, her eyes cast up to the sky. 'I wish I had euthanasia.'

'It's *synaesthesia*, Maeve. Euthanasia is when you kill someone who can't cope with being alive.'

'Sorry,' says Maeve.

'I'm trying to really harness the synaesthesia. I'll be getting started on my portfolio soon and I want to blow their minds.' Evelyn has decided that she wants to go to art college after we finish school and become an artist. Specifically, a famous artist.

'You will blow their minds,' I tell her. When I'm generous with Evelyn, she's generous with me. 'Don't you think there's something special about Glenbruff? It's interesting. Someone should make a film here or something.'

Evelyn sits up and rests her jaw on her fist. 'No fucking way. It'd be a shite place to make a film. There's nothing going on here worth filming. The whole point is to get out of here. You go to where the action is happening. The big cities.'

'Okay. Alright.'

'You can stick around if you want but I'll be long gone.' She lands a soft punch on Maeve's upper arm. 'Have you decided what you're going to do, Maeve?'

Maeve's tugging stems of grass out of the ground and laying them in a pile. 'I don't have much of an interest in anything.'

'What sort of an attitude is that. You're surely interested in something.'

'Not really. I'd say I'll just stay local.'

'You actually want to stay in Glenbruff. Like, for the rest of your life.' Everyone else will be going on to college or have something lined up. Maeve's the only one with no plan.

'I'll be grand as I am.'

'You will not. You'll be making a big mistake, stuck down here scratching your hole while we're off gallivanting,' warns Evelyn. 'You'd better go in to Pearl Powers on Monday and have a talk with her.' Pearl Powers is the school guidance counsellor, head of the girls' choir and enforcer of the school corridor transit policy.

Maeve twirls a stem of grass between her fingers as a slow wasp veers around her. 'I was already in talking to Pearl. She said she'd phone them up in Amperloc with a recommendation if I want.'

'You'll be counting tablets and putting them into brown glass bottles. Is that what you want?'

'They've machines to count the tablets,' I interject, and Evelyn rolls her eyes.

'*Obviously* I know they've machines for counting tablets.' I bet she didn't know about the machines for counting tablets.

41

Maeve blows on the pile of grass stems, sending them askew. Maeve is good at maths, especially accountancy, and chemistry too. Maeve is capable of going to college and doing alright. I can't help but feel some relief at her disclosure, however, because it means that myself and Evelyn won't have to mollycoddle her wherever we end up. Say if we were chatting to fellas in a nightclub and Maeve was standing there looking gormless, we'd lose our allure entirely. I'll be glad to leave Maeve behind in Glenbruff. It'll be great to have her out of the way.

'If you could choose to be anyone else alive, who would it be?' she says in a faraway voice.

'How do you mean?'

'If you could choose to be someone else. Anyone at all. Who would it be?'

'God almighty. Why in the world would I want to be someone else,' Evelyn snorts.

In recent times, Mammy's become friendly with Maureen Cooney. She invites her up to the house, and Pamela along with her. 'Why don't yourself and Pamela go out to the good room with the dancing tape,' Mammy suggests. 'We'll come in and watch ye in a while.'

We don't light the fire in the good room unless there's visitors coming or it's Christmas. The room even smells like Christmas, like pine and spice and oranges. I roll up the rug and push back the furniture to make enough room for the dancing. There's cold moisture in the air, and Pamela briskly rubs the tops of her arms.

The videotape is wrapped up in a plastic bag. It's called *Urban Beatz IV*, and the cardboard sleeve is decorated with fluorescent triangles and squiggles. I turn on the television and the screen goes *whoomp* and rustles with static. The tape is sucked into the video player and it clicks and whirrs and a lady comes on the screen in a lime-green bodysuit. '*Welcome to Urban Beatz. Get ready to bounce.*' Half of my brain is trying to keep up with the dance routine and the other half is taken up with the presence of Pamela Cooney. It's like being in the room with someone famous. She has that sort of charisma about her.

When the dance is over, we pause the video and seat ourselves down on the couch. 'Where'd you get the tape?'

'Desmond Duignan got it for me. He got it in America.' America's the most glamorous place in the world. America's paradise.

'Have you been there?' I enquire. I'd love to go to America, but I can't see it happening.

'A few times,' she says, like it's no big deal. 'Who would you say is better-looking, Peadar Morley or Aidan Morley?'

'Oh. They're both nice-looking. One of them fair and one of them dark.'

'Peadar was phoning me nonstop for a fortnight,' she says proudly. 'He's mad after me.'

'Is he really.'

'And Aidan must be gay. I've been to all the matches and still nothing. Who do you like? You must like someone.'

I shake my head. 'There's no one.' I haven't kissed anyone and I've no one to be talking about. 'How d'you like living down the country?'

'It's only alright.'

'Oh.'

'Like, you have to make your own fun around here. You've to find ways of keeping yourself occupied.'

'Mm.'

'I'm bored a lot of the time. Desmond Duignan offered to bring me down to Galway to the dance school but Mam said no.' There's a pause, and then she says, 'I'm looking for someone to do the dancing with and enter competitions. Would you be interested?' Myself and Pamela could be backing dancers for a pop band. We could have a wind machine, and a make-up artist and hairdresser going around with us on a tour bus. 'Why don't you keep the tape for a while and have a think about it.'

'Alright. Thanks, Pamela. I'll try it out.'

Pamela lies herself up on the good couch with her shoes still on her. We're not allowed put our shoes on the couch but I don't say it.

'You're friends with Evelyn Cassidy,' she murmurs, smiling out of one side of her mouth.

'I am.'

'How come?'

'I don't know.' How do you answer a question like that. 'I've always been friends with her. We've always been friends.'

'Don't you think you'd have more friends if you weren't?' she says, laughing and waggling her shoes, but the thing is that myself and Evelyn were born friends and that's just the way it is.

The pitch in Glenbruff is lopsided, higher on one side than the other, and the players from Saint Malachy's Parish poke fun at it, and poke fun at Glenbruff. 'Have they never heard of a spirit level round here, lads. This is some backwards spot.'

Myself and Evelyn and Maeve are huddled in the concrete shell, our nerves already jangled. The old men have fold-out stools and they're sitting as close as they can to the pitch. The clubhouse is an old shipping container painted white on the outside with lights strung on wires on the inside and old school benches to sit upon. I can see Pamela Cooney tucked in with the supporters from Saint Malachy's Parish, wearing a pale pink coat with a furry hood. The Glenbruff boys stream out onto the pitch, their breath coming in plumes of fogged air.

Aidan's the team captain. He's shouting across the pitch, pointing at and directing the other players, a fierce determination on his face. There's a sharp whistle and the roars rise up. Aidan is pelting up and down the pitch, and we can sense the force of the kicks, the acceleration of the ball hurtling through the air and up, up, up between the high bars. His shoulders gyrate in his jersey. His legs have a nice and even covering of honey-coloured hair and the skin beneath is tanned and supple.

The day after the match, appreciative talk of Aidan's legs reverberates around Saint Dymphna's Girls' Secondary School. 'Those thighs could crack walnuts...' Almost overnight, Aidan has become the most eligible seventeen-year-old boy in the locality, surpassing even Dylan Hartigan, who's been up to Dublin to do modelling shots for a clothes catalogue. Geraldine Dobson takes a funny turn with all the excitement. 'He has the sexiest pair of legs in Roscommon,' she says, her eyelids heavy with lust. 'They're rock solid and they've veins like wires running across them.'

'You're some horndog,' says Evelyn, in precarious humour after certain goings-on at the match. Peadar had been roving around in the crowd, asking girls for their phone numbers and getting the shift from Stacey Nugent behind the clubhouse.

There's a celebratory disco in the community centre. Geraldine Dobson is doused in glitter, wearing shoes like stilts that she can't rightly walk in. She's holding on to the backs of chairs like a first-time ice skater, afraid to let go for fear her legs will give way. Meanwhile, up to twelve girls are leaning against the wall by the entrance to the gents' toilet, awaiting Aidan to happen in their direction. 'Imagine trying to catch a fella's eye when he's heading for a shite,' says Evelyn, shaking her head. I'm seeing Aidan in a new light. It's not only the legs, but the firm jawline, the ever so slightly oversized white teeth and the way he furrows his eyebrows when he's deep in concentration. If I myself was to get a kiss from Aidan, or even a slow dance, I'd be made up, but the competition is fierce.

Maeve has to borrow clothes from Evelyn to wear on nights out, and she looks all wrong in fingerless gloves and velvet tops with draped sleeves. The black lipstick makes her teeth appear yellow and unscrubbed. 'What in God's name is Maeve Lynch wearing. It looks like she fell into the bargain basket in a charity shop,' says Jennifer Graham, who's touching up her mascara in the girls' toilet.

'Yeah. She looks like Courtney Love threw up on her,' chimes Stacey Nugent.

A toilet flushes and Maeve emerges from a cubicle, her face animated with microscopic twitches. She's moving towards me, her eyes blinking rapidly as Jennifer and Stacey scurry out the swing door. 'You didn't stand up for me,' she says. 'You let them trash me.'

'I didn't have time to think. It happened so fast.'

Maeve hunches over the sink. The water coming out of the tap is very hot and there's steam rising off it, but Maeve allows it to run all over her hands. As she soaps and rinses, soaps and rinses, I worry that she's going to tell Evelyn, and Evelyn will think badly of me, but it works out that I get to tell Evelyn my side of the story first.

'It's not our fault if Maeve looks like a tool on nights out,' Evelyn says.

Pamela is standing alone by the dance floor. She turns all the lads down. 'I'm too shy,' she says, giggling, when Peadar tries to catch hold of her hand and when the other lads attempt to pull her elbow to bring her for a dance or out the back into the dark. And then Aidan approaches her, and we can see the whole thing happening in slow motion. There's a collective wave of upset. The girls stop dancing and begin whispering furiously behind cupped hands. They text their parents to come and collect them from the community centre without delay.

You have to put like with like, and the likes of Pamela Cooney will always end up with the likes of Aidan Morley. I revert my attentions to Dylan Hartigan, a fella with an irresistible high-fashion sneer and poor eye contact. I've never seen his legs but they're surely better than average.

Aidan and Pamela are oblivious to myself and Evelyn and Peadar and Maeve all gaping out of Angelo's window at them, Aidan delicately brushing a strand of hair out of Pamela's face, and Pamela touching the soft skin on the back of his neck with her fingertips, her mouth stained with the pop of pomegranate lip gloss. They're like a pair of ancient statues intertwined.

'Would you look at the two virgins,' Peadar sneers. I had thought we were all virgins.

'Everyone knows girls from Dublin are only sluts,' Evelyn says, and Peadar snorts with amusement. I don't think Evelyn once met a girl from Dublin before Pamela came along, and what makes her the authority on girls from Dublin, I'm wondering.

'Are they?' enquires Maeve. 'Every one of them sluts?' Maeve has taken a notion and sewn a fur trim onto the hood of her own coat.

'Any I've met in a personal capacity,' Peadar says knowledgeably. 'The thing is that Pamela was after me first. She'd her eye on me first. We'd a few chats at the matches and a good long conversation on the house phone there not so long ago. Herself that rang. We were planning to meet up.' Evelyn pushes the chip carton away from herself across the table. 'I never thought a woman could break the bond between brothers,' Peadar adds. 'But there you are.'

Evelyn curls her hands. 'Can we not talk about something else,' she says in a hard voice. 'I'm bored of talking about her. She isn't the least

49

bit interesting. She's nothing to say for herself. She's the most boring person I've ever known. Who is she anyway? She's no one.'

'Aidan's on the phone from the minute he's in the door from school. I was waitin' for a call from a girl over in Shrule the last night and he wouldn't get off the fuckin' line so I fuckin' cut it. He'd to go down to the phone box and phone her from there.'

'What can they be talking about every evening?' asks Maeve. 'What would they have to be saying to one another?'

'Nothing. Shite talk. I wouldn't mind but I've business to be dealing with. Women waitin' on me, like.'

'I wonder why he doesn't call over to the house to see her instead,' muses Maeve.

'Would ye shut up talking about her,' Evelyn cries shrilly. 'I'm going the fuck home if ye don't shut up talking about her.'

'She's not allowed out during the school week. And the brothers are two knacker thugs. If Aidan takes a wrong step with her, they'll kill him stone dead.'

'Maybe we should give her a chance,' says Maeve, craning her neck for a better look. 'Get to know her. She could be nice. She looks nice.'

'She's not as good-looking as I thought she was,' Peadar says. 'Not when you're up close. She's plain-looking up close.'

In a flash, Evelyn tips her carton of chips over Peadar's head, and he grabs her wrist in the air and shakes it roughly. 'The fuck is wrong with you,' he snarls. Evelyn bursts into tears. She yanks her wrist free and flees from Angelo's as Peadar shakes the salt out of the front of his hair and onto the table before him. 'Let her fuck off home for herself. Contrary bitch.'

Maeve is laughing away, having a great evening's entertainment. It's all happening with Pamela Cooney in town. 'Life is very exciting at the minute,' she gushes. 'Wouldn't you agree?' she says to me.

I'd better go after Evelyn. I need to find her and comfort her. That's the expectation. I have to leave Angelo's unattended and pelt up the street, and she's at the church by the time I catch up to her.

'I hate everybody. Nobody in the world loves me.'

'Would you stop that talk. Your mother loves you. Your father loves you. Myself and Maeve.'

'My mother doesn't love me. She slapped me across the face. She slapped me so hard my father slapped her after so she'd never do it again. And now she only pretends to love me.' Jesus. She never told me that. She turns her face to the wall and sobs into her palms. 'It's Peadar I love but he doesn't love me back.'

'Oh.' It's Peadar she loves. How could I have missed it. 'Maybe he does love you but he doesn't realise it. He might go on to realise in a few years' time.'

'Will he ever come around?' she says, her voice wrenched with anguish.

'I'd say he will. And if he doesn't you'll meet someone better. Think of all the places we're going to go and the people we're likely to meet.'

She turns her tear-streaked face and hiccups. 'Will you go back and make an excuse for me?'

'I will. I'll tell him your favourite actor died in a car crash and you're in bits over it.'

'Thanks, Katie,' she says appreciatively, and wiping her eyes with the back of her hand. 'That's a good one.'

The guilt is rising up within me. I'm as well off to own up to everything. 'Mammy invited Pamela up to the house. She brought the dancing tape up with her. She asked me if I wanted to get matching tracksuits and do performances.'

Evelyn's subdued for a moment, and then she says, 'People would only be laughing at ye.' Laughing at us. I hadn't envisioned people laughing at us. 'You don't want to associate with the likes of her, Katie. Haven't I warned you before about girls from Dublin.' She narrows her eyes. 'I heard the father is in prison. I heard he's a contract killer.

51

It mightn't even be safe for you going around with her. You could be shot dead in the night.'

'Shot dead.' What would I be shot dead for? It doesn't make sense.

'I'd say she'll try and get between us. You won't let that happen, will you? You wouldn't choose Pamela over me, would you?' she says, and now I wish I hadn't gone after her to see that she was alright. I could have learned a thing or two from Pamela. She could have shown me how to get a fella, since she has so many of them interested in her. And I could have looked phenomenal in a lime-green bodysuit, but now I'll never know. 'I wouldn't like that, Katie. I'd hate that. I couldn't be friends with you after that.'

Myself and Evelyn were born friends. I'd do anything to keep her feeling friendly towards me. I won't dance along to the tape any more, pretending I'm an American.

Pamela's spending the Tuesday night. Our mothers have arranged it. I've never before had anyone spend the night. Evelyn won't sleep anywhere but in her own bed.

I've a freshly laundered bedspread and I've hidden away anything that Pamela might consider to be childish. The room is looking fairly sparse afterwards. I've to go around the house and collect up things to make it appear more sophisticated. A decorative bowl of potpourri and a lampshade with feathers on it.

She has a purple rucksack crammed full with clothes. 'Where are you going with all the gear?' I ask her.

'I'm going out for a while but I'll come back,' she says. 'I'm meeting someone.' She drops the rucksack and takes position in front of the full-length mirror, cross-legged and perched upon her tailbone, her copper hair cascading behind her.

'Oh. Aidan, is it?' She *is* plain-looking when you look at her up close. 'How are ye getting on?'

'I can get nothing done with all the phone calls. It's too much.' She pulls opens the drawstrings of the rucksack and yanks out the tops and jeans and shoes. 'I don't know what to be talking to him about. It's painful.'

'Is that so.'

'We went up to the cinema in Adragule the other night. Did you know they've fleas in there. I was scratching all week after it. Anyway,

I'm not sure if I chose the right one, Katie. He isn't my type. He's boring.'

'You're hardly meeting Peadar this evening, are you?'

'I'm keeping it private for the moment. If you don't mind.' I do mind. It isn't fair of her withholding Aidan from the rest of us if she isn't keen on him. And she has some audacity interfering in Evelyn's pursuit of Peadar, not that Evelyn owns Peadar outright or anything. 'Would you put on the radio there while I'm getting ready.'

I sit down on the bed and observe her preening herself along to the pop songs. She hasn't much to say, alternately absorbed in her own reflection and rattling through her make-up bag. I'm not as taken with her now as I was before.

'How is it you moved down from Dublin?'

'The brothers were getting in trouble up there. They were on their last warning.'

'What's it like in Dublin anyway?'

'It's like a different planet, Katie,' she says wistfully, and daubing her eyelids with eyeshadow using her index finger. 'You'd love it, I'd say. It's all happening up there.'

At ten to nine, there's a soft car beep outside on the road. After she's gone from the room, I look through all the things in the rucksack and the make-up bag. It's nice to be looking through the things. The disc of pink blusher and palette of eyeshadow. The small tin of lip gloss, nearly new. I wonder did she rob the things or did she have the money for them herself. She has Sun Moon Stars perfume that must belong to Maureen. I spray it on my wrist and take it in. I try on lip gloss and eyeshadow as well but then I think better of it and rub it all off. She could be back any second and I don't want to be caught and look foolish.

This is no fun at all. She's been gone now for hours. I lie awake in the dark, listening to the radio at a low volume. I wouldn't have minded going for a spin too if she would have asked me. I'm thinking now that she's only using me for cover. I'd say she might only be passing the time with me until she meets the right people. Mammy taps on the door. 'Are ye alright?' she says softly.

'Yes, Mammy.'

'Is Pamela alright?' Should I say something? Should I be concerned? What if Pamela was to never come back? I want to confide in Mammy but I don't. It's Mammy and Maureen engineering things between myself and Pamela, and undermining myself and Evelyn's friendship.

'She's asleep,' I call out, and Mammy pads away from the door and down the hall. I roll over in the bed, fold my arms and sigh out loud.

It's very late when the headlight beams sweep through the room. There's a rustling at the window and Pamela's leg swings over the sill. I lean out of the bed and turn on the feathered lamp. 'How'd you get on?'

'Oh my God. Amazing.' She drops the furry hood down from over her head. Her face is flushed and her copper ponytail has loosened out about her. She has a cool, moist aura from being outside.

'Where'd ye go?'

'We just drove around talking.'

'Tell me who you were with,' I press her. 'Go on.'

'I'll tell you another time,' she says. A friend who tells you nothing is no friend at all. I'm altogether gone off her. 'Take a look at this. I got a present off him. He says he's never before met a girl like me.' She holds out a navy box and there's a necklace inside on a bed of velvet padding. The necklace has a ballet slipper pendant on it. 'I might fall in love with him yet. It's about time I fell in love with someone. I'm seventeen.' I'm seventeen myself. Is it time I fell in love too?

'You can't fall in love over a present. That's only a cod.' You wouldn't mind but the necklace isn't even expensive-looking. It's only sterling silver.

She considers this. 'It's not just the present. It's the way he makes me feel. He knows the dancing is everything to me.' It's clear that I don't feel as strongly about the dancing as Pamela. I don't think I'm destined for dancing after all. 'It might be better if I just do the dancing on my own, Katie. He'll only give me the lift to the competitions and no one else.'

'That's grand. I don't mind.' That's it so, and just as well.

She turns her back and hurriedly gets into her pyjamas. 'Don't look.' I can hear her kicking off the high-heeled shoes and unzipping her jeans.

I knock off the lamp and turn over on my side. Pamela clambers into the bed and tugs the duvet over herself. 'Katie,' she whispers after a minute. 'Could you go out and get me a glass of warmed-up milk.' I pretend I'm asleep. The potpourri smell is pervading my nose from the bowl on the bedside locker but I don't budge.

I'm cycling home from Angelo's the Friday night following, and I spot Peadar inside in the phone box, and him yakking away.

'I want to work in films.' I feel a golden thrum in my chest just saying the words aloud.

'Come again?' says Pearl Powers.

'Films. I've decided I want to work in films.' I haven't been many places, and my world is small, but I often feel that life is so much like a film. If only I could take the pieces, string them together and make something wonderful out of them. The sun on closed eyelids. The eternal bike rides of summer, a girl's hair whisking in the wind, and her sitting on a wall and kicking her heels against it.

Pearl Powers looks at me concernedly in her beige woollen suit and orthopaedic shoes. She has a fuzzy face dusted with compact powder and jowls that judder when she speaks. There's a powerful scent of talcum and Yardley perfume in her poky office, and a rotten sweet smell wafts from her mouth. 'It's very competitive. And I've heard it's not as glamorous as you may have heretofore assumed.' What about it, I think to myself. Life is competitive. Everything is competitive. Myself and Evelyn will crack it. The two of us together will make the dream a reality. 'In all my years working in the school, we've never had a girl from Saint Dymphna's wanting to be in films,' she says, making notes on an index card. I can read the handwriting upside down: *Phone parents*.

'I don't want to be in the films. I want to make them,' I say, pressing the tips of my fingers into the armrests of the chair and looking over at the stacks of pamphlets Pearl Powers keeps bound with elastic bands on her old-fashioned roll-top desk. *A Girl's Guide to Montessori Teaching. Type Your Way to the Top. Career Girls Choose Cosmetology.*

'I had you in mind for a secretary.'

'I don't think I'd like being a secretary. I want to work in films.' When Daddy is finished with his Sunday newspaper, I go through it and look for the successful people working in the Arts to see how they've done it; most of them say it was hard work, and only some of them say it was luck. Daddy says that most of these people start out with money, or with relatives and connections who've already forged a path. It'll be the likes of Evelyn who'll get lucky, and I'm the kind who'll have to put in hard work.

'I'm not sure how you would go about it. Getting into films. I suppose you could write a few letters to well-known personalities and see if they write back to you. You might be lucky.' Pearl Powers smooths her hands over her pleated wool skirt. 'Out of interest, Katie, what do your parents do?' She's scrawling on the index card, her head bent down like an impersonal doctor.

'My father is a maintenance man in Amperloc. My mother is an aide in Saint Fintan's Psychiatric.'

Pearl Powers looks disapproving. 'Isn't that a pity. You'll have an uphill battle trying to get a career going in films. A well-to-do family tends to have connections in unusual places, but you won't have that advantage.' She thrusts a handful of pamphlets at me. 'I don't like to dissuade young ladies from following their desired path, but you might want to have a read of these. In case the films don't work out.'

'Thank you, Miss Powers.' I come out of the office and the door clicks shut behind me.

Evelyn has her shoulder hoicked up against a wall of steel lockers. 'Give us a look at those. Fuck's sake. Did she give you any decent advice at all?'

'She said to send letters to well-known personalities.'

'What good would that do. Fucking Pearl.'

'She's some dose.'

'Never mind her anyways. Leave it with me and I'll come up with something.'

It's later the same day when Evelyn ducks out of her typing class with a freshly typed sheet of paper. 'Here it is. Here's what we'll do,' she says, waving the paper about. I catch hold of it and read it aloud.

Ten-Step Career Plan

1. *Get into college*
2. *Finish college*
3. *Get any sort of job at all*
4. *Save up like mad*
5. *Move to London, New York or Los Angeles*
6. *Work internships during the day*
7. *Get a job in a cool bar at night*
8. *Get to know the right people*
9. *Everyone falls in luv with our art and ideas*
10. *Take the world by storm*

'I wish we could go right away. Life is moving at a snail's pace,' I say, gazing at the plan, my heart thumping wildly.

'Time moves slower in Glenbruff. It's a proven fact,' she says, and then her voice takes on the lilt of suspicion. 'You won't change your mind, will you?'

'Of course I won't. You'd think I didn't want to go.'

'I'm only making sure. There's more to life than Glenbruff, you know.'

'The graveyard is full, and there hasn't been a house built in the place for over a year, and what does that tell you,' I say, echoing Daddy. I fold up the sheet of paper and put it in my pencil case for safe keeping. I'm all buoyed up by Evelyn's plan. If it wasn't for Evelyn, I might have applied for the teaching, like Mammy and Daddy were advising me to, but instead of that, myself and Evelyn are going to unleash ourselves upon the world, and everyone's going to take notice of the pair of us.

'Come over to the house this evening. I've something for you,' she says, grinning.

'What is it?'

'Come over to the house and find out.'

There's a commotion at home before I leave for Evelyn's house. Daddy and Mammy and Robert are gathered around the kitchen table and scrutinising the college application form I filled out the night before. I have an Arts degree at the top of my list, and Daddy especially is ashen-faced. 'What'll you do with a degree like that,' he says, and it sounds like a rhetorical question.

'I'll go into the Arts and all that.'

'The Arts are only for rich people,' Mammy says forlornly. 'I've seen it all before in the theatre business.' I always feel that things aren't right for Mammy. It doesn't suit everyone to be holed up in a small place. She seems happy enough, but that might be a sort of a performance too. I don't want to end up like Mammy, going through the motions.

'I'll be alright. I'll figure it out.' Myself and Evelyn will crack it. The pair of us together will make the dream a reality.

'It seems that you've given little consideration to anything else. People like us have to be sensible,' Daddy appeals. *People like us.* He's always saying that. It makes me feel sad and trapped.

'You're headed for a rude awakening. I'll be earning the big money and you'll be scraping away,' Robert drawls, sitting into a chair and cocking his feet up on the table. His school shoes skim the clean pages of the form.

'Down. Now,' Daddy barks and Robert takes down his feet.

'All I'm saying, Katie, is you have to go where the jobs are.' Robert's palms are turned out and his black eyes are glinting. 'There are plenty of shiny jobs that pay fuck all and go nowhere. If there are good jobs going in banking and finance, you go into banking and finance. If there are jobs going in manufacturing, you go into manufacturing. Otherwise you'll be left behind.'

'Would you listen to his lordship,' Mammy says irritably.

'Please ye're selves. If ye don't want to listen to sense, I can't make ye,' he says, before sauntering out of the kitchen and turning up the television in the sitting room.

'Would you not do the teaching,' Daddy says. 'You'd have a guaranteed job and a pension. That mightn't sound like much, but when you're our age you'll be glad of it.' I can't imagine myself as old as Mammy and Daddy. *Pensions.* Sure, that's light years away.

'He's right,' says Mammy, and she looks to be troubled, but I'm full to the brim with the belief that myself and Evelyn are going to lead an exhilarating life together, the likes of which you couldn't begin to imagine. Still, there was something in Mammy's eyes that caught me in the heart like a hook.

Evelyn takes me out to the big garage at the side of her house where there's a skip full of dusty electronics and other odds and ends. Inside the skip I can see the hoop of a wedding dress and an unopened box of paints I once gave her as a present. 'I found this and thought you might get use out of it,' she says. It's an SLR camera in its original box. 'Have it. It's only going to the dump if you don't want it.'

I touch her sleeve excitedly. 'Are you sure?' I've never before had a camera of my own.

'Take it. It's yours.' Evelyn is the best friend that anyone could hope for. If there was ever a sign that things are going to go well for us, surely this is it. 'It's your birthday present, Katie, so don't be expecting anything else.' It isn't my birthday until the summer but what about it.

'I couldn't sleep last night,' she says as I sit up on the seat of the bike and place the camera carefully into the basket on the front. 'I was worrying that I'm going to die before I get to do all the things I want to do.' Evelyn's always saying mad and unusual things, and she's always thinking a step ahead of me. I've never even thought about dying before, and how we might not get to do all the things we want to do.

'That's not going to happen. We've loads of time to do it all.' I push down on the pedals and hit off in the direction of home. 'I'll see you in school.' I've every confidence that myself and Evelyn are going to live forever.

It's the day before the Christmas holidays from school. Pamela's at the vending machine sending a pound coin into the slot, and Evelyn makes a bold approach towards her. 'Pamela,' she says, her smile effervescent. 'Everyone's getting bored of your dancing. No one else would say it to your face, but I offered to do it out of niceness. It's time to hang up the dancing shoes.'

A can of Coke thunders into the metal receptacle, and Pamela reaches in her hand and removes it. She turns about to us and snaps back the tab on the can. *Ksht.* 'Would you ever fuck off,' she says.

'Why don't you fuck off yourself. Why don't you go back to Dublin and stop annoying us with your stupid-looking hip hop.'

Pamela smiles and sups off the can. 'No one likes you, Evelyn. Everyone says you're a contrary bitch.' It was Peadar calling Evelyn a contrary bitch the other evening in Angelo's. He's been talking it over with Pamela evidently. She looks to me. 'You must be finished with my tape by now, Katie. You've had it for ages. When are you giving it back?'

'It was stolen. Someone took it. I don't know where it went or who might have it.' The tape has been languishing at the back of my school locker.

'Stolen.' She's eerily casual, supping on her can. 'You'd better find it.'

'We've things for doing and you're holding us up,' Evelyn declares. 'Just stay out of our way. I mean it.' She barrels along the corridor, and I follow after her. 'Maeve. *Come on*, you dickhead. Come *on!*'

Myself and Evelyn go into the girls' bathroom. We mash up the plughole with wads and wads of toilet paper. We toss the dancing tape into the sink and turn on the hot tap. Evelyn pushes down on the soap dispenser and a glop of liquid soap falls into the hot water. The tape floats to the surface and Evelyn pushes it down and suds form around her wrists. She bends the plastic shell in her hands until it snaps. She digs her fingers in and loosens out lashings of shiny black entrails. The entrails are disgorged all over the sink and all over the floor and we wind them around and around the taps on the sink and around the plumbing. It's Evelyn gives rise to the daringness, who helps me see who I can be. It's Evelyn gives me power I never thought I had.

We walk about the school and the town with a buoyancy in our step, and the phrase 'It's time to hang up the dancing shoes' causes us to erupt in fresh laughter, over and over and over again.

I wonder if it's true, that no one really likes Evelyn, and if that's the case, where does it leave me? I suppose that Pamela is right, and I'd have more friends if I wasn't friends with Evelyn, but the thing is that you can't be friends with everyone, and I'm not to feel too badly about it. Even Mammy says, 'If you're everyone's friend, you're no one's friend.'

Maeve is in the sick bed with glandular fever, and so myself and Evelyn hit off to the New Year's disco by ourselves. We spin around with our arms in the air, dappled by coloured lights, the music sustaining us and leading us about the floor. It feels as though everyone's watching us admiringly. I end up kissing Dylan Hartigan at midnight, and at long last, Peadar throws the lips on Evelyn. I can sense the swell of pride within her. I can sense that it's the release of a great tension that had been building. 'I just hope it doesn't hurt myself and Peadar's friendship,' she says about the kiss. She might only be saying it because Peadar is as likely to forget it happened at all.

Dylan Hartigan is more than a bit of a let-down. In addition to the modelling, he's a keen amateur golfer, and he talks at length about the set of custom golf clubs he got for Christmas. I notice he has a tiny golf caddy embroidered on the pocket of his shirt. He doesn't ask me a single question about myself, but sure, what have I to tell him in any case. All that being said, there's many a girl who'd love to be in my shoes and kissing Dylan Hartigan on New Year's Eve. It's some achievement for a first kiss.

Myself and Evelyn dissect the events of the New Year's disco. Evelyn reminisces about her slow dance to 'Runaway' by The Corrs with Peadar, when he slid his hands all over her bottom on the outside of her jeans. All the while, Maeve sits slumped on the bed, or paints her stubby nails silently, or rummages through the clothes in Evelyn's wardrobe. 'Who else was there? Did Aidan go?'

'He was there with Pamela,' Evelyn says contemptuously. Pamela steered clear of us at the disco, and Geraldine Dobson was hopping around her like a fly on shite until Aidan brought Pamela into the dark corner for himself.

Maeve is turned to the wardrobe, is ordering the clothing by colour. The wire hangers clatter together.

'Hey. Don't move stuff around in there. I have a system.'

'Sorry.' Maeve returns to sitting on the bed. 'I think I'd better go home. I'm not well enough yet to be out.'

Evelyn and myself write out a list of all the songs we heard at the disco and resolve to buy the singles the next time we go to Galway. Evelyn gets her mother to bring her to Galway all the time, and sometimes they take me along too. The small bit of money I have from shovelling chips keeps me in trendy tops, body spray and contact lenses. 'Where's Maeve?'

'I think she said she'd to go home.' Maeve has slipped out of the room without either of us noticing.

'Isn't it awful funny how Maeve got glandular fever. She must have caught it off the water fountain at school,' says Evelyn.

'Or else she licked the monument after Johnny Grealish pissed on it,' I say, and Evelyn cackles and slaps her thigh. No one can make Evelyn laugh like I can. I love hearing her laugh. 'Do you think we'd be friends with Maeve if Mary wasn't your mam's sister?'

Evelyn cranes her neck, looking to see that the bedroom door is closed. 'Mam wants me to keep in with Maeve to make sure she's alright. Why do you think I have so many clothes and CDs and stuff?'

'She's paying you to be friends with her?'

'Sort of. Mam said Maeve had an awful start in life. She said it was like something from Dickens.'

'*A Christmas Carol?*'

'No, you dope. More like *Oliver Twist*,' she says, and after a pause she adds, 'with drugs.'

'Jesus.' I don't press for additional detail. I don't care too much for Maeve one way or the other.

'Maeve's my little project. I'm going to polish her up and pull the string and set her going.' Evelyn has her work cut out for her.

It's all over the news. Only a few days into the New Year, and Pamela Cooney has disappeared without trace. She went out to meet Aidan by the handball alley on a Friday evening, but she never arrived. Aidan got cold standing around waiting for her, took it that he'd been stood up and made his way home. When Pamela failed to materialise at her own house, Maureen phoned the guards, and it wasn't long before talk of the missing girl hit the streets and households, Donovan's Bar and Angelo's Chip Shop. Pascal said I could shut up the shop and go home, and Daddy came down to collect me.

There were guards called in from all over the county, and they walked up and down the roads and poked around in the grass. They put empty wrappers and bottle caps into see-through bags. An old man called Bertie Halligan said, 'These are lonely roads to be on by yourself. You could be taken off them just as easy, and no one would be any the wiser.'

Desmond Duignan headed up a search party comprised of his former students, but they were only covering the same ground as the guards. He said the scene of a crime could blow away in the wind, and the guards would need all the help they could get, but within a half an hour, a senior detective instructed Desmond and his cohort to clear off. And then a rainstorm rolled in and stayed for the full week, and people were less inclined to go out and search in the wet weather.

'You must tell the guards everything you know. Even if you think it's not important. You must say it anyway.' What do I have for telling the guards? Why is it all on me? I said to Mammy that I don't know Pamela as well as she thinks, but she didn't listen. She got on to Mary Lynch and Alma Cassidy to see if Maeve and Evelyn will be going up to the station too. Mary says Maeve is too emotional to speak, and Alma says Evelyn won't go up unless she's called to go up.

Jarlath Quinlan is the sergeant in Adragule. There's so little to keep him occupied under normal circumstances that he owns and operates a small farm as well as breeding greyhounds. 'Katie and Pamela were becoming friendly. Isn't that right?' Mammy says, looking over at me. I wouldn't have got caught up with Pamela at all only for Mammy's interference. I would have observed her from a distance, and carried on wondering about what it was like to be her, and that would have been enough.

Jarlath grunts something unintelligible. His pen isn't working and he goes out searching for another one, and I sit looking around in the interview room. The room doubles as a kitchenette with a travel kettle and a microwave set out on a sideboard.

Jarlath returns and tests the new pen by scribbling on his jotter. He licks the ball of it and tries again. *Bingo.* 'It appears that your new friend has wandered off. Do you've any idea where she might have gone?'

'No.'

'Why don't you tell me a bit about her.'

What am I to say. She was a girl who never seemed real. A girl you couldn't relate to. 'There wasn't enough going on for her down the country. I'd say she might have been bored.'

'Bored, is it. Did she want to return to Dublin at all?'

'I don't know. Eventually. She said Dublin was like a different planet.'

'Did she have friends in Dublin that she talked about? People she might have gone up to visit.'

'No. She didn't mention any friends in Dublin.' She'd no friends that she ever spoke about, and I suppose I was no good of a friend to her in the end, but who says you have to be friends with people even if they want to be friends with you. Who says she was any good of a friend to me, sure. She was only alright of a friend as friends go. Still, we shouldn't have ruined the tape. I know now that we shouldn't have done it.

'What kind of form would you say she was in?'

It's a hard one to answer. I've to make a guess. 'I don't think she was in great form.'

Mammy cocks her head sideways.

'Why was that?'

'It was hard for her making friends and keeping them.' I should have returned the tape to Pamela, but how could I go against Evelyn? You couldn't go against her, but the black mark is on me now.

'This young fella. Aidan Morley. What do you make of him? What did Pamela make of him?'

'She thought he was alright. She was going to break up with him.'

'Is that so.'

'She lost interest in him. She stayed over in our house and she snuck out and met up with someone else.' There's not enough air in the room. I'm seeing coloured stars.

Mammy leans forward, and Jarlath too. 'Who?'

'She wouldn't say who. She said it was private.'

'A secret suitor,' Jarlath says, looking over at Mammy. 'Isn't that interesting.' He flicks over the jotter cover and leans back in his chair.

'Is that it?' I ask him, my voice shrill. 'Can I go?'

'Go on so, good girl. Off with you,' he says jovially. 'That wasn't so difficult, was it.'

'That's everything, Jarlath? You've no other questions?' Mammy says, sounding surprised and flustered.

'We've a fair idea of what happened. We don't think there's anything sinister to it.'

'Sure, we can come back if you need us for anything else.'

'Mammy. Come on.' I pull her on her coat sleeve. My stomach is heaving and roiling. I've to get out of the dank room quick.

The rain is lashing down and beating off the windscreen. I roll down the car window and gulp in cold air.

'Did you tell him everything?' Mammy says. 'Everything you could have told him.'

'I did.' I did, I think.

'Wasn't she bold leaving the house like that? Wasn't it ill-mannered? What sort of girl is she at all.' I press my head back against the headrest and close my eyes tightly. 'You did the right thing telling us, Katie. You've done your bit. We can tell Maureen we've done our bit and there's nothing more we can do.' She pauses for a minute. 'You wouldn't ever slip out of the house on us like that, would you?'

'No.' I can feel Mammy's eyes are still on me. Can she see the black mark? Is it indelible, or will it ever wash away?

'You'd better close up that window or you might get a palsy.'

There hasn't been a customer in Angelo's in over an hour. The black-and-white television on the wall bracket is fixed on the horseracing highlights from Leopardstown, and the remote control is missing.

I can sense a shadow falling over me and I look up to see Desmond Duignan standing at the glass counter. 'Robert tells me you're a friend of Pamela's.' His eyes are a crystalline, Rasputinesque blue, and he's a towering six foot seven in height. He's so tall he could reach over the counter with his long arms and lift me out from behind it. 'Have you heard from her at all?'

'No. I haven't. If I heard from her I'd go straight to the guards.' She's gone now two full weeks. It's frightening to think that she was here one day and gone the next. It can't be that long ago she half stayed the night.

'I was very fond of her. Did she ever say anything about me?'

'No,' I tell him, though I can't entirely recall.

Desmond Duignan nods thoughtfully. 'Very good. Very good.' The fluorescent ceiling light is flickering. *Spink, spink.* He reaches his hand up to the ceiling and pushes the loose tube back into its casing. 'You'd want to be careful in here on your own.'

'It's okay. We've a security camera.'

Desmond Duignan takes the camera down off the top of the television. He turns it over and shakes it, and it turns out that it's only a hollow box with a false lens and a red light on top powered by a battery. Pascal bought the dud security camera from a travelling salesman.

'This is an imitation. It wouldn't be much good to you.'

'Oh.' I have a wave of fear that leaves me feeling weakened. 'Would you like me to get you anything, Mr Duignan?'

'Desmond. Des,' he says, grimacing and rubbing his strong chin. 'Something quick.' He clears his throat and inhales deeply through his nose. I do up chips and a piece of cod for him and pass him the bag over the counter as Pascal is making his way in the door and him cleaning out his ear canal using a hairpin.

'Des,' says Pascal.

'Pascal,' says Des, doffing an invisible cap.

Des glances back into the shop before crossing over the street. He scans up the way and down the way, and then he folds himself into his silver Toyota car. He throws the hot paper bag onto the dash and hurriedly drives away. I don't think there's one ordinary person to be found in Glenbruff, but sure, the same could be said of any place.

Mammy and Daddy have advised me to leave the job in Angelo's. The exams will be coming up in a few months' time, and it isn't safe to have a teenage girl working alone in a chip shop at night. You wouldn't know what sort of an oddball would take a shine to you over his fish and chips, and it isn't safe to be cycling around afterwards in the pitch black.

There's a vigil for Pamela organised at the church in Saint Malachy's Parish and we're all let out from school to attend. There are undercover detectives present and talk that the vigil is their idea, the purpose being to pay close attention to the people in attendance, eavesdrop on conversations and keep an eye out for abnormal behaviours. The other schoolgirls weep dutifully, but neither myself nor Evelyn nor Maeve shed a tear. There's a tense moment when Aidan enters the church, flanked by his father, Terry, and Peadar too. Heads turn and tut. Up at Saint Ambrose Boys' College, everyone's talking about him and eyeballing him. Pamela's brothers, Daithí and Donnacha, shoulder him in the corridor, and they beat him up after a match because it's something they feel the need to do. Aidan's right eye is blackened and half shut, and Evelyn had had the idea that we'd sit next to him to show our solidarity, but when it comes to it, we stay put.

Maureen stands up on the altar wearing a stained blouse, and says a few short words in a wavering voice. 'Pamela isn't the least bit of trouble to us. She's a happy, pleasant girl. If anyone knows anything, please talk to the guards. Someone must know something.'

74

Myself and Evelyn and Maeve make our way through Saint Malachy's Parish in the direction of Glenbruff, and pass the boundary wall of the Cooney household. There's a colourful display of cuddly toys, bouquets and cards, and even a figurine of a ballet dancer. Everything is sopping wet after the week's rain. Maeve shivers to see the gaudy items resting by the wall, and then she sticks her face forward and picks up her stride. She whistles the melody to *The Great Escape* as we skip around the big puddles. The three of us are afraid, but we're exhilarated too, because this is the most exciting thing that's ever happened in the locality.

'The guards are shite,' says Evelyn with her nose in the air.

'Why d'you say that?'

'They've no arrests made. Not even one.'

'Sure, there isn't even a body. Where would they get evidence from?'

Evelyn watches a lot of true crime documentaries, and espouses the theory of a serial killer, a man taking and killing women all over the country. 'Or…' She pauses for dramatic effect. 'It might have been someone she knew.'

We walk along for a small while, and then, with some reluctance, I say, 'Do you think it could have been Aidan, like people are saying?' Aidan was questioned by the guards but released without charge. It was Peadar told them Aidan was in the door at ten past seven and they watched television together for the whole evening. Aidan was able tell the guards who had been the guests on the *Late Late Show*.

'Aidan's our friend,' Evelyn says sternly. 'If he says he didn't do it, then he didn't. He's fed up explaining himself.'

Maeve's eyes are round, like she's been suddenly disturbed. 'It wasn't Aidan,' she says. 'He'd never hurt anyone.'

'I was watching a documentary on Sky Television the other night about portals to other dimensions,' Evelyn says. 'I'd say it's entirely possible that she walked through a portal to another dimension, and now she can't get back.'

I burst out laughing. 'You're having me on. Serial killers and portals. Whatever next.'

'Here. There's plenty of unexplained stuff that goes on in Glenbruff. It's a queer old place. You should hear some of my dad's stories.' Dan Cassidy has a few strange stories. One of them is about a ghost dog that came along the bog road and ran right through him on a winter's evening. Another is the story of his own father, who was lost in a field at night and became possessed by 'the hungry grass', a residual hunger from the Great Irish Famine that hangs like mist in lonesome places. 'I'll tell you who they should bring in and string up by the toes.'

'Who?'

'Desmond Duignan. He's been front and centre since the news broke.' Maeve's mouth makes an 'o' shape, and Evelyn continues, 'A killer will often infiltrate an investigation by offering to help out. They think they'll avoid suspicion but they end up drawing attention to themselves. It's textbook.'

There are several journalists knocking around the place and annoying people. We're approached by a whippersnapper girl in her twenties with blonde hair and cracked lips. She introduces herself as Sheena Sheppard from the *Connacht Press*. A young man with a big camera and a flash on the top of it is with her. We look about instinctively, in the hope that an adult will come along to shoo her away, but there's no one in sight. 'Girls. What do you think happened to Pamela?'

'We don't know,' I begin, and then Evelyn says, 'She might have just wanted a change of scenery.'

'I see you're all walking along together. Are all the young girls travelling in groups until Pamela's found?'

'We're well able to look after ourselves,' says Evelyn haughtily. 'We're getting on with our lives in the same way. We won't allow it affect us.'

Sheena Sheppard looks to Maeve and asks, 'Were you friends with Pamela? Tell me. What was she like?' Maeve's lower lip quivers, and suddenly she's bawling hard. Sheena reaches forward and hugs her and gestures at the photographer. He snaps photographs from different angles. *Tsch. Tsch. Tsch. Tsch. Tsch.* Maeve is awful upset. You'd forget she has feelings at all sometimes.

'Stop taking photographs of my cousin. Leave us alone,' Evelyn protests. The photographer persists, and Sheena Sheppard is patting Maeve's hair. 'This is exploitation.'

A picture of Maeve's crumpled face is featured in the paper the following week, with the caption: *Distraught classmate of missing girl attends vigil in Roscommon.*

'Everyone loves a story with a missing girl in it. There'll be another one next week, and the whole thing will be forgotten about,' Evelyn says, as though she's tired of the world and everyone in it.

'I was told the banshee was heard in Glenbruff the night that girl disappeared,' Daddy announces in the kitchen at home, and Mammy throws him a cross look. She doesn't want me feeling afraid in my own hometown. Mammy and Daddy both are wary of me going out in the evenings and at the weekends, and I'm to be dropped off and collected for the time being. Evelyn can go out whenever she wants as long as she's with Peadar. She'd throw a fit if she wasn't allowed come and go.

'What daft person said that?'

'Tom Lynch said it.'

'Arrah, Tom Lynch, my eye. He's still leaving bread on the doorstep for the fairies.' Tom Lynch has a hawthorn tree at the side of his house, and he swears up and down that there's fairy activity attached to it.

'What do you think about Aidan Morley?' I pipe up. Aidan's been standing by the side of the bog in the evening time and staring blankly across the horizon. The bog goes on for miles and miles, and it could be a thousand years before they'd find a person in a bog, if they're even in there at all.

'I never knew a bad person to come from a good household,' Mammy says.

'That's soft talk.' Daddy's always giving out to Mammy about soft, sentimental talk.

'Says the man talking nonsense about banshees.'

There are still no clues as to Pamela's disappearance. She left no diary, no letters, 'no nothing', says Maureen when she's up to see Mammy. Mammy tells me to stay put in my room until she's gone home or the sight of me might set her wailing. Why was it Pamela taken and no one else's daughter?

Some of the girls at school are saying that Pamela might have done away with herself in a secret place, for some unknown reason. There might have been trouble at home, sinister and mysterious in nature. It comes to light that Pamela had no close friends with whom she could confide, but the circumstances of the vanishing don't add up to suicide.

Evelyn wants to study fine art at the Institute of Art and Design, a prestigious institution where art is taken very seriously. It's the best programme in the country, according to Evelyn, and it's the only programme she's applied to. She has an interview at the college before our final exams, and I accompany her on the journey up to Dublin. She clips open her big portfolio case and withdraws her art for me to have a look at. I haven't seen the art before as she's been uncharacteristically shy about it. She's been toiling away in her bedroom for two whole years, she says. 'What do you think?' The truth will never suffice. Evelyn's art is both eccentric and mediocre. She's drawn a crude self-portrait that's off-centre: eyes set too far to the left, and nose too high on the face, almost emerging from the forehead. There are pencil sketches of people with no faces at all, their bodies all out of proportion. Another canvas features a cat wearing a suit and holding a pocket watch.

'I don't know how you come up with this stuff,' I say in reference to the cat in the suit, and she takes it in the best way possible, beaming from ear to ear. But I don't think there's any merit in what I've been shown, and I've a sinking feeling the administration at the art college will reach the same conclusion. The last piece is a painting of Maeve done in watercolours. It's so strikingly accurate that I'm quite startled: Maeve's big grey eyes tilting at the outer corners, her translucent skin, the unusual floating quality of her thin bistre hair like a trick of the light, the shoulders hunched and the head drawn down like a tortoise

mid-retreat. 'That's exactly Maeve. That's exactly what she looks like.'
The only difficulty is that Maeve doesn't resemble an artist's muse.
She's odd-looking. To the stranger's eye, the painting could be deemed
to be totally unrealistic. Still, there's nothing to be done but admire
the portrait, for Evelyn's sake. 'You're some trickster, doing all this
work without any of us knowing.'

'There's more where that came from. Stacks and stacks of paintings
and drawings going back forever.' She returns the papers and canvases
to the portfolio case.

'Have you had any hassle at home? About wanting to go to the art
college.'

'They couldn't give two hoots. I said to Dad that I was looking to
do art and he said the house could do with a lick of Dulux.'

'You're lucky. I'm being pestered with aptitude tests and career
coaches and all sorts.' I sit back in my seat and watch the landscape
wash past me. After all our big talk, I might be moving up to Dublin on
my own. I can hardly contemplate it. I'm anxious because I remember
Mammy telling me about her old school friend Hillary Bowman. She
said they were as thick as thieves. The two of them were mad into the
acting. Hillary Bowman moved to New York and married a stockbro-
ker and herself and Mammy lost touch. After twenty years, Hillary
called the house phone unexpectedly, and Mammy was so tongue-tied
she could hardly string a sentence together. They'd nothing at all in
common to talk about, and she never heard from her again after that.
Mammy got into a fit of befriending local women as a consequence,
but there was none could compare to Hillary Bowman.

I sit and wait in a nearby café as Evelyn goes to meet with the
interview panel. She joins me after forty-five minutes, sliding onto the
wooden chair and clattering the portfolio next to a radiator.

'Well. How was it?'

'Sure, it's impossible to know.'

'What did they ask you?'

'About my influences, where I see myself going as an artist, that sort of stuff. I didn't get much of a reaction, but I think that's how it's supposed to go. I'll find out in a few weeks whether I've got in or not.'

'Try not to think about it too much.' It's important in life to know the right things to say at the right times.

'I'm not in the least bit concerned about it. It's done now. I'm going to leave the portfolio here and head off.'

'You're going to leave your portfolio. After all the work you put into it.'

'I only needed it for the interview. Come on and we'll go for a few drinks.'

'We'll miss the train.'

She fiddles with the plastic carnation in the small vase on the table, and then peers out the window at passers-by. Two young fellas lope along on the street with portfolio cases slung over their shoulders and Evelyn watches them with her lips pressed together. The boys are likely to be competing for a college place too. Her place, probably.

'I'm bored. Let's go,' she says suddenly, rising to her feet and scraping the wooden chair away from herself. The art portfolio remains propped up next to the radiator. I'm relieved that the ugly drawings and paintings won't be accompanying us, like evil spirits traipsing along in our midst. I'm relieved to abandon the uncanny painting of Maeve. It has the feel of bad juju emanating from it.

Evelyn wants to inspect the pubs close to the college and have a drink in each one. It's a Thursday afternoon, and there are art students with unruly hair, wearing shirts and overalls covered with flecks of paint, standing about and chatting animatedly. Some wear angular glasses, some smoke hand-rolled cigarettes. Their shoes are scruffy, with dried tidemarks of dirty water, but their accessories are expensive and copious. 'These are my kind of people,' she breathes, leaning on the counter as I order two beers. 'I can't wait to come back here when college starts.'

'Hopefully it will all work out,' I say, feeling deceitful.

'Peadar says he might come to Dublin too. He might be up after us after a few weeks.' I can feel my heart sinking. That wasn't a part of the plan at all. There isn't room for Peadar in the dream.

As the afternoon turns to early evening, Evelyn takes a phone call from the owner of the café, who says he has located the portfolio against the radiator, with Evelyn's phone number on a sticker on the front. She tells him he can keep the pieces and put them up in his café or sell them if he wants to. We do end up missing the train, and we stay out all night until the station reopens in the morning. We sit with our backs against the cold exterior wall, eating cheeseburgers, and I watch out for creeps as Evelyn dozes for short stretches. As long as we get a story out of it, it's worth doing. I'm feeling buzzed and contented resting against the cold wall, until the thought strikes me: I wonder why it was Maeve that Evelyn painted, and not me.

We're celebrating after finishing our school exams. Evelyn has us trampling after her through the woods. 'Would you ever come on, Katie,' she calls, rolling her body over the top of a vertical cliff riddled with tree roots. 'You're awful fucking slow.' Aidan and Peadar have gone up ahead of us with carrier bags of beer. Clouds of midges are papping my face and cluttering my sight, and the strap of the camera is raising a welt on my neck. Maeve's made an easy job of the climb, already peering over the edge.

The front door of the cottage is forced inward and bulging with damp. Great sheets of paisley wallpaper have rolled off the walls, a surge of mud has reached the foot of the stairs and there's a wide, gaping hole in the roof as though an almighty boulder has been dropped through it. Someone has gathered five musty armchairs in a circle beneath the gaping hole. 'Ta-da,' says Evelyn, sweeping her hand before us. 'Secret IRA hideout. I told ye.'

'How'd you know about this place?' asks Peadar, impressed. He runs his fingers through his heavy fringe.

'Dad told me about it when I was young. It belonged to his uncle. We'll be watching the stars soon,' she says proudly. We sink into the damp, stinking chairs. As the minutes roll by, the starry sky emerges in its fullness, and we can see thousands of white stars from our unusual vantage point. 'Isn't this unreal,' she says, clinking her beer bottle against all of ours before regaling us with the story of her great

84

uncle Timothy, who beat two Black and Tans unconscious with a yard brush. It's Evelyn who's brought all of this about. I could never think to do something like this without her. She has a way of being magical and unexpected. What would I be doing with myself if I didn't have Evelyn for a best friend.

Even Aidan has some amusement out of the evening. 'You've some gift for storytelling,' he says, chuckling lightly and taking a sip of his beer. It's good for him to be having a drink and taking his mind off things. I catch myself looking at him, to see if guilt can manifest in a person's face, to see if you can read it in a person, but there isn't the least hint of malevolence.

Evelyn has a good one about Maeve. When Maeve was small, Evelyn says, she was a friend of the crows. Tom taught her to make the habit of leaving a crust of bread or a piece of raw meat out in the yard. Up to ten crows used to come into the yard at a time, and Maeve would venture out with an offering of one kind or another. She kept it up for a few weeks, and the crows began to leave things in the yard for her: a raffia bow, a half crown coin, a bent nail. Maeve nods excitedly as Evelyn tells the story. 'It's true,' Maeve says, perking up, confident now. 'They're clever that way. They bring presents to keep you generous. I've all the bits and pieces in a tin box. They're keepsakes.' Maeve likes to be drawn into the conversation; it doesn't happen too often when we're with the two lads.

'That's gas. I'd love to see them,' I say, bemused.

'Did you keep on feeding the crows?' enquires Aidan.

'I didn't. I left it a few days and they came onto the window sill in the kitchen and started hammering on the glass with their beaks. Mam got afraid of them so I had to stop.'

'Jesus,' says Peadar disinterestedly. I can tell by his tone that he thinks it's a dry, daft story, and Maeve clamps her mouth shut after that. Evelyn makes a face at Peadar, raises her eyebrows meaningfully, and they announce that they're going around the back exploring. They're gone a while. On their return, Peadar is holding a lit cigarette and drawing off it before passing it over to Evelyn.

'When did you start smoking?' I say, gawping at her.

'I've been smoking for years,' she says. The cigarette suits her, like a new hairstyle or a set of earrings. The blue smoke curls up around her face.

'You have not.'

'I have, I said. You don't know everything I do be up to.'

Peadar has a flashlight with him, and we walk from room to room. The paint on the walls is chalky and leaves a residue on our hands. There's a scalloped orange fungus attached to a stack of books, a gigantic tree root shifting the floor tiles in the kitchen, and the windows are laden with silt. *Tsch.* I tug on a cupboard door, revealing enamelled bowls and plates stacked carefully for their next use. *Tsch.* The cutlery on the countertop is crusted arsenic green. The clock in the hallway is stopped at half past three and the glass dome holds droplets within it. The curtains are paper-like and full of jagged holes. *Tsch.* I want Evelyn to see me getting good use out of the camera. I had to get a special book out of the library to learn how to use it, and I've only just got the hang of it.

'Would you say there are any guns left lying around the place?' asks Aidan, meandering about in the hallway. Evelyn opens her mouth to reply, when all of an instant we hear loud clomping strides across the wooden landing above.

'What's that?' Maeve cries, clutching her palms to her face. Peadar's flashlight whirls in the darkness, picking out our whitened faces. He spins the beam to the top of the stairs, where Mickey Cassidy's hobbling from one soft wooden step to the next, clutching the loose banister for support. He's wearing a sleeveless vest and checked skate shorts, and his white-blond hair is sticking out all over his head. His red wet mouth is contorted with gross amusement, the force of his laughter like a possession.

'This is a nice comfortable spot ye have here,' he gurgles, his shoulders shaking with giddy mirth.

'You fuckin' tosspot, Mickey,' rails Peadar. 'We should tie you to the banisters and leave you for a week.'

'I gave ye a good scare,' Mickey says, jubilant. 'Didn't I give ye a good scare?'

'You did, Mickey. I thought I was going to die with the fright,' admits Maeve.

'How did you follow us?' asks Aidan. 'How'd you get upstairs?'

'Is there a rope in the place?' Peadar's neck is turning hard and red. 'I'll soon tie him up.'

'Give him the torch and let him off.'

I can sense the fury emanating from Evelyn, the air charging about her. Her face gains a serenity that masks the rage beneath, the faintest of smiles appearing and crinkling the corners of her mouth. 'Go home, Mickey. Go home now or I swear to God.' It must be hard-going for Evelyn having Mickey for a brother. At least Robert has a semblance of sense.

'Take your time,' Aidan advises as Mickey makes for the bulging door. 'Don't fall.' Peadar fires an empty beer bottle at Mickey's ankle and misses, and we hear Mickey blathering away to himself out in the woods and then nothing.

'What's wrong with him anyway?' spits Peadar. 'What's he diagnosed with?' Evelyn looks humiliated, looks to the ground, and Peadar fumes, his shoulders rising and falling with the heavy breathing. Aidan hands him a beer and he wrenches the cap off it with his teeth. We all flinch. 'Fuckin' special. That's what he is.'

'Does that not hurt your teeth?' I blurt.

'Your teeth get used to it. It makes them stronger.'

'That's bullshit,' mutters Aidan.

'What did you say?'

'I said that's *bullshit*.'

Peadar puts his hand in his shirt pocket, paws around and pulls it out again. 'I've something for you, fella. I found something you'd be very interested to see.' He opens his hand to reveal a writhing collection of worms and woodlice. 'Behold. The remains of Pamela Cooney.' He lets out a strong, cruel laugh that comes from deep inside him.

Aidan smacks the underneath of Peadar's palm and the worms and woodlice go flying. 'Fuck you, Peadar. Fuck you anyway,' he cries, choking back emotion, and my heart fills up with pity and love for him.

We have a big job to convince Aidan to come to the Saint Ambrose Debs' Ball. Evelyn and Peadar and Maeve gather around him and squeeze him about the shoulders. 'Don't mind people being nasty. All that talk is dying down,' Evelyn says.

'It won't be the same without you,' Maeve says.

'Everyone's got a date already. Who'd want to go with me?' Aidan says, his blond head hung low, his shoulders narrow with dejection. I'm emotionally wounded myself to see him in such a way.

'I would,' I say, my pulse quickening. 'I'd go with you.' There's a moment's pause as Aidan lifts his eyes to me.

'I'll go, so,' he says with a grateful expression. Evelyn and Peadar cheer loudly, and Maeve smiles with her teeth clamped together.

I'm wearing a lavender satin dress one of my cousins had for being a bridesmaid, and I'm pleased enough with how I've dolled myself up. Evelyn's steady hand has applied my make-up, and we've copied a hairstyle from a magazine: a crown of twists embedded with crystal pins. It's been sprayed with a full tin of Mammy's hairspray, and Evelyn is certain that no amount of dancing will disturb it.

Aidan lands down in a silver Toyota, looking gallant in a rented tuxedo. Terry bought the car off Desmond Duignan, who's gone to California for the summer, and Peadar and Aidan have the use of it whenever they want. 'You scrub up well,' he says to me, rolling down the window, the flicker of admiration on his face.

'Thanks,' I say shyly, slipping into the passenger seat, and hoping the fake tan will disguise the red flush creeping up my chest and neck.

He takes a deep breath and holds on to it as we enter into the ballroom. The sensation of my arm in his is electrifying. I'm aching to know if this is the commencement of a relationship, the cusp of something momentous. I'm aching for Aidan to know my heart, and for me to know his.

Several people come towards us as we make our entrance. Fellas from the football team and their girlfriends. 'Good man, Aidan,' one of them says, giving a light punch. 'When are you coming back to the team?'

'I'll be back one of the days soon.'

Myself and Aidan are gazing across the bedazzled crowd in search of Evelyn, Peadar and Maeve, when Kenneth Geraghty comes bounding over towards us. Kenneth has a gap in his front teeth and a widow's peak, and he always smells of decaying bananas. His father owns Geraghty's Newsagent's, where they sell overripe bananas for half price. 'We thought you might unearth Pamela Cooney for the Debs' Ball,' jeers Kenneth.

Aidan rears up at him. 'I'll kill you.'

Evelyn stumbles into the fray wearing a red bustier and flared floor-length skirt from a boutique in Galway. 'Don't engage with him, Aidan. He's only messing with you. He's only rising you. Don't give him the satisfaction,' she calls out as an alcopop slips from her hand onto the tiles, the fizzing liquid shooting out in a spray against the mahogany panelling.

Aidan is full of agitation, his face straining, his eyes watering with emotion. Peadar wrestles him clear of Kenneth, straightens his jacket and tie for him. 'Keep it together, man. Keep it together. What am I always telling you? Kicking off will only make things worse.' Aidan clenches his jaw, and forces Peadar away from him.

'Poor Aidan,' I murmur to Maeve, who's suddenly materialised in a pink high-necked creation. 'No matter how much time goes by, people won't let him get on with his life.' We attend to the dance floor for 'Rock the Boat', and our dresses soak up beer and dirt.

'He's gone,' Evelyn shouts in my ear.

'Wha'?'

'Aidan's gone home.' I've deluded myself. I'm not enough of a draw for Aidan to stick it out and stay on for the evening. I feel like a sham in the old bridesmaid dress, and the crystal pins have begun dropping out onto the floor. The hairstyle couldn't even withstand 'Rock the Boat'.

The rest of the night is a washout, and I'm disturbed to see Peadar drinking shots with Daithí and Donnacha Cooney at half past midnight. You get the feeling that Peadar would say and do anything to keep the right people feeling friendly towards him. I feel badly for Maeve too, who's pinned to the wall with Kenneth's tongue down her throat, and him mauling her. The state of the pair of them. It's a pity she doesn't have much going for her, but what can be done about it.

'Katie.'

My stomach tightens. My heart gadunks.

'I'm here to say sorry. About the other evening.' Aidan's called to the house to see me and he's standing under the porch looking sheepish. 'I'm sure you had a line of fellas waiting to ask you to go with them. And you went to so much trouble. I fucked it all up.'

'It wasn't much trouble.' I'm smiling apologetically, as though I'm the one in the wrong.

'You didn't have to take me along but you did, and all I could think about was myself.'

'I had a great night, sure.'

'I wouldn't mind, but I know exactly what he's like. He's an arsehole with drink on him. He's an arsehole without drink as well.'

'It was natural to react as you did.'

'I'm sorry anyway. I shouldn't have stormed off,' he says, grimacing and scratching his ear. 'It won't be long now until we're all going our separate ways.'

It hasn't really struck me before now. We're hurtling towards the end of it all. We're about to embark on a new adventure, and take a new trajectory.

'It'll be strange alright,' I say.

'You're going up to Dublin.'

'I am. I got the letter this morning. What's on the cards for yourself?'

'Sports science. Sligo. Peadar said he'd batter me if I didn't apply for something.'

'What's he hoping to do himself?'

'You wouldn't know by him. He's changeable. He's even thinking of joining up with the Cassidys, like Dad, and driving for them. He said the money is decent and he'd get to see a bit of the world. He might go on to college in a few years' time.' Is he only stringing Evelyn along with talk of going to Dublin? He mightn't go at all yet. It'd suit me fine if he didn't go.

'Each to their own. I think he'd enjoy it.'

'We must all make the effort to meet up from time to time,' he says wistfully.

'We must. Good luck, Aidan.' He opens his mouth, and closes it, and then he turns his back and he's gone. I suppose he only sees me as a friend.

Mammy says I'll never feel as intensely as I feel now, at the age that I am. She says the emotion gets worn out of a person. It sounds like a comfort to have the emotion worn out of you.

I hadn't heard from Evelyn in three days. It was most unlike her, as she was always phoning me up and wanting me to call in to see her. It turned out she got a letter telling her she hadn't been successful in getting into the art college. Alma offered to go up to Dublin to try and sort it out. Mammy heard from Alma that Evelyn had threatened suicide. She'd been screaming and crying, wouldn't eat or sleep, and was out of her mind. Alma said she had to call Doctor Fitz to go into the house and sedate her. Doctor Fitz is the doctor in Glenbruff, an old man who never formally retired, and the elderly people still go to him, but anyone with a bit of sense goes out of the town to the medical centre in Adragule.

It's a hot day, but Evelyn is lying in bed wearing a tracksuit and a dressing gown over it. She's spun herself around in the sheets and she's facing the wall, her long hair splayed across the pillow. She looks small and vulnerable and bundled up. Your heart would break for her. 'Evelyn,' I say, kneeling gingerly by the side of the bed.

'Mm.'

'I heard the bad news.'

'Mm.'

'It's not the end of the world, you know.' I place my hand on her shoulder, and she turns and has a glassy look in her eyes. She's been put on something awful strong. It's like she's been hit with a poison dart.

'My life is over,' she whimpers, dry-mouthed.

'Don't say that. You can still do everything you want to do. You can apply again in a year.'

She takes a deep breath. 'I'm not spending a year of my life fucking around trying to get onto a fucking course. I don't even want to go there any more. The facilities were shit. The interview people were dicks and the pubs were shit. Fuck them all.'

'Okay, well, what do you think you'd like to do instead?'

'I don't fucking know, do I. I can't have a conventional life. I'll die.'

'What about the teaching?' I quip.

'Fucking teachers,' she cries and laughs and hiccups all at once. 'Totalitarian bitches.'

'Do you know what, I'm not a bit worried about you, Evelyn Cassidy. I know you're going to figure it out. You're going to surprise us all. You're going to make it one day.'

'Do you think so?'

'I know so. You're pure magic, so you are.' She's pure magic. I've always felt it. I've always believed in Evelyn Cassidy.

'Thanks, Katie. Will you go out and get Mam to make me a cup of tea and bring in the Rich Tea biscuits.' I still believe that Evelyn will achieve greatness in one guise or another. Once the sedatives wear off, and she shakes off the pain of rejection, she'll go on to do something unexpected. Something outlandish. Remarkable. She has that sort of an aura about her. You couldn't help but believe in her.

It happens some days later that Pearl Powers phones up Amperloc on Evelyn's behalf, and they offer her a contract in the customer care department. 'I'll do it for a short while. Put a few bob together and move up to Dublin. I won't be long after you.' I think Evelyn has plenty of money for moving up to Dublin. All she has to do is ask Dan. Any time Dan was in Angelo's he had big rolls of money stuffed in his trouser pockets, and he'd make a scene out of peeling off a fresh, crisp note.

'Fantastic.'

'Don't be kissing anyone's hole while you're up there. And don't get into any five-year lease or anything because we'll be getting our own place.'

'Alright, boss.' If the dream means as much to Evelyn as it does to me, I've no need to worry.

Evelyn has decided that she wants to go and see the Vaudeville. 'We'll only go for an hour. Come on,' she pleads. 'We'll pull up, and we'll walk around, and then we'll head off again. Sure, what else are we doing. I'm bored stiff.'

'How are we getting there?'

'I'll get Peadar or Aidan to take us,' she says smugly, having triumphed over me.

'Is Maeve coming?'

'Ah no. She'd shit herself.'

My parents had met at the Vaudeville, the only dance hall for miles around. Hundreds of young people used to come there from all over the county and beyond. Daddy would cycle to the Vaudeville all the way from Glenbruff, and Mammy would get a lift over from Adragule when she was down home from Dublin and visiting her family. 'People got very dressed up,' Mammy told me. 'They had a photographer taking pictures of couples and gangs of friends. He used to develop them in a darkroom out the back and you could buy them at the end of the night. Myself and Hillary were in our element.' Mammy hasn't kept any of the photographs, and Daddy won't talk about the Vaudeville at all. On a Saturday night in December 1980, there was a tragic fire killing eighteen young people. Daddy was there, and a cousin of his, Bríd Devane, had died. Bríd was a wilful girl of fifteen who hadn't permission to go out for the night, but she went along anyway when her parents were gone up to bed.

'Where's Peadar?' Evelyn enquires, and Aidan shrugs. *Dunno.* Aidan's not nearly as friendly as he used to be. He's gone awfully sullen. Something of him has been lost. Only last week Father Christopher postponed all upcoming football matches between Glenbruff and Saint Malachy's Parish. The rivalry between the two communities has taken a sinister turn: Donnacha and Daithí Cooney have been hoicking gobs of phlegm at Aidan on the pitch, and a fifteen-year-old forward has had his collarbone broken. The clubhouse has been broken into and the wiring torn out of it, and someone did their business on top of a bench.

A fence has been erected around the Vaudeville, a rectangular block with scorched walls. The roof is burned away, or fallen in. I can't tell from where I'm standing. The casing on an old neon sign is still attached to the front wall, though the lettering has faded off it. A notice says: PRIVATE PROPERTY NO TRESPASSING.

'Come on. We'll go in,' Evelyn says, gazing at the blackened building beyond the fence. I can feel my heartbeat in my throat. A cold sweat rises across my shoulders and in the dip of my back.

'We'll be trespassing,' I say weakly. I imagine Daddy as a young man running for the exit and colliding with flailing limbs, and flames leaping over the fabric ceiling. I imagine desperate people fighting to get into the building to find siblings and friends and neighbours and being restrained. I imagine bodies covered with coats laid out on the gravel.

'It's only an aul sign,' she says. I walk behind her, hyper-aware of every step I'm taking. The gravel in the car park is wild with papery red poppies and assorted weeds. I'm fearful that I'll see a flutter ahead of me, the flash of a spectre.

'I'd prefer to stay out here. Ye go on ahead. Don't be too long,' Aidan mutters, jamming his hands in his pockets before stalking briskly to the car.

Myself and Evelyn make our way inside the Vaudeville. We trudge about the space, the sunken floor like a green lagoon. Ferns have sprung up, dock leaves with burgundy stems, and ivy-like plants straggle along the ground, all emitting a green glow. Our footsteps snap broken glass. I lean down and take a picture of the melted sole of a shoe set in a scrap of old lino. *Tsch.*

'You must show me the pictures when you get them developed. There might be orbs.'

'What's an orb?'

'It's how a spirit looks when you take a picture of it. Like a ball of light. This is the sort of a place that'd be a portal to another dimension. It's a place of significance.' She strolls about, nonchalantly kicking the ground. 'I'd be watchful of him, you know,' she says, like an afterthought.

'Who? Aidan?'

'I'd say he had something to do with it. With Pamela's disappearance.'

I look at her, puzzled. 'Sure, we know Aidan wouldn't have done anything like that.'

'I think we should be careful under the circumstances,' she says, darting her eyes and lowering her voice. 'A cold-blooded killer doesn't require a motive.'

'He has an alibi, hasn't he?'

'Alibi, my hole. It's only Peadar saying Aidan came in the door at ten past seven. Saying they sat down together and watched the *Late Late Show* from beginning to end. They're brothers anyway, so it doesn't count.' A bird flaps out of a hollow in the wall. 'You've a thing for Aidan. You don't see what everyone else can see. You don't know what he's really like.'

'I do not have a thing for him. I never said I had a thing for him.' What is it that everyone else can see? What's Aidan really like?

'You don't need to say it. You're a pure spa when he's anywhere near you.'

'I am not. Go away out of that.'

As we drive away from the Vaudeville, inching along the ruined road, I think of the people rushing over fields, leaping over ditches and raising the alarm at houses nearby. I think of the Ford Granada squad cars coming at speed, their sirens wailing.

From the back seat, I can see the reflection in the rear-view mirror. I see Aidan's face, intent and watchful, and Evelyn dipping her head to inspect her split ends.

There's an old story about the Vaudeville. That if you're driving by at night and look into your rear-view mirror you might see a phantom passenger in the back seat. Someone looking to get home after the big fire. There's people who've sworn to have had the phantom passengers and they've never been right after it.

We've a banger of an olive-coloured car that takes a few goes to get started. Daddy has to *wom-wom-wom* with his shoe on the accelerator, and it's a risky manoeuvre as the car has been known to shoot off unexpectedly. We can't park in car parks in case the car bolts forward and hits another car, or even a person, and it goes without saying that it's too much of a gamble to go all the way up to Dublin in it. I end up saying my goodbyes to Mammy and Daddy at the train station in Glenbruff.

'You're just as good as any of them,' Daddy says. 'Let nobody think they're any better than you.'

'Have a fresh start, Katie,' Mammy says. 'Go off and enjoy yourself. And no matter what happens, don't be rushing home. There's nothing here for you.' I peck Daddy on the cheek and I embrace Mammy and then I board the train. I spy Dylan Hartigan a few seats ahead of me and take a magazine and raise it up in front of my face. There's nothing worse than being trapped in conversation with a dry person on a train.

With the journey underway, I think about Evelyn staying behind and going to work in Amperloc, the same as Maeve is doing. It's a pity she couldn't come up to Dublin at the same time as myself, but it looks like she'll be up before long. I think of Aidan going to college in Sligo, starting a new life for himself, and Peadar getting a licence to drive an arctic truck around France and Spain. And I think of Pamela Cooney, who's either someplace and dancing, or no place and dead. I wonder if we'll ever know one way or another. It's a full eight months since she vanished, and the more time that goes by, the less she crosses my mind. Her name is as flimsy as 'Princess Diana'; when I hear mention of Pamela Cooney, the words glide past me with little effect. The only hint of her now is a cellophane cone of crispy brown roses left down by the handball alley.

I'm regularly lost on the university campus. I have to consult a map with minuscule triangles and tiny shoe prints, and I end up in the wrong place. I feel like a blood cell rushing in a vein, coasting past countless faces and bodies. A crescendo of noise bookends each lecture, and the halls are enormous caverns, with rows upon rows of broad-smiling strangers. I turn to three or four people and say that I didn't catch the bit about the exam, or ask what was the name of the book mentioned, and I get to know the odd person that way, but I feel a bit daft for doing it. Most of the girls at university have come up in big numbers from the same Dublin schools and go around in ready-made middle-class gangs of friends, and it seems they've their friends already made and don't need any more.

I share an apartment with the Creighton twins, Nuala and Norma, in a high-rise in Stillorgan. Their father is a big dairy farmer and he bought the apartment for them. The place reeks of the chemical scent of hair removal cream and the vinegar tang of cheap synthetic clothing. They'd another girl in the room for a week before me, but she turned out to be a safety hazard. The girl left a boiling egg on the hob until it exploded and blew a hole in the plaster ceiling. 'It went off like a grenade,' Norma said as she was showing me around the place. 'We couldn't trust her after that. We had to show her the door.'

Nuala and Norma are from New Ross, and they are thin, anodyne girls with curly hair and pointed noses who never have any luck meeting fellas. Norma has a high forehead and a Filofax and Nuala has neither. They're humourless. Like a pair of wet logs in a fire, the spark of devilment won't catch. Nuala and Norma say that country girls have to stick together up in Dublin, and look out for one another, which is a nice sentiment but borderline forceful. Nonetheless, they're good-natured girls and Nuala in particular is easy to talk to. 'I don't know if I belong up here at all. I feel like I don't fit in,' I find myself telling her.

'Everyone has that feeling. Myself and Norma are in the same boat. You're only up a wet week. You have to give it time.' Nuala's ironing a pair of jeans inside out. I've never known anyone to iron their jeans. I can't see the point of it.

'I don't want to give it time.'

'That sort of thinking is no use to you. You can't live in...where did you say?'

'Glenbruff.'

Nuala screws up her features and sets the iron aside, a heft of steam rising from it. 'Didn't a girl turn up missing down there not so long ago?' I don't know how could a person turn up and be missing as well.

'I don't know too much about it.'

'Well. As I was saying. You can't live in Glenbruff for the rest of your life. You left for a reason. This is a new chapter. You have to make the most of it.'

'I don't know, Nuala. I'm finding it hard.'

'That's why us country girls have to stick together,' she says resolutely, heaving the iron back and forth. 'You can hang out with myself and Norma. We're going to go out every week. We'll be the ones in demand, wait and see.' I can't see how Nuala and Norma will ever be in demand.

'It's just weird being here without my friend. We're supposed to be up here together.'

'She hasn't died, you know. You'll make plenty of friends yet. Haven't you made friends with myself and Norma?' I nod out of courtesy. It'll be great when Evelyn moves up to Dublin. We'll find our own place, and get the show on the road for once and for all.

'How are you getting on?' Mammy enquires on the phone. 'Have you made any nice friends?'

'No. I haven't. Not one.'

'Ah, sure. You just haven't met the right people yet.'

'Mm.'

'I suppose you're missing the Cassidy girl.'

'Mm. I am.' I'm missing her badly.

'Evelyn Cassidy is the sort of a person who likes to be a big fish in a small pond. The likes of her will never leave Glenbruff. She'd be too afraid of becoming a nobody.'

I hope Mammy's wrong, but she's often right.

'When are you coming down to see us?' Evelyn's phoned between lectures. It's bad timing. They're after changing the lecture hall to another building, and they won't allow us in if we're late.

'Christmas, I'd say.'

'Christmas,' she exclaims. 'Jesus. That's ages away.'

'I'll never settle in if I'm always running home.'

'I suppose,' she says, sighing. 'I'll come up to you, so. I'll tell them I'm sick.'

'Do that. I'd better go anyway. I've a lecture.'

Dry autumn leaves skate around our feet. Evelyn and myself meander through the campus amidst thousands of students milling about in their new college outfits. 'Look at them all,' she says disdainfully. 'Look at them all dressed the same and thinking the same thoughts.' The student bar is thronged with fresh-faced first years yammering in excited registers, and everywhere there are student union representatives in fluorescent T-shirts passing out flyers for societies and foam parties. Evelyn rams her index fingers in her ears. 'Let's just go into town and have a real night out,' she says, shuffling from one foot to the other.

'I told the twins I'd head out with them tonight. Why don't you come with us?'

'I'm not going out with that pair of fannies.' She's handed a flyer, which she promptly scrunches in a ball and drops onto the ground.

We take the bus into town and go to a few of the upmarket bars, the likes of which we've never been to before, all velvet damask wallpaper and electronic dance music. 'This is more like it,' she says loudly, flicking her hair over her shoulder and looking around the place. It is more like it, in fairness.

In the course of our conversation, I'm careful not to make too much of my new university experience. I don't tell her that I'm learning about art history and film history, and I don't talk to her about the mind-bending complexities of criticism, and how it seems to me that some film-makers and artists only come up with their rationale after having created their films and art in order to make themselves out to be intentionally adroit rather than accidental geniuses.

I don't tell her that I've signed up for the Film Society, and that I attended a screening of a Tarkovsky film called *Mirror*, and I've never seen anything like it. The woman sitting on the wooden fence, gazing out at the pastel pastoral and smoking a cigarette. The sound of country silence that isn't silence at all, only nature's whisper and the breathing of the ground. The film has me thinking of Glenbruff. Panoramas of navy-green trees and irresistible meadows vibrating with life. Evelyn won't have heard of Tarkovsky, and I hadn't either until last week. If I told her there's a difference between a movie and a film, she'd say I was raving.

It isn't long before Evelyn relays something that's happened Maeve. Maeve left a note under the statue of Saint Jude in the church in Glenbruff, asking him to help her to find her mother, and just last week Maeve's birth mother sent her a letter saying she wanted to see her. This incident makes Maeve more intriguing to us. We think it would be good for her to meet her mother, and it might change Maeve for the better. It might bring her *closure*, and help to bring her along socially. 'She hasn't got a lot going for her. It could be the making of her,' Evelyn says.

'At least we have a bit of get-up-and-go to us,' I say, feeling sorry for Evelyn still saddled with Maeve in Glenbruff. The bond cemented with Maeve might be altogether inescapable. 'How are the lads getting on?'

'Aidan's gone up to Sligo. We haven't heard from him. Peadar's working for Dad for a few months to see if he likes it.'

'Right. Good.'

'I wish you'd just come back to Glenbruff with me,' she says after a few drinks, jabbing a slice of lemon at the bottom of her glass with a straw.

'I can't go back,' I say. 'I'm in college now.' She can't think I'd give up the whole lot to return to Glenbruff. There's nothing for young people down there.

'You're missing out. We've trips organised. We're going ghost hunting at the famine workhouse. We're going out camping on Doona Island.' I've never even heard of Doona Island. It sounds made-up. I'd say there's no trips organised at all. 'I never ask you for anything. I'm always doing things for you. Taking you places. Giving you ideas. The camera.' What can she mean, *giving me ideas*?

'I thought you were to come up here.'

'I'll come up when I'm ready to come up.' She crosses her arms and turns to face the lit-up display of vodka bottles behind the bar. 'You've changed since you've been up here, you know. I used to get a buzz off you but I don't any more.' The words are like stones flying out of her mouth and belting my skin. How have I changed? I wonder. Is it bad to change? Is it wrong to follow the dream after all we've discussed? And whatever about the art college, couldn't she still get the job in a cool bar at night and work an internship during the day? And how is it that she had a way of making you think you could do anything at all, but she hasn't managed to do very much or go very far herself?

Might it be too soon for her to be up in Dublin, confronted with all the young people embarking on new lives, or might it be that the flame of friendship is beginning to sputter. I have a magnificent terror that she's saying goodbye to me in her own way, and there might be no coming back from it.

The student grant doesn't stretch too far. I take part-time work as a chambermaid in the Liffey Hotel in the city centre, a budget hotel catering to all and sundry. I have to turn around eighteen rooms on the fourth floor in three hours on a Saturday, and again on a Sunday. It's back-breaking work, lugging heavy bath towels and vacuuming deep under beds, pulling fresh sheets taut across mattresses and scrubbing toothpaste spittle off bathroom sinks, mirrors and even walls. I have to wear a bright blue tunic with a name badge on it, and wide-legged pants, and wide-fitting shoes with metal toecaps. The weekend work prevents me from heading down home to Glenbruff, but Mammy and Daddy don't appear to mind. 'We're all fine here. There's no news, nothing happening. Keep the head down.'

Not long after I start the job, I'm pushing a cart loaded with cleaning products along the corridor when I see Dan Cassidy coming out of one of the rooms. I dip down and bend my head and pretend to rummage through the detergents, and he walks past me with an attractive young woman holding several shopping bags. The young woman isn't much older than myself and Evelyn. I had an inkling that Dan Cassidy might be that kind of a person alright.

I'm on Grafton Street, drifting by the flower sellers and dodging a glut of Spanish students wearing matching backpacks. I double-take. Is it…? *Yes*. It's Maeve. Just a few feet away, in a chic camel-coloured coat, and gazing in the window of a jewellery shop. A woman joins her. A tall woman. This is no Mary Lynch. This woman is coiffed, and younger, and more radiant than any of the mothers I know. Blonde in a long black coat with black spike-heeled boots. I can see a close resemblance between the pair of them. Even a brief sighting gives it away. Maeve is flushed and healthy-looking, as though she's imbibed some kind of elixir. She seems altered to me, poised by the edge of the street. Her grey-blue eyes are flashing and rimmed with black pencil. Her hair is thick and long, a dark shining auburn shade. Maeve and her mother enter the jewellery shop together, and a flare of winter sun strikes the glass door.

I can't get over it. Maeve, of all people, in a beautiful coat, drifting into a jewellery shop on Grafton Street with her regal-looking mother. I've seen it all now.

It's Christmas Eve. Glenbruff is judderingly cold. The sky is crossed with clouds like wildebeest, and the air tainted by the wide-scale burning of turf.

Robert lands down to collect me from the train station. A tangerine sliver of sun rests on the horizon as we course along roads lined with bare black trees, the fields and bogs waterlogged beyond them. 'Anything strange or startling?' I ask of him.

'Fuck all,' he says, twirling the volume on the car radio. 'How's Dublin treating you? How's the course?'

'It's tough-going. We've to watch an awful lot of films, and write about them and talk about them.'

'Jesus,' he says, giving the side eye, and it's there and then I resolve not to discuss the course at all while I'm down home if people are so inclined to be dismissive. 'I was talking to Peadar Morley. He's invited us up to the house on Stephen's Night.'

'I'm on for that. Will you go yourself?'

He shrugs his shoulders. It's doubtful he'll go to the party. He's never had much in the way of Christmas spirit.

In a low voice, he asks, 'How's that friend of yours?'

'Who?'

'Maeve Lynch. Is she seeing anyone?'

'I don't think so. I doubt it,' I say, shifting uncomfortably in the passenger seat. 'I thought you said she was a head-the-ball.'

'I don't remember saying that. She's a nice-looking girl these days.'

'Is she not a bit old for you?'

'Sure, there's only a year between us. I can't see a problem.' The thoughts of Robert meeting up with Maeve. Stepping out with her. Falling in love with her and marrying her. I have the feeling that someone's stepped over my grave.

I'm not long in the door when Mammy informs me that Johnny Grealish had a stroke the day prior, and he's lost the power of speech. He's been put in a spotlessly clean room in the regional hospital, and after that he's to be put up at Saint Fintan's Psychiatric Hospital on a permanent basis. 'They only agreed to take him in because he's lost the speech. Can you believe that.' Mammy is well acquainted with Johnny Grealish. She says that everyone's a bit mad, it's just some people are better at keeping a lid on it. Johnny Grealish has been in and out of Fintan's several times over the years. He's offended the nurses, the chaplain, the other patients and their visitors. On his most recent stay, he soiled himself deliberately and leapt about the ward laughing as the nurses chased after him. Mammy says he loved the attention. At night-time Johnny cried over his two brothers who burned to death at the Vaudeville, and his arm and his ear that he lost in the fire. The nurses took him to the therapy room, but it was a futile exercise; he could never make sense of his life and all that had happened to him. Johnny was only spouting the same tragic stories on repeat. The stroke will put an end to the stories.

Aidan's at Midnight Mass, holding a candle embedded in a cardboard circle. The wax is falling on the fronts of his shoes but he doesn't appear to notice. People are whispering that he looks shook. They're saying he dropped out of his college course in Sligo, and went to a rave in a warehouse at Halloween and fried himself and didn't sleep for a week after it. He'll end up in Fintan's too if he's not careful.

On Stephen's Night, I push the white, shrieking iron gate at the front of the Morleys' bungalow and make my way towards the front door. I recognise the familiar cracked flower pots either side of the porch, the dried scrub poking out of them, and one pink flower vibrating in the biting air. I press the doorbell, hearing the low rumble of conversation within the house, and I rap on the window too, unable to hold myself back, wanting to get inside and have my entrance over with. I'm anxiously scuffing my shoes on the rattan mat when Peadar answers the door. He's lanky and cross-looking, dark circles under his eyes, but still good-looking. He's in black jeans and one of his father's old Thin Lizzy T-shirts. 'Peadar. Happy Christmas.'

'Katie. You're lookin' well,' he says, and then Kenneth Geraghty barges his way in in front of me, closely followed by a whooping Mickey Cassidy.

'Where are the *oars-derves*,' Mickey says, rubbing his hands. He has no coat, and his arms and hands are mottled purple with cold.

The house isn't entirely slovenly, but has a sort of a careless look about it; there are clothes drying on radiators and pink-grey towels tossed over the backs of chairs. Crusted casts of dried mud fallen from football boots speckle the hallway. There's hardly a decoration about the place, just a few skimpy Christmas cards slung on a string.

Inside in the sitting room, a gallery of familiar faces turns towards me. They're neighbours, people from school, fellas Aidan used to play football with and their girlfriends. Not one of them rushes forward to greet me.

My face aches with the smiling. It's hard work to look as though you're enjoying a party. Maeve emerges from the kitchen. 'Katie. You're here.' She's like a different person. Her body has lengthened, unlikely as it is. She's had her ears pinned back, and grown her hair long. Her eyebrows and nails are impeccably groomed, but nevertheless, I feel the swell of a familiar, unpleasant sensation: the recoil I've always experienced in her presence.

'Hello, Maeve. It's good to see you.' We lean together and I kiss the air by her cheek, taking in the citrus perfume on her clavicle.

'Can I get you a drink?' she asks demurely.

'Yes. Is there any white wine?' I've become used to drinking white wine with Nuala and Norma on Thursday nights. They call it 'wine o'clock'.

'I don't think so. There might be vodka or whiskey maybe.' I follow Maeve into the kitchen and lean against the sideboard as she takes a glass from the cabinet and a bottle of vodka from the counter. I notice a chic little black-strapped watch with a white face and roman numerals on her ivory wrist. She hands me my drink; it's warm, and the Coke is flat, but I drink it graciously, and another after that. Maeve tells me she's enjoying the work at Amperloc, but she lives for the weekend. 'You know how it is.' She goes on to tell me that she's been meeting with her birth mother, Amanda Dowling, over the past two months. Amanda had Maeve when she was a teenager. She owns a property company called Dexon Green, and she's very involved in philanthropy. Her partner John is very involved in sailing yachts and Maeve's gone out on a yacht with the two of them several times.

'Isn't that unreal. Good for you, Maeve. It's done you the world of good meeting up with Amanda.'

'I know it has. I feel like a different person. I've been spending an awful lot of time with her.'

'I saw you on Grafton Street a few weeks ago. You were with a blonde woman in a long black coat.'

Maeve looks as though she could just die and go to heaven. 'That's Amanda. Isn't she lovely? She got me the watch for my birthday.' She holds up her wrist and the face of the watch catches the light.

'Amanda has a glamorous look about her. You're taking after her, if you don't mind me saying.'

'Thank you, Katie,' she says, before placing her hand on my arm; my skin rises with prickles. 'Will you call up to see me before you go back to Dublin? I want to talk to you about something.'

'Okay. I could call up tomorrow.' I hope to God she won't be asking after Robert.

It's late when Evelyn shows up. She's wearing a denim jacket and a tight black dress, and a black velvet choker round her neck. Her hair whisks around her with every movement, and a cigarette hangs languidly from her lips. I rise from the couch and await her approach. She works her way about the room, hugging the local lads, smashing their cider cans against hers and hooting. Perhaps she hasn't noticed me yet, I try to reason, but deep down I know that she has. Eventually, she turns about and comes to me. 'Katie. I'm so fucking glad to see you.' All at once, we're back as we were, and over the hump. All the agonising for nothing. 'How are the two spastic sisters?' she says, smirking.

'Nuala and Norma.'

'Who else.'

'They're actually fairly sound when you get to know them.'

She lifts her gaze and her eyes rest on Peadar, who's standing by the doorway with Kenneth. Kenneth is enquiring about the result of a match, and Peadar can't remember, but he knows it was Connolly kicked the final point. Peadar says the barriers were broken and there was a bit of a scuffle but it resolved itself after that. 'You can blame Saint Malachy's Parish. They're like caged animals over there.' The matches have recommenced.

Peadar is coaxed to take out his guitar, and he plays and sings 'Working Man's Hero' with an awkward sincerity, perched on the armrest of the couch. Everyone's gathered round, smiling inanely, hoping he'll do himself justice. I can't think of a song any less jolly than 'Working Man's Hero'. Nonetheless, Peadar isn't bad at the old crooning, and he certainly looks the part.

'Myself and Peadar are really close. We hang out all the time. He says I've no need for college at all. He says some people are all they need to be.'

I clear my throat. 'I don't know. I mean, for a lot of people college is like a training ground for specific things.' Evelyn doesn't know what she doesn't know.

'That time I gave you the camera. How'd you learn how to use it?'

'I got a book out of Adragule Library.'

'That's my point. It's about a person's initiative more than anything else. There's a thousand scientific studies saying the same thing.'

Someone unexpected has entered the room during Peadar's performance. It's Stacey Nugent in a faux-fur cropped coat and jeans with a diamanté seam. Stacey's had a weakness for Peadar ever since the glory days behind the clubhouse, and she gives an impassioned cheer at the end of Peadar's playing. 'That was powerful, Peadar,' she gushes. I can sense the upset off Evelyn, her mood curdling.

Kenneth is looking to steal away some of Peadar's acclaim. He rests one elbow on the mantelpiece and opens his mouth. He can't hit the high notes, and he can't hit the low notes, and only barely manages the ones in the middle.

'There's always some gobshite at a party who thinks he can sing,' Evelyn mutters in a choked voice. She slinks out of the doorway and out to the front porch. I follow her, drawing my coat around me and buttoning up to the neck. She takes a box of cigarettes from her denim pocket and lights up with a rasp. The light from a curtained window shows up the fine wrinkles emanating from her eyes and the new creases in her forehead. 'Why don't we just book flights and go over to London?' she says, her lower lip trembling. 'Just me and you. It's what we've always wanted. What's stopping us?'

'Ah no, Evelyn,' I say, swallowing. 'I can't just drop everything.' I'm more committed to university than I realised before. The dream needs a strong foundation.

'Will you not even consider it?'

'No, Evelyn. I can't.' I have the frightening, momentarily exhilarating idea that I may have outgrown Evelyn, and that she's already peaked. I'm the Hillary Bowman in the equation. The idea is immediately followed by the fear that if myself and Evelyn happen to go about the dream separately, it will bring us into competition with one another.

She mashes her cigarette off the pebbledash. 'No problem, Katie. No problem at all. I only thought I'd ask.'

Maeve's small voice pipes up from behind us. 'Stacey Nugent is all over Peadar.'

'Go away inside and don't be annoying me. You're an affliction.' Maeve stands there gawping at the pair of us, and Evelyn pushes past her into the house, cursing under her breath.

I find Aidan sitting in one of two bamboo chairs, the kind with a big fan shape at the back of it, like a shabby tropical throne. He has blinking Christmas lights in a loop around his neck, and the aura of torture about him. He beckons me towards him with a jerk of his jaw. 'Katie. Katie Devane. Come here and sit down until I talk to you.' I've always felt comfortable in Aidan's presence. It was Evelyn set out to plant a seed of doubt about him, but I never allowed it germinate.

'How are you, Aidan? Happy Christmas.' My heart lurches out of its socket as he drapes his left arm over the back of my bamboo chair, and places his right hand down on my thigh.

'You're the best of all of them. You've always been the nicest girl in Glenbruff,' he says, slurring, and his eyes are running all over me. 'The day I called to see you. I wanted to say it then. I hadn't the courage.' He takes a sharp intake of breath, and in a hard, constricted voice, he says, 'I'm losing the head over Pamela. Did she ever say anything to you? Did she ever talk about going somewhere or doing herself in?' I notice the empty bottles scattered about the floor and beneath the chair, and it occurs to me that I'm only a sideshow to a missing girl, and all the life force seeps out of me.

It's later now, and it's dark in the house, except for the twinkling embers in the grate. The sandalwood-scented football players and their girlfriends are long gone, and someone's heaved Aidan off to bed. Evelyn's waiting for Stacey Nugent to clear off, but Stacey's still here, waiting it out. It's clear to all that Evelyn's reluctant to go home for fear of what might happen if Stacey and Peadar are left to their own devices. I wonder now if Peadar's the source of Evelyn's reluctance to move up to Dublin. 'Will you have another drink, Evelyn?' asks Stacey in a simpering voice.

'Don't trouble yourself, Stacey. Have you organised a lift home yet? It's getting on.'

'I'm in no rush, thanks.' Stacey clacks her plastic nails on the side of her glass. 'Will you be heading soon yourself?'

'Oh no,' Evelyn says brusquely, 'I'll be sleeping over.' Stacey has a face on her like she's chewing a wasp.

Kenneth says we're in luck. He has time for one more tune before he hits the road. He takes position by the fireside once again, and he opens his mouth and then his elbow knocks a porcelain deer off the edge of the mantelpiece. It dashes off the tiled surround of the fireplace, and the head topples in on top of the sparkling ash and embers. Aidan appears in the doorway, and he lunges at Kenneth, and takes him by the collar of his shirt. Mickey Cassidy laughs a hair-raising laugh as Kenneth writhes and splutters. Aidan tightens his grip around Kenneth's neck, and Peadar makes a dive for Aidan, wrenching him away from Kenneth. Aidan glares about the room, breathing hard and fast. 'Let them lock me up. Get it over with,' he shouts hoarsely. 'Isn't that what ye're all thinking?'

'That fella's tapped,' Kenneth proclaims, rubbing his neck. His face is wet with tears and snot. 'Ye're all witness to it.'

There's no use picking up the pieces of the porcelain deer. It's shattered completely, the small white pieces lost in the thick carpet pile, and the head turning grey in the hot ash. It was an ornament belonging to Louise Morley, but that doesn't warrant Aidan losing his mind over it.

It's all gone haywire in Glenbruff. I'd have been as well off watching *Die Hard* on television with Robert for the evening.

I take the long way round to Maeve's house on my old bike. I spin through Glenbruff, scanning the weather-worn shop fronts, faded bunting and chipboard stapled onto window frames. I make my way through the monotonous countryside, with its pastures of thick glossy grass and endless stone walls crumbling into ditches. The air is fresh and clean and cold, shocking my lungs and heart with every intake, and the wind whistles past my ears.

I'm wondering why I've been summoned to see Maeve. I suppose I could have made an excuse, but it isn't in my nature. 'I wanted to talk to you about something,' she says, leaning forward, peeling the insipid peach nail varnish off her fingernails and leaving the remnants on a plastic table covering patterned with golden bells and holly wreaths. There are all sorts of Christmas gewgaws on every surface. Holy angels in gaudy muumuus. Silver sleighs with foam parcels.

'Oh-kay,' I say, sitting ramrod in the chair. 'What is it?'

'I feel like it's time for me to move on from Glenbruff. I'm thinking of moving to Dublin in the New Year,' she says, smiling. 'I'm ready to be a different person. Have you ever felt that way?'

'I h-have,' I stammer, before taking a big slug of tea and burning the roof of my mouth. Holy Mother of God. It's like the blood is draining out of my head, like my face is going to slide off with the fright. *Maeve foisted upon me in Dublin!*

'What's it like up there? Do you think I should make the move?'

'Th-that's up to you, Maeve. I mean, Dublin is…it's very different. It's not like walking around Glenbruff and everyone knows you. That's the nice thing about a place like Glenbruff. Everyone looking out for everyone else and asking after you.' It's the last thing I could have anticipated, Maeve moving up to Dublin.

'Right,' she says.

'It's a whole different ball game up in Dublin. I'm telling you. It's full on. Getting used to the public transport and the crowds of people. And the t-tourists all over the place. Not to mention the price of rent.' I can taste iron in the roof of my mouth.

'There's plenty of country people like ourselves up there,' she says, furrowing her eyebrows.

'There are,' I say slowly, 'but it's lonely for the likes of us.'

'I'll have Amanda, sure. And you. Maybe you can introduce me to a few people.'

'I could do that. Still and all, I wouldn't be in a mad panic to uproot your whole life up to Dublin. What does Amanda have to say about it?'

'She doesn't know yet.' Maeve laces her fingers together in her lap and turns her eyes to the kitchen window. The view beyond is of the pine trees and the dirt yard and Tom's tumbledown shed. 'It's not just about Amanda. It's hard to explain. I don't think I'll ever come right in Glenbruff. You know?'

'Mm.'

'Evelyn's caught up with Peadar. You're in university. I feel like it's my turn to do something. Be someone.'

'It sounds like you've your mind made up.'

'I think so. I've the bit of experience in Amperloc under my belt now, so I'll apply for a few jobs and see how I fare out.' We move towards the front door and she opens the latch, and we go out onto the concrete step beneath the hood of the porch. 'It might be wise not to mention anything to Evelyn. She's a bit sore with the way the year has gone for her.' I nod in agreement.

Out on the porch, I can hear the *ark-ark-ark* of the crows beyond in the pine trees, and it reminds me of Evelyn's story, the one she told us in the old cottage. 'If you move up to Dublin, you'll be leaving your good friends the crows behind,' I say, and Maeve laughs. She's not the worst, sure. Going up to Dublin could be the making of her. I'll hardly be seeing her that often, and going for a coffee every once in a while wouldn't kill me. I've been overthinking it entirely. Maeve is harmless, sure.

'I wish Evelyn hadn't told ye that. In front of the lads and everything.'

'Not at all. We found it very interesting. Do you still have the things they left for you?'

'They're out in the shed.'

'Go on and show them to me.'

'They're only bits of rubbish,' she says hesitantly.

'It doesn't matter. I'd like to see them.'

'Alright so.' Maeve pulls on Mary Lynch's woollen coat from the coat stand inside the door, and then we stroll around to the dirt yard and across to the shed. It's smaller than I remember. There's a rusty padlock on the door but it's unlocked.

Inside in the shed I have the sensation that we've disturbed something or someone. Maeve pulls a cord by the door and a single light bulb dangling from the rafters comes on. I notice an old coal sack flung in a corner, the white roots of tubers creeping out of it. I could swear they're moving.

'The tin is around here someplace,' Maeve says, reaching for a high shelf with old paint pots on it and grasping around with her fingers. She takes down a small tin box from the shelf and clips it open. Side by side, we look inside the tin. I see a red raffia bow, a bent nail, an old coin and a small silver pendant. It's a ballet slipper in the midst of the trinkets, with a loop for fixing it onto a necklace. I lean forward, pushing my face closer to the tin.

'Where did you get that from?'

'Get what?'

'The ballet slipper. It's Pamela Cooney's.' My heart is banging behind my ribs.

Maeve turns slowly, her face reddening, her mouth moving like it's full of marbles. 'It's not.'

'It is.'

'We've the same one, so. It must have come from the same shop.' She snaps the tin closed and shoves it deep in the pocket of Mary Lynch's coat. She goes to the door of the shed and yanks the cord, knocking out the light. I follow her out to the dirt yard.

Maeve is harmless. Maeve the Mope is harmless as a dove. I begin walking across the yard and making for the road. 'I'll be seeing you in Dublin, so,' I call shrilly, and wave.

'You will, Katie. The two of us are going to have a great time.'

2
Dublin

I'm wearing one of Norma's polyester blouses and sweating profusely under the arms. It's taken two bus journeys and a taxi to get to Pyro Productions, a production company situated in a sprawling industrial estate to the west of the city. The interview takes place in a room that appears to be a sort of a storage area; there are long cables in primary colours swept into loops and hanging on wall hooks, stacked hard drives with dings along the sides, and tripods draped with spider webs. The ground is strewn with curling yellow call sheets, old clipboards and empty mousetraps.

Bernard, the person who replied to my email enquiring about internships, sits on a metal chair with his legs spread wide. He looks to be in his early thirties, and he's wearing a beanie hat, a black polo-necked jumper and a shark tooth on a cord around his neck. He presses his nicotine-stained fingertips together. 'We're looking for a high-energy individual. Someone who's willing to go the distance.' He has a sort of pout that comes on him intermittently.

'I'm definitely that kind of person. I'm definitely ready for an opportunity like this.'

'The hours are long, Katie. In this industry, that's what we contend with. But there's a real sense of camaraderie here at Pyro. It keeps us pumped. We're all incredibly driven and working towards the same goal. We're here to make high-quality television programming for a discerning market. Is your passport up to date?'

I nod eagerly. 'Yes. Yes it is.' I can't recall the last time I saw my passport. I've never had any use for it. I'll have to ask Mammy to post it to me in a Jiffy bag.

'I like to tell the newbies to keep their passport in their back pocket. That's the way it works around here. Everyone's got to be primed and ready. Up for it.' Bernard clasps his hands behind his neck, arches his back and thrusts his paunch forward. 'I've a good feeling about you, Katie. Come back in on Monday. Early. I'll give you the tour and get you started on the basics. Filling the coffee pot. Sorting the post. We'll bring you in on the production meetings. You'll get a handle on how things are done. Meet the producers. The directors.' Holy God. I'm after doing what I set out to do. 'Once you know the ropes, it's easier to branch out into research, or directing if that's your thing. It takes time, but it's entirely possible.'

I've done it. I've actually done it. I'm in. 'Brilliant. Brilliant, Bernard,' I say, unable to conceal the elation.

'You know, a lot of people at Pyro started out as interns. Myself included.'

'That's very encouraging. What do you do here now?'

'I, uh, work across several projects. Lots of stuff in development. Lots of stuff waiting to be green-lit,' he says, rubbing the side of his nose with his thumb.

'Right. Brilliant.'

'Any questions for me.'

'I suppose I'm wondering what made you want to meet with me over anyone else. You must get lots of emails like mine.'

'I can always tell who's keen and who's not. I can always tell who's got a lot to offer.'

Holy God. 'That's amazing. Thank you.' I'm reeling with delight. 'Thank you so much.'

'I've been around the block a couple of times. Worked on a lot of the big productions over the years. I can make things happen for people like you.' Make things happen. Holy God.

'Thank you, Bernard.'

'Pleasure.' He proffers a warm, damp handshake. 'And so you know, it's fine to wear jeans on Monday, or whatever you're most comfortable wearing.'

I saunter out of the building and into blinding sunlight. I can feel my soul lifting out of my skin. The dream is underway. I get straight on the phone to Nuala. 'I'm in. I got the internship.'

'That's unreal,' she squeals. 'You're going to love it. You'll be on the up from here on out.' We're only a few months finished college, and about to launch ourselves on the world. Knowing Nuala, there'll be a cake from the supermarket on the table this evening and a soppy card about following your heart.

'I know. I'm sick with excitement. I'd better ring home.'

Daddy answers the phone. 'Hello.' I can hear a political debate on the television in the background.

'I got the job.'

'Good girl yourself. Is it well paid?'

'No, Daddy. It's more of an internship. There's no pay involved.'

'I can't see how that will be much use to you.' It would have been better if I'd caught Mammy on the phone instead.

'It's how people start out in the creative industries, Daddy. You do an internship for the experience. Something proper might come out of it afterwards.'

'Is that it. I must be behind the times.'

It's important when you've good news to tell the right people. People who understand the dream or have a dream of their own. Otherwise you end up feeling deflated.

I've made attempts to coax Nuala and Norma to the more eclectic bars and clubs in the city, but it hasn't worked out. Nuala said she didn't mind it too much, but herself and Norma clung to the edge of the bar counter like they were in the deep end of a swimming pool and unable to swim. 'Everyone's out of their minds on drugs in these sorts of places,' Norma exclaimed fretfully, and Nuala appeared to be somewhat afraid of the other patrons: shifting her posture, compulsively glancing over her shoulder, her eyes full of uncertainty. She tried to dance along to the bleeps and bloops, in fairness to her, the curls bouncing up and down like springs, but she couldn't make time with the beat.

'Is the music supposed to do that?'

'Do what?'

'Give you palpitations. I think I'm going to have a heart attack.'

There's no use in pretending. If Evelyn was up in Dublin, we'd be out every night of the week and going to all the best places. The nights out would feel different. They'd be manic and unrestrained. We'd be meeting vibrant people, going to endless parties and rolling in at all hours of the morning. We'd be high as the roof in one another's company.

I often think of her, especially when I'm attending the bad parties with Nuala and Norma. I wonder had she a big party for her twenty-first birthday. I'd say she did. I'd say she went all out, and not a penny was spared. She might have had a caterer and live music, and people might have wondered if I was coming too, or not have wondered at all. In any case, the day came and went, and I only thought of it after, and it was too late then to be ringing up and wishing her the many happy returns.

I suppose I'm fearful that we might have fallen out of the groove of getting along with one another. The easy humour having become strained. It seems to me that the more you experience in life, the more you are distanced from others. Your experience alienates you. I'd say it'd be tough-going trying to get back in with Evelyn now, and she'd make me work hard for it. She'd be resentful that I haven't phoned, though she herself hasn't phoned. It could be that I intentionally forgot to phone on her twenty-first birthday out of fear of a reckoning or a rejection, or even both.

Myself and Nuala are heading out to celebrate the internship. Nuala has the first shower because her curly hair takes longer to style. After Nuala's out of the shower, we lay an array of outfits on the bedspread and have an asinine conversation about what goes with what. 'I haven't worn this yet,' she says, picking up an embroidered top with woollen roses sewn onto it.

'It's a bit granny.'

'Norma got it for me. She bought it at a craft market.'

'Why don't you put a big lump of cotton wool inside it and sew it all the way around and you'll have a lovely cushion for the couch.'

'You're full of cheek,' she says jovially. She always ends up in the same outfit anyway: a plain navy top, jeans and sturdy wedge shoes. Nondescript Nuala.

I'm in next for the shower, and by the time I've emerged, Nuala's poured me a glass of chilled Prosecco. Then she sits on the edge of the bed in a pilled dressing gown and pumps a pavlova-sized wad of hair mousse into her hand before massaging it into her hair.

When the mop of curls is set, Nuala's still hemming and hawing over the outfits on the bed. She tilts her head to one side. 'Do you know what. I think I'll just wear something comfortable.' Once she's dressed in the navy staples, she spritzes herself all over with a dusty bottle of perfume she's had on the go for three years. Then she looks at herself in the mirror from different angles, sucks in her cheeks, turns around and looks at her own backside. 'Have I too much make-up on?' she says, frowning.

'No. You're perfect.'

'Is the hair too big?'

'No. It's lovely. It's spot on.'

'Should I brush it all out?'

'Do not.'

'Do you think we'll meet anyone nice tonight?' she says, patting her lipstick on a piece of tissue paper. She asks the same question every Saturday evening, and I always answer the same way.

'Tonight could be the night, Nuala.'

'I haven't met anyone nice in ages. If I see someone nice tonight, I'm just going to go for it.' She's never said anything of the sort before.

'How do you mean, *go for it*? What have you in mind?'

'I'm going to take a fella home with me and give him a night he'll never forget,' she says. 'I'm over this wallflower business altogether.' I'll have to see it to believe it. As for myself, I've no difficulty catching a fella's eye. I'm far better at pulling than Nuala, but I haven't managed to keep a hold on anyone yet. I've trouble with fellas asking me questions about myself. *So tell me. What do you do?* I always feel that if I'd a better story to tell, they'd be more keen. That being said, it's going to be different now; come next week, I'll be talking nonstop about the dream that's underway.

I go into my own bedroom, the box room, and I put on my own outfit. I don't like having the box room and sleeping so high up. I'd prefer my bedroom on solid ground like it is at home in Glenbruff. I think of myself as being unnaturally suspended up in the sky, and I've a fear of the bed plummeting through the floor and into the apartment below and the one below that and the one below it again, even though that sort of an incident is virtually unheard of.

After I've done my make-up and straightened my hair, myself and Nuala prance around to a rotation of pop songs. We dash out to catch the last bus into town at the side of the dual carriageway, and it isn't long before we're standing and shivering in the queue for Club Dynasty. Nuala wants to meet a fella from the country, not from Dublin, and she says there's a higher likelihood of finding a country fella at Club Dynasty than at the likes of Electric Jake's Basement, or technofunk night at Gristle. She says the talent is better at Club Dynasty. The fellas are dressed better and they're a more decent sort. 'Evening, ladies,' says a drunk fella in a checked shirt and square-looking shoes who's trundled up behind us. He hiccups close to my ear. 'I said, *evening, ladies.*'

'Evening,' says Nuala. Nuala's compulsion for politeness is bordering on disorder.

'Ye're looking well,' he slurs, his stout breath on my neck.

'Thanks,' says Nuala, high-pitched. The drunk fella stumbles on his feet, bumping up against me, and I shudder.

'What's wrong with your friend?' he says to Nuala. 'Is she stuck-up?'

'There isn't a thing wrong with my friend.'

'There is. She's fucking deaf.' A finger pokes me hard in the shoulder. 'Here. You. I'm talking to you.' I take a step forward. 'I was right,' he says. 'She is fucking stuck-up.' He reaches out and pokes me in the shoulder again.

'Don't touch me,' I hiss. Nuala looks anxious, like a rabbit in headlights.

The drunk fella does a clumsy dance, waving his hands. 'Oh, I'm a little stuck-up bitch. I love myself.' His hand is on my shoulder now, tugging at it and catching strands of my hair in his beefy fingers.

'Don't fucking touch me.'

'Hey.' A fella ahead of us turns his head. 'Don't be an asshole, man.' He sounds to be Spanish or Italian or something.

'Me so sorry,' says the drunk fella, bowing from the waist.

'Leave the ladies alone, okay.' There's something of the Peadar Morley about the fella ahead. The thick black hair and the almond-shaped eyes. The lean body and the air of confidence. I look at Nuala and she looks at me and she sets about licking the pads of her fingers and smoothing over her eyebrows.

When myself and Nuala slip into the dark, pulsing warmth of the nightclub, we overhear the drunk fella being turned away at the entrance. 'Not tonight, son.'

'Hah?'

'Not tonight.'

'You must be fucking joking me. I'm after getting the bus up from Galway,' the drunk fella protests.

'Isn't that nice,' says one of the bouncers, and the other one says, 'I hope you got yourself a return ticket because you're not coming in here.'

'You're a comedian, is that it. I'll remember your face, pal.'

'You will in your hole, you culchie prick.'

Nuala says she'll go inside into the club and find us a table. I hand the coats in to the cloakroom and shove the paper tickets in my bra for safe keeping. I wander into the darkly lit area next to the dance floor and spot Nuala conversing closely with the good-looking fella from the queue. Wasn't she very cute making a beeline for him while I was handing in the coats. 'Katie. This is Luc. Luc is from France. He's French.' Luc is gorgeous. What can he be doing in a place like Club Dynasty? He must be the only man in the place not wearing any socks.

'Hello, Luc.' Luc gives me a kiss on each cheek like a real-life French person. 'Thanks for your help outside.'

He gives a small shrug. 'Sure.'

'So. What brings you to Club Dynasty?' purrs Nuala, winding a sticky curl around her finger, her eyes lit up like the moon.

'I've just moved here. Someone recommended it,' says Luc, sounding nonchalant. 'I'm not sure it's my kind of place. It's a little, uh, *burrring*.'

'Have you heard of Electric Jake's Basement?' says Nuala, and she has a micro-glance over at me. She hates Electric Jake's Basement. She swore she'd never return. 'You'd love it. I could take you there some time.'

'Why not,' he says coolly, and now Nuala's sliding a hand up onto his chest, but it won't be long before Luc turns his attentions away from Nuala and towards me. That's how these things tend to go. I've the more compelling personality, and a nice small mouth and symmetrical eyebrows. I wait, and I sort of shunt around a bit, and I scan the club as though I'm interested to see who else is here, and then I look over again to see Luc with his phone in his hand and Nuala calling out her number to him. 'Oh. Eight. Seven...' I suppose she's changed her mind about country fellas. 'Nine. Two. Four...'

In the morning, Luc's sitting backwards on a kitchen chair in the apartment, resting his chest against the wooden frame, the tanned forearms hanging and leather bracelets encircling his wrists. 'Nuala tells me you're working in television. Cool.'

'I'm starting an internship on Monday. A place called Pyro Productions,' I say casually. I have the ironing board out, and I'm ironing my jeans. If there's one thing I've learned from Nuala it's that jeans look better when they've been ironed. 'I want to make films. I just have to build up a bit of experience.'

'Nice. I just took a job as a barista. But I freelance as an illustrator.'

'Is that so.'

'I'm working on a portfolio to bring in commissions. It's on my website.'

Nuala lands into the kitchen in fresh make-up. 'I'll walk you to the bus stop,' she says breathily.

'LucDuret.com. L-U-C-D-U-R-E-T. Maybe you could take a look,' he says to me, slowly rising from the chair.

'Sure. Yeah.' A website. I've never met anyone with their own website before.

After they've gone, Norma comes into the kitchen with a glossy magazine rolled up under her arm. 'Well. What do you make of the foreigner?'

'I think he's nice. Why, what do you think?'

'No.' She shakes her head. 'It won't work.' She fills up the electric kettle with water and plugs it in. She rattles around in the cupboard and takes out two mismatched mugs.

'Why won't it work?'

'God knows who he is or where he's from. We know nothing at all about him. He could be a raving madman for all we know. He mightn't even be French.'

'I don't know why he'd pretend he was French.'

'I always say you're as well off meeting someone from down home. At least then you know the parents and the aunts and uncles and cousins and all of that. You know what you're dealing with, and there are no unpleasant surprises.' That's all well and good, but the only fella I ever loved from down home lost his mind, and there's no way of knowing if he ever found it again. 'Will you have tea?'

'No, thanks, Norma.'

'Please yourself,' she says, returning the two mugs to the press. She doesn't like drinking tea on her own.

I fold up the jeans and take them into the box room. I pull out my old battered laptop and go on to Luc's website, where there's a gallery of illustrations of lunar landscapes and three-dimensional characters brandishing futuristic weaponry. I lie back on the bed and mull over the conversation myself and Luc had in the kitchen. It's great having a new story about myself that I never had before. I wonder what Evelyn would think of the story. Would she be admiring?

Minutes later, I hear shrieking from outside in the hallway and the sound of high-heeled boots jumping up and down. It's Nuala, returned from the walk to the bus stop. 'He'll never forget Nuala Mary Creighton! Never! *Never!*' We'll hear all the ins and outs of it over the days to follow.

'I'm Katie Devane. I'm starting my internship today.' The woman at reception with the septum piercing, faded green hair and headset with a tiny mic looks down at a worn black diary. 'I was told to come in and ask for Bernard. He said he'd get me started.' The woman smiles a confused smile before lifting her head.

'Bernard's not here. He's left the company.' I stare at the woman and she stares back at me. 'He didn't leave us any messages about an intern,' she says, matter-of-fact.

'He offered me the internship last week. I can show you the emails. We had a meeting and everything.'

'Let me talk to someone. Give me a minute.' She slips out from behind the reception desk and enters a room along the corridor, half closing the door behind her. I look around the foyer. There are several screens secured to the wall, each showing a different Pyro Productions television programme. A travel show called *Away and Abroad*. A programme about casserole cookery called *The Heat Is On*, and a new detective drama series, *Shanley and the Shades*. A cluster of snappily dressed people meanders past the reception desk, chatting about actors and schedules and contracts. As they clear the foyer, I can overhear the conversation between the woman with the faded green hair and a man inside the room down the corridor.

'What the actual fuck. We've interns hanging out of the lampshades at this stage,' the man says.

'Bernard arranged it. I could wring him. The poor girl is standing out there in reception. She's waiting for an answer.'

'We'll have to put her off. Tell her we're after bringing in someone else.'

'She'll be upset, Jason. She's only young, and up from the country.'

'God almighty. Give her something. One of the mugs or a hoodie. It's as much as we can do.'

The woman returns to the front desk and hands me a cellophane wrapped hoodie branded with an *Away and Abroad* logo. 'I'm sorry about this. It's Bernard. He's been organising meetings with young women and promising things.'

'How do you mean?'

'He's just trying to get off with them. With girls like yourself. He's caused all sorts of trouble.' She leans over the desk and says, 'One of our runners has a restraining order out on him.'

'So there's no internship.'

'No. There isn't. We already have someone. We've a few people. There's a form on our website that you can fill out, but I have to tell you, we get hundreds of applications every month.' I nod and draw my bottom lip into my mouth. 'I hope you haven't travelled too far. Will I call you a taxi?'

I shake my head. 'No. It's okay.' I haven't the money for splashing out on taxis. I walk out of the building and a forklift whips past me, barely missing my nose. It was all too good to be true. Who's going to hire me, or offer me any sort of an opportunity, when all I've done is wrapped up chips and scratched toothpaste off mirrors and I've the same education as hordes and hordes of other young people? Now I know how Evelyn must have felt, not getting on her course. She must have felt dreadful.

As I shuffle towards the bus stop, I think about having to phone Mammy and Daddy and telling them the internship hasn't worked out. After pleading with Daddy to give me the money for rent and everything. He won't hear of me going after another internship after this. And I think about having to go back to the apartment and facing Nuala and Norma. Relaying disappointments to others always seems to magnify them. If Norma so much as says *I told you so*, I'll wallop her.

According to Nuala, who works in recruitment, all the production companies are damned with graduates sending in applications. 'Supposably there's a company that gives out the number for an old fax machine they have sitting someplace in a prefab. They haven't filled the paper tray in five years. It's become a sort of a running joke.' I wish Nuala wouldn't say 'supposably'. It's not even a real word. It drives me mad when she says it. It makes my blood boil.

The story has disintegrated, and with it, a hatch opens in my mind, unleashing an unsettling thought. The dream will never come to fruition without Evelyn. And though I tell myself that it's illogical, superstitious even, I can't seem to shake the idea that myself and Evelyn are supposed to pursue the dream together. I won't be able to make it on my own. I'm only special by association.

Myself and Nuala and Norma are out for a hot chocolate at a shopping centre close to the apartment, and I have the sneaking suspicion that this is a sort of a prearranged intervention. Norma's strongly recommending that I go forward for the teaching diploma, like she's some sort of evangelist for doing the teaching. She has all the details tucked into her Filofax. 'Just apply for it, Katie,' she says firmly. 'You can decide later. Give yourself the option.' She's like a dog with a bone.

I'm staring sullenly into the glass of hot chocolate, swirling a long-handled teaspoon in the lukewarm sugary gloop. 'Norma. I don't want to do the teaching. How many times have I to say it.'

'You have to be realistic, Katie. Everyone gives up on their dream eventually. Holding on to it is a bit childish if you ask me.'

'Norma,' says Nuala. 'You're very harsh.'

'I'm only saying. It's human nature to think we're all here for some big purpose. But most of us aren't. Most of us are ordinary, and it's important to accept it. A person has to be content to lead a normal life. There's no shame in it.' The three of us sit in terrible, awkward silence. The worst thing that could happen would be for me to fail, to never make something of myself, and I've the anguished feeling that failure is fated. I haven't Evelyn's self-belief. I haven't Norma's pragmatism. I'm not a natural Pollyanna, like Nuala. *Polly-fucking-Nuala.* Maybe it's the usual thing for people to give up, and it's a part of the fabric of life. Look at Mammy, sure, existing with the spectre of the unlived Self.

I wonder should I relent and apply for the teaching. The prospect of it is making more and more sense. I've the impression that Nuala and Norma are only keeping me on in the apartment out of charity: the rent hasn't increased since I moved in. My tweed coat is four years old and fraying at the cuffs. There's a hole in the left pocket and coins have slipped into the lining, ringing against my leg.

Nuala puts her hand on my forearm and rubs it. 'It wasn't your fault it didn't work out,' she says in a kindly tone. 'You must put this incident behind you and have another go when you're feeling better.'

Norma shakes her head, closes over her Filofax with a slap. 'There'll be more torment where that came from.' She sits back and folds her arms. 'I'm only saying.'

'You've said your piece, Norma. It's no one's business only Katie's what she does next.' It's a pity Nuala can't get me a job herself, but she only recruits door-to-door salespeople.

It isn't too hard to get back my old job. The Liffey Hotel has a revolving door, and it's common enough for former staff members to return when they're in a tight spot.

I have an email from Bernard. He says he's sorry he had to leave Pyro Productions so suddenly. He's done so for personal reasons, he writes, and he's exploring new horizons. It was very nice to meet me. Would I be interested in going for a drink sometime?

I'm beginning to wonder if I want to work in films at all. Am I able for it? Am I cut out for it?

I've a good photograph of myself and Evelyn and Maeve and Peadar and Aidan all in front of the cottage in the woods. It's one I set up on a timer. We're sitting together on the low wall as the sun is setting, and there's solar flare in the upper left corner of the frame. Aidan has his arms wrapped around one leg drawn tight to his chest. Peadar's blowing smoke. Maeve is captured licking the corner of her mouth with one eye closed, and Evelyn's dead centre staring sourly at the camera. As I cast an eye over the photograph, I'm seeing something I never noticed before: there are two orbs above Aidan's left shoulder.

'Who're all these people?' enquires Nuala, leaning over.

'Friends of mine.' I've come to recognise that a photograph can never capture the essence of a person, or a friendship. The way that certain people provide an exhilarating sense of life's possibilities, and make your heart sing. That can only be held in a space within you, and photographs are inadequate by comparison.

'Tell me what I'm looking at here,' Norma says testily, knotting her forehead as she shuffles through the photos and carelessly fingerprints the edges.

'It's the ruin of an abandoned cottage. In a wood down home. It's full of interesting things to see.'

'I don't get it. It's just junk. Broken clocks and dirty curtains and filth.'

'It's art,' Nuala says wistfully, half closing her eyes. 'It has meaning. It's supposed to move you.'

'It gives me the creeps. I've never liked old places. I prefer new places.' Norma hasn't the least proclivity for the Arts.

'Does it not make you wonder about the people who used to live there, and the kinds of lives they had, and how they died, and why doesn't anyone bother with the old cottage any more,' Nuala sighs as I gather up the photographs and return them to an envelope for safe keeping.

'You can't have much to do with these friends any more if they've never been up to see you,' Norma says.

'That girl has. The girl with the long dark hair. Do you remember?' says Nuala. 'She had the half an hour shower. We nearly broke down the door thinking she'd collapsed inside in it.'

'That one.' Norma tsks, raising her eyes. 'Smoking in someone else's bathroom, as if she owned the place. She'd some neck.'

My phone is ringing from inside the locker in the cleaning office. I've applied for a hundred jobs and so I'm hoping it's someone important looking to speak to me. 'Hello.'

'Katie. It's Maeve.' The hairs spring up on the back of my neck and along my forearms. What in the hell is Maeve Lynch phoning for? Is there some bad news concerning Evelyn?

'Maeve. What's going on? Is everything alright?'

'I'm very well, thank you for asking.' The line is full of static and echoes. It's like she's phoning from another time and place. 'You're setting the world alight above in Dublin?'

'I am.' I laugh in a false way. 'What's happening, girl?'

'I felt badly for not getting in touch when I said I would. I'm only after realising that you might have been waiting to hear from me.'

'Oh. Yes. I was wondering.' I was in my hole.

'It was better for me to stay in Glenbruff in the end. I got a promotion in Amperloc. I'm an assistant manager now on the supply chain end of things.' A promotion. How in God's name did Maeve get a promotion? 'Amanda said I'd be mad to turn down the opportunity.' Surely be to God but Maeve Lynch hasn't outdone me, though I suppose she was always clever in her own way.

'Is that so. A promotion. Congratulations.'

'What are you up to yourself these times?'

'Arrah. Nothing to write home about.'

'Have you a job in films?'

'I don't. I must have applied for a hundred things but I haven't the right experience for any of them. I'm not sure what I'm going to do with myself.' I even joined up to a few message boards and enquired about jobs working on films. It seems I need to have the experience first, but you only get experience out of working for free. The dream has never felt so distant, and not for the likes of me. Hard work or otherwise.

'If you were down in Glenbruff, I could get you something in the company,' she says. I wouldn't go working in Amperloc in a fit, but isn't she very considerate all the same. I've always felt there's an inherent loveliness in people from the country.

'Ah no. Thanks anyway. Maybe my ship will come in one of the days.'

'You must pray to Saint Jude. He'll take care of it for you. All the other saints are a pure waste. They'd do nothing for you. No good at all.'

'Is that so.'

'I'll talk to Amanda for you. She's well in with all sorts of successful people.' My ears prick up. 'You must come to the next fundraiser. You wouldn't know who you'd meet.' There might be something in it. 'As soon as I'm off the phone I'll text you on the details.'

'Thanks, Maeve. I'm glad to hear you're keeping well. I'd better go anyway.' It just goes to show that people can surprise you. And if the fortunes of a person like Maeve Lynch can change, surely anyone's can.

We're sitting in a veritable fort of drying laundry and watching the RTÉ News. Desmond Duignan is being interviewed as acting spokesperson for the Cooney family. The camera is tilted up at him, he's so tall. Maureen Cooney is standing to the left of him wearing Jackie O sunglasses, and Daithí and Donnacha are standing either side of her like two pillars. 'To say the Cooney family are sorely dissatisfied with the investigation would be an understatement. Cadaver dogs were never engaged in the critical days following the disappearance. Local people were actively deterred from getting involved in the search. A reported sighting in a shopping centre in Belgium two years ago has never been followed up. The time has come for a fresh investigation into Pamela's disappearance, and we await formal communication from An Garda Siochána on this matter.'

When the segment has ended, Norma mutes the volume on the television. 'You must tell us about Pamela Cooney. What was she like?' I have a twinge of contrition to think of the dancing tape in the sink of steaming suds, and the black entrails wound round the taps. *It's time to hang up the dancing shoes.*

I puff my cheeks and blow out slowly. 'She's about my height. She has two brothers, and she likes hip hop dancing.'

'Noo-oo. What was she *reaaallly* like? Was she good at school?'

'She was okay at it.'

'Was she a simpleton?'

149

'No. No, she wasn't a simpleton.'

'Was she popular?' asks Nuala, squinting.

'Sort of.'

'She had a boyfriend, didn't she. He did an interview with one of the papers.' An interview? I must ask Mammy or Robert to locate it and post it on to me. It might even be on the internet.

'It was only a few months they were together.'

'Did the boyfriend snap, I wonder,' muses Norma.

'No.'

'It's always the boyfriend.'

'He's not the type. He's harmless.'

'Harmless,' snorts Norma. 'God. Do you know, I always think it's an awful insult to refer to a person as being *harmless*. Like they're not worth treating the same as other people. Like they're only to be tolerated.' I've never given the word much thought before now. I suppose there are a few ways of being harmless. You'd readily define Mickey Cassidy as harmless, in that he intends no harm. He's the sort that's tolerated. You'd label Aidan as harmless too; he doesn't have it in him to harm anyone, not in my estimation, and so there's nothing derogatory intended in calling him harmless. 'Do you know him? The boyfriend.'

'Everyone knows everyone in Glenbruff. It's a small place.'

'Go on,' urges Nuala. 'What's he like?'

'He's a good person. An ordinary, down-to-earth person.'

'Well, what happened her, so?' says Norma impatiently.

'There's something strange about Glenbruff. Strange things happen there.'

'Don't be feeding us *ráiméis*.'

'I'm not.' How else am I to explain it?

'She vanished into thin air. Is that it? You're no good to us.'

FIVE-YEAR MYSTERY OF VANISHED
SWEETHEART HAUNTS AIDAN MORLEY (22)
by Gráinne O'Gorman-Flynn

There's something raw about Aidan Morley. It's all in the throwaway remarks. 'I'm happy to have a quiet life. I'm happy just going out for a run or meeting up with a few of the lads for a quiet drink or a kickabout.' Aidan is an attractive young man with dark blond hair and blue eyes. As the former captain of the local football team, he's well known in the town of Glenbruff in County Roscommon. But although he's in the prime of his life, Aidan doesn't go to nightclubs any more. He's been recognised several times and it wasn't pleasant. People pointed and whispered, 'There's your man,' and even squared up to him.

'It's been a living nightmare,' Aidan confides. 'I've been diagnosed with post-traumatic stress disorder. I've had hours and hours of therapy over it. I'm fed up of people judging me without getting to know me. I've often thought about leaving Glenbruff but I can't let bad people get the best of me.' He's currently single, hesitant to seek out romance. 'It's always hard when you meet a nice girl. You're not sure when is the right time to tell them about a former girlfriend going missing. You can't tell them on the first date, that's for certain. So it's been hard for me to judge when is the right time.'

In the spring of 1998, Aidan's girlfriend Pamela Cooney (17) vanished. Pamela was making her way to a handball alley in Glenbruff to meet with Aidan on a Friday evening, but he says she never arrived. The alarm was raised when Pamela failed to return to her home in nearby Saint Malachy's Parish. A search was undertaken of the local area, but to this day, no trace of Pamela has ever been found. 'I believe that the spotlight that's been put on me has detracted from the search for Pamela. The media always puts the focus on the boy-friend or the husband or whatever, and I'm an easy target.' Aidan was even asked to take a step back from his football pastime when the hostility between Glenbruff and Saint Malachy's Parish escalated into violence on the pitch. 'I've been verbally abused during football matches. Spat on. Tackled with excessive force. One of my team-mates had his collarbone broken. It's gone too far.'

Aidan lives with his brother Peadar in their childhood home. Their mother Louise passed away from cancer when the boys were aged ten and eleven respectively. 'Peadar's been a great support. Our dad was away a lot working when we were young. We had each other for company. Peadar was there for me when I reached breaking point. We're the best of friends.'

Aidan is studying sport science at college in Sligo, and intends to become a school sports coach or personal trainer. When he's asked about the future, he says, 'I'm determined to build a life for myself on home turf. I feel I have to stand my ground. There isn't one ounce of evidence against me. I've cooperated with the guards. What more can I do? I can't let the rumours deter me from living the life I've wanted for myself.

'I just want to share my story and tell people what it's been like for me. My hope is that Pamela will be found, and that we can all achieve a state of closure. It'd be great if she was found alive some-where, but the more time that goes by, it's seeming fairly unlikely.'

Do you have information on this missing persons case? Call the Missing Persons Helpline on 1800 324 791.

The sky is grey and heavy, and fat warm rain spatters the pavement. Colourful pinwheels blur in a rising wind that carries the deranged shrieking of seagulls. The sea hurls and heaves, and down by the marina, boats bob and sway disconcertingly.

All at once, I'm apprehensive about the whole thing. All at once, I'm anticipating the end of the evening, scurrying away to the apartment and as far from Maeve as I can get. I pinch the collar of my coat tightly round my neck before turning into a side street. And there she is. Over there. Over the road, standing at the railings in front of a smart townhouse. I cross towards her at a slow pace. As she catches sight of me, her face breaks into a goofball grin. 'Katie,' she calls, waving frantically as the damp wind catches tendrils of her wispy hair and whips them about her head. She's wearing the camel-coloured coat but it's seen better days, and the buttons are drooping on it. Her lips are scabbed, lipstick congealed at the corners, and the dark semicircle mouth has rubber strings suspended within it.

'You're after getting braces.'

'I am. I've had them nearly a year.' Her speech is laboured, punctuated with the slurking of excess saliva. *Hluk.* She has a child's breath that smells like sweets. 'They're coming off in a few weeks' time.'

'Thanks for inviting me. I've never been networking before.'

'Sure, we go way back, Katie. Old friends always help each other out.' *Hluk.* 'Come on anyway. We'd better go in. Amanda's waiting for us.'

I follow Maeve up the stone steps, and we come into a plush-carpeted reception area where warm light pools from beneath mosaic lamps, and muzak plays over the speakers. Beyond the reception area is a function room full to capacity with Amanda and John's wealthy acquaintances. They're well-dressed people, back-slapping and laughing loudly with their mouths wide open and heads thrown back. The kinds of people who personify what the media is calling the 'Celtic Tiger'. I feel like an alien in the room, a misfit, but networking is a way of getting ahead, so Nuala says, and if I don't get ahead one of these days I don't know what I'll do. I might have to do the unthinkable. I might have to do the teaching.

Amanda Dowling, deeply tanned and sinewy, glides towards us in a black velvet gown as though she hasn't any feet, only a big wheel beneath her dress. She has Maeve's oversized grey eyes framed with two sets of false eyelashes. Gold jewellery drips from her ears and bounces on her wrists, and her neck is unnaturally smooth. She has a short forehead, and I suspect she's wearing a sort of a hairpiece. 'You're late,' she says tersely, flashing veneered teeth. 'You're not dressed.'

'This is my friend from Glenbruff. Remember I told you,' Maeve announces. 'She's looking for a job in films. Remember I asked if you could introduce her to the right people.'

'Go out in the back and change. And tie up that hair.' Maeve's smile falls away, and Amanda Dowling turns to me. 'There's a change of clothes in the utility. Maeve will show you.' I follow Maeve out through a concealed wallpapered door and into a small utility room, where she proceeds to hang up the camel-coloured coat and her banjaxed-looking handbag.

'What's going on? Why do we've to change our clothes?'

'Amanda wants us to serve drinks and help out,' she says, and she unbuttons her blouse. 'You don't mind, do you?' It makes me nauseous seeing Maeve in such a way, standing before me in the grubby bra.

She proceeds to unwrap two white shirts from dry-cleaning plastic and holds one out to me.

'Hold on now a minute. I thought I was here for the networking. I thought Amanda would get me talking to the right kinds of people. I wouldn't have come if I'd known.'

'Will you just help out for an hour or two?' She looks at me pleadingly, her eyes pinkening. 'Will you help me keep Amanda happy? You can do whatever you want after that.'

With seething reluctance, I yank my top over my head and put on the white starched shirt. To think I've come all this way to be handing out canapés. I've enough of being a lackey at the hotel. The pair of us go out and take position behind a trestle table laden with minuscule edibles. 'So. How's Evelyn?'

'Oh. She's hot and cold with me these days. I think she's jealous of me.' Evelyn has far more going for her than Maeve. Maeve must be stone mad if she thinks Evelyn is jealous of her. 'Things are going well for me and she doesn't like it.'

'Is she still in Amperloc?' I wonder if Evelyn is coming up with big ideas without me. Coming up with big plans that don't include me. There's no doubt but that she'll have made strides since we last saw one another.

'She is. Evelyn has high expectations for her life but she never follows through. I've never had anything handed to me, Katie, but look at me now. Amanda's going to make me a director of her property company.' She throws up her chin. 'You know, I thought we could be good friends by ourselves. The two of us. I'm up in Dublin a fair bit, doing the sailing and helping Amanda with her accounts and so on. I thought I'd call you up now and again and we could go shopping or on nights out.'

I can feel Maeve sucking me into the black hole and drawing the vitality out of me. 'It's nice of you to think of me that way,' I say, squirming inwardly. I haven't a notion of going shopping with her, or on nights out. I can't bring myself to say any more to her about it. 'Have you read Aidan's interview?'

'I have. We all thought he did very well. We were very complimentary.'

'What's he doing with himself? How is he getting on would you say?' I wonder does he ever think of me. I wonder are himself and Evelyn feeling my absence.

'He's in good health. I'd say he'll end up doing the teaching. He's filling in the forms, he says.' He must have got his mind back, so.

'You won't recognise yourself when Amanda makes you a director of her company. It'll be a whole new start.'

'Oh, I'd just love to be working with Amanda. I'd love to be just like her. When the time is right I'll have a job in Dexon Green, buying up properties and turning them around like she's doing. One of these days Amanda will tell me I'm ready for it.'

'What's this fundraising for anyway?'

'It's for a boat. John's father's boat. He was a well-known sailor. He won a lot of races in the boat and it needs refurbishing.'

'A boat. All this for a boat. You couldn't call that charity. An old boat needing refurbishment.'

'It is charity.' *Hluk*. 'It's a good cause.' She hands a glass of champagne to a man in a mustard linen suit, who neglects to say thank you. It's an awful waste when a person with money has poor taste, throwing cash and cheques at undeserving causes and wearing mustard-coloured linen suits. It's only Dublin people who do be carrying on like that, I've realised.

'I think I'll head on, Maeve.'

'You're leaving?'

'I'm not feeling well. It came on me all of a sudden.'

Maeve considers what I've said. Her expression softens. 'Alright. I'm sorry about Amanda. She's normally very friendly. I don't know what got into her.'

It takes an age to get home to the apartment. I've to take a train and a sticky damp bus, and I become increasingly despondent with every passing minute. It was a pure waste of an evening, not to mention the full hour spent earlier on doing the wing-tipped eyeliner. And I'm not one bit impressed with Amanda Dowling. She doesn't strike me as the altruistic sort. She never introduced Maeve to anyone all evening, like she was ashamed of her or something.

The pursuit of the dream alone is no good. It doesn't work. It's only anguish. I remember the white ball of fire under my ribs, the excitement of all that was to come. I used to think my imagination would end up taking me places, but instead I'm like the girl that fate forgot.

I'm sitting on the toilet seat and looking in my mouth with a compact mirror. The dentist says I have two wisdom teeth requiring immediate extraction. I can overhear Nuala and Norma consulting with one another in the kitchen. 'We'll give her a break from the rent so she can get her teeth done,' Nuala says in a loud whisper. 'Daddy won't mind. He won't even notice.'

'How will she learn the hard lesson if we do that?'

'We must overlook all that and do the right thing.'

'Do you not think it's getting a bit old, all this talk and notions about films. If she had a right job she'd have health insurance along with it.'

'Never mind all that. This is an emergency. We can surely forego the two months' rent.'

'There's plenty of smart, sensible girls who'd only love that room, who'd be only delighted to pay the rent on time and in full. You're too soft, Nuala.'

'Katie's our friend. She needs our help. The teeth must be dealt with.'

'Let you be the one who deals with the fallout. Let you be the one who explains it to Daddy if he rings up asking. I don't know how she'll get on the property ladder or anything with the way she's going. Do you know, I think she likes being poor. Doesn't it suit her now to be poor.'

I spend Christmas Eve and Christmas Day on the couch in the apartment with a mouth full of cotton padding. Nuala gets the early bus back to Dublin on Saint Stephen's Day with a block of frozen turkey soup for me, but it isn't the same sucking up Christmas turkey through a straw.

Mammy rings. 'Where did you get the money for the teeth?'

'I hadth the money.'

'You should have asked us. We're not in the poorhouse yet, you know.'

Nuala's back in work the first week of January. 'Sit down, sit down, sit down,' she says excitedly, patting the cushion.

'What is it?'

'My remit's after changing in work. I'll be doing media recruitment from now on. I'll be able to help you get a job.'

'What sort of a job?'

'I need someone for an entry-level role in an agency. An advertising agency. Will you do it? Do you think you'd like it? I'll tell them you're the best candidate on the books.' Advertising is all stories, pictures and words. I could manage that, I think. Coming up with ideas and being paid for it. And I could badly do with the money. I swore I'd pay back the two months' rent to Nuala and Norma after having the wisdom teeth taken out.

'Would they take on the likes of me?'

'Of course they'd take on the likes of you. Why wouldn't they? You'd be well able for it.'

'Go on and put me forward for it, so. What have I got to lose.' I give her the most enthusiastic heartfelt hug I've ever given anyone in my whole life, and I feel her shaking with laughter underneath. 'Have I ever told you you're unreal, Nuala.' This could be something. This could really be something.

'This calls for a hot chocolate,' Norma declares.

'This calls for Pinot Grigio,' insists Nuala.

'It's only Tuesday,' Norma says. 'You'd better make mine a spritzer.'

Despite her best intentions, Norma gets tipsy on the spritzers. When Nuala leaves the room to use the toilet, Norma leans over, looks at me screwy-eyed and says, 'I feel like you're only watching us for stories. You're only listening to us to get stories out of us. Why don't you own up to it?'

'I don't know what you're talking about.' She's some wagon.

There's all sorts of mental gymnastics to contend with, working at the agency. My brain is firing off every second of the day with trying to keep up. It's a whole new departure, getting to grips with the jargon, learning how to follow the planning charts. Knowing when to say something and when to say nothing.

According to Mervin Magee, advertising isn't a career but a way of life. Mervin Magee has a flat nose, dyed black hair sculpted into a ridge and a ripple of fat at the back of his head. He wears tight jeans, his shirtsleeves rolled up to the elbows, a complicated-looking chrome watch with multiple dials and hands whirring around inside it, and a signet ring jammed on his fat baby finger.

Mervin Magee doesn't have a single thought without relaying it to an audience. He summons us to the boardroom, and it all gets a bit Jim Jones; client calls go unanswered, fresh emails stack high, and we sit tight as he blusters ad infinitum about advertising trends, predictions for the future of the industry and, more often than not, the pitch that got away. I'm only a month in and I've heard the anecdote three times. 'I'm not sure if I've ever told you all about a little pitch we were invited to back in the day. We were a small outfit. Out on our own, doing cutting-edge stuff. Ambient. Experiential. We were getting noticed. I got a call out of the blue from Pete. We used to play rugby together. Pete was on top of the world. Heading up HighTail Airlines. He brought me in. He said, "Mervin. I want you guys to handle our brand. Full creative command." I said, "Pete. I don't know. I need to think about it." Pete looked me in the eye. He said, "Mervin. I want you. I won't trust anyone else." I said, "Pete. I'm scared." He said, "Mervin. This is the big time." I said, "Pete. What do I need to do?" He said, "Mervin. Come and meet with the board. It's just a formality. I've already made my decision." I was all set. I went in. I met with the board. But Pete didn't show. Pete was dead. Shellfish poisoning. Caribbean cruise. What do you think happened next?'

'The board went traditional,' answers Edwina, account director at Intuition 2.0. Edwina has a small frame, a head as round as a marble and thin hair. She has a bullhorn ring in her nose and wears ugly and expensive clothes: a cardigan that drags off the floor, a jumper shaped like a square, shoes with stacked rubber soles, a skirt that flares out and then tapers at the knee like a lantern. I've never seen her eat, and she only drinks a very specific pineapple-flavoured energy drink. She takes great pleasure in sitting it out until late in the evening, long after the rest of the staff have guiltily slunk out the office door under her powerful, belittling glare.

'That's right. They went for some old fogey agency. Let me ask you. Where do you think HighTail Airlines are today?'

'Bust. They went bust.'

'That's right. But what do you think might have happened if everything had gone according to plan?'

'You would've become lazy. You would've become complacent.'

'You've got it. Now tell me. Do you think I have any regrets?'

'No,' Edwina says firmly. 'It made you who you are today.'

The day slides into evening. The lights in the surrounding buildings are switched off. People on the street are clutching convenience meals and yoga mats and making their way home, and the cleaner comes in and hoovers about our feet, but Mervin Magee is just getting warmed up. He's sketching complicated spindle shapes and funnel diagrams on a whiteboard denoting what he likes to call 'Weapons of Mass Disruption'.

My stomach growls forlornly. My bladder throbs. I've got pins and needles in my arse. At a guess, I have four hours of work to do before returning to the apartment. I'm going to be mad late again, and relying on another hodgepodge meal for sustenance: tinned tuna with a side of beans. Nuala and Norma will turn to look pitifully at me from the couch, three episodes deep into *Sex and the City*. 'You look like shit,' Norma will say. 'You're like one of those people over in Japan, working themselves to death.'

'You poor *créatúr*,' Nuala will say. 'You're working far too hard. You're gone as thin as a rake. You'll end up with rickets if you're not careful.' Nuala's even bought me a pepper-spray canister for the late-night commute, and a small one on a key ring to put on my bunch of keys.

But haven't I done well for myself. I've a story now that I never had before. If I'm to encounter an old neighbour in the street or someone I was at school with, I can tell them I've a job in advertising, and they'll be taken aback. *How did you get into that line of work?* And if there's a gathering of young people in Glenbruff and they happen to enquire about what so-and-so is doing, and what such-and-such is up to, and if I happen to come up in the conversation at all, people will learn that Katie Devane is up in Dublin and she's doing well for herself.

Nuala's skittish, checking her phone. 'Are we ready to go? We'd better head.'

'I just got here. Let me talk to your friend. At least say hi or whatever,' says Luc. 'Katie,' he says to me. 'How are you?' He picks up a chair, spins it in his hands and sits with his chest against the back of it in his signature pose.

'I'm very well, thanks. It's nice to see you.'

'You work in advertising now, right.' He's watching me carefully, as though he intends to sketch me from memory later on.

'I got a job in an agency in town. I'm an account executive.'

'I helped her get the job,' Nuala interjects. 'I told them she has a good eye.' She hoicks her handbag over her shoulder and presses her elbow in against it.

'A good eye. What is that?'

'It means she's a natural for putting pictures together,' Nuala says frostily, eyeballing the pair of us from the kitchen doorway and tapping her foot.

'I taught myself photography before I came up to Dublin. I must have hundreds of good photos taken.'

'I'd like to see them. You think we could do that?' Unless I'm sorely mistaken, Luc has a soft spot for me, and he's doing a poor job of concealing it.

'Next time, sure.' I peep up at Nuala, and she has a tremendous sulk on her. 'How are your illustrations coming along? Is there much freelance work for you?'

'A little here and there. Not enough. But I'm just starting, right.'

'It'll get better. It'll improve.' Nuala looks like she could burst.

'I'm just happy to do what I love. You know, people talk about sexual frustration. But they never talk about creative frustration, and it's a real thing. It's actually unhealthy for a creative person not to create. It makes us ill.' It's Nuala who's the third wheel. It's Nuala with nothing to add to this sort of a conversation. She goes down to her room under the pretence of searching for an umbrella.

'Yeah. I totally get it.' I do. 'I think I'd go mad if I didn't get to do creative things. It's a part of who I am.'

Nuala returns promptly, stomping into the kitchen and holding up a flowery umbrella with bent spokes. 'Now. Are we all set?' Luc's eyes drop to the floor. 'I've often got caught in a shower waiting for the bus. You can't be too careful,' she says.

'Well. Have a nice time. Are ye going to Electric Jake's Basement?'

'We're going for a Chinese,' snaps Nuala. *Oof.* Luc gives a backwards glance at me before himself and Nuala make to leave the apartment. The front door wallops shut with an almighty force, the picture frames rattle on the wall and the clothes horse slumps in the corner. Whatever about before, but Luc has a hold of me now. It's clear he went home with the wrong girl on the night out, and doesn't he know it himself too.

Mervin Magee stands by the window, gazing out at the cityscape by night as though he's the suave lead in an aftershave advertisement. 'How can we describe the attributes of a moisturising lotion without using the word "moisturising"?'

Edwina and Neil put on their best thinking faces. 'Plumping,' suggests Edwina.

'Firming,' says Neil. 'Rejuvenating.' Neil has poor posture and beady eyes, and resembles a prawn. He's an account executive too, like myself, and he's just completed the six-month probation. He looks altogether worn out. He has bags beneath his eyes, and bags beneath the bags.

'No. Definitely none of those. Come on, people. It's your job to be smarter than me.' We continue in this excruciating vein until Mervin comes up with the correct answer himself, and we bear witness, held hostage to his inherent genius. 'I've got it.' He comes away from the window, presses his palms down on the boardroom table and takes in all of our faces. 'The word is…"enlushing".'

I know I'm better off saying nothing until I know the lay of the land, but it's hard to contain myself. 'I suppose I'm wondering why we can't just say "moisturising". I mean, "enlushing" isn't a word. And everyone knows what "moisturising" means already. It's like, why reinvent the wheel?'

Mervin glares at me as though I'm the shit smeared on his designer shoe. His face turns white, and I can see the terracotta-tinted concealer dabbed beneath his eyes. 'It doesn't *have* to be a *word*. I just *made* it *up*.' I shrink down in my chair, my cheeks blazing and hot. 'There's a lesson in this for you, Katie. Creators get to bend the rules. Creators get to invent new words. It's how language evolves.'

'Yeah. I mean, originality is absolutely critical to this agency,' Edwina says self-righteously, her eyes swivelling towards me. 'If people aren't willing to take risks, then we just won't survive. It is that important.'

When we're eventually released from the boardroom, I decide to go out for a coffee someplace, with the intention of returning to the agency afterwards to work on some reports. Bean & Gone is an independent coffee shop some thirty yards from the agency building, and I've walked past it several times but never been inside. Luc is deftly chalking up the specialty coffees on the board behind the register. 'You work here,' I bleat. He turns his face from the board and looks pleasantly surprised.

'Hey. What are you doing here?' He's wearing a T-shirt with chic little holes scattered throughout, hinting at the tanned skin beneath.

'This is so weird. I work really close by. Like just around the corner.'

He smiles and wipes the chalk from his hands on the barista apron slung around his hips. 'What would you like?'

'I'll have an americano, please. To go.'

'Milk and sugar?'

'Yes. Please.' There's another guy strolling around and between the small round tables, collecting cups and saucers and stacking them precariously in the crook of his arm. He has a mostly shaved head with a nub of plait and he's wearing a loud-coloured poncho made out of scratchy-looking woven material.

'That's Marco. He has the best weed, if you want to buy,' Luc says, pressing the plastic lid down on the paper cup. 'You should hang out here with us. After work.'

'I work late.'

'Us too,' he says. 'Marco and I have a lot of friends who come here at night. You're welcome to join us.' I hand him cash for the coffee, and Luc takes hold of my hand and closes it over.

'On the house. Is that correct?'

'Oh. Thanks,' I say. 'Thanks a lot. I'll call in one of the days soon.'

'Cool. Don't forget. I want to see your photographs.' He winks, turns his back and clanks about with the coffee machine.

'Hello.'

'Who is this?' the voice demands in an American accent.

'It's Katie. Katie Devane. I'm the new account executive.'

'I'm calling to speak with someone about the proposal. I tried to reach Mervin but it's gone straight to voicemail.' Mervin is gone to the gym, where he says he has his best ideas. 'We've all sat around and had a conversation. I mean, everyone agrees that the artwork is great, but there's this really strange word emblazoned on everything. I've tried looking it up in the dictionary and it's not there. It's not an actual word. I have to say, I'm super confused right now.'

'Yes. "Enlushing". Mervin came up with it.'

'We hate it. It doesn't make any sense, and it's totally pretentious. We can't launch a product off the back of a word that doesn't exist. We'll lose all credibility.'

'Do you want it taken out?'

'Without delay. It's not working for us whatsoever.'

'If you wouldn't mind putting it in writing. We have to have things in writing.' The employee manual says we're to have everything in writing.

Within a half an hour, Edwina storms over towards me clutching a sheaf of papers and shaking them. 'Who changed the copy? Who's responsible?'

'The client said to change it. She sent an email to the whole team. Look.'

Mervin, Edwina, et al,

Enlushing? Do I need to FedEx a thesaurus? Our brand trades on science, not claptrap. Please switch to the copy I signed off on last week, and stop being so damn ridiculous.

Cindy

Edwina glares at me for a long moment before settling down on the rubber exercise ball she uses instead of a chair. She pinches the bridge of her nose, inhaling slowly and loudly.

'When you have a chance there, Edwina, you might help me find the budget for the TuffOats account. I've looked all over the system and I can't find it.'

'Fuck's sake. The budget was set up in Q2 when we won the contract. It's obviously in the Q2 file drive.' She bobs up and down on the exercise ball, making *scuff-scuff* sounds on the carpet. 'I don't know what you're doing here, Katie. You're incredibly green around the gills. Even for a beginner.' She flips her face back to her computer screen. 'All the country people coming up to Dublin should be turned back at Kinnegad,' she says under her breath, all the words strung together, and it'd make a person feel awfully unwelcome. It'd make a person want to turn back for the familiarity of home.

Neil reaches over and taps me on the arm. 'Come with me.' I walk in his wake through the open-plan office, past rows and rows of pale-faced account executives. The other account executives have their own exclusive scene going on where they quote from obscure television shows at one another in the kitchenette, and swap the punchlines of dead comedians, and you couldn't say that any of them are especially friendly. I learned long ago that people from Dublin have their friends already made and haven't the need for new ones, and country people would nearly knock you over with the friendliness by comparison.

Myself and Neil take a flight of stairs to the unoccupied floor above the agency, where there's a rusted door with a sliding bolt. Neil draws back the bolt and we walk out onto a neglected terrace with a thick-crusted layer of pigeon droppings on it. He takes a joint from his shirt pocket and crouches away from the breeze, lights the joint effortlessly and tosses the used match over the side of the building. 'There are some things you need to know,' he says, toking off the joint. 'About working here.'

'Like what.'

'You need to stop being friendly. It makes you look weak.' He moves to pass the joint to me and I decline. 'It's always the country people who come in trying to be friendly. It tends to backfire.'

'Uh, okay.' He might be right. The friendliness hasn't endeared me to anyone. The friendliness has sent people scattering. 'Can I get your advice on something? It's just I think I've got off on the wrong foot with Edwina.' It seems I never know whether it's better to be saying something or nothing.

'It looks like she's got it in for you.' Neil gazes out across the drab, colourless cityscape. 'She likes to, uh, break people.'

'What? Why?'

'She wants to prove to herself that she's the best at everything. The only way she knows how is to bring other people down.'

'Jesus. What can I do to improve things?'

'First, you've got to pass your probation. But it won't be easy.'

'How'd you pass yours?'

He blows out. Grimaces. 'I'm not gonna lie. It was really rough. One time I had keyhole surgery to have my gallbladder taken out, and that night I was on a conference call with the guys at TuffOats. I had to be at my desk at seven the next morning, and I had to pay a nurse to come to the office and take out my stitches. But I got through it.' He smiles a sad and desperate smile. 'And it's all worked out. I passed the probation and now I'm a part of something that's cool and worthwhile and a lot of my friends are pretty jealous to be honest.'

I think I'm after ending up in the wrong place.

The three of us are up late and talking about what we're earning at work. Norma's completing her diploma to become a schoolteacher, and says she feels secure in the knowledge that her salary can only rise as the years progress, even if she has no job at the present time. Meanwhile, Nuala's earning seven grand more than me as a recruitment specialist, and she has health insurance and a pension out of it. 'That's a very poor salary,' says Nuala to me. 'If you're going to stay on in that place, you should ask for a raise.' It's a bit rich coming from her mouth, herself being the one who got the job for me in the first place. I'd say she got a tidy commission out of it. The resentment is beginning to rise up within me. I could do with having more suitable, like-minded friends, and neither Nuala nor Norma has the special ingredient.

'I'm only on probation. I can't ask for a raise.'

'You're cracked in the head,' Norma says, and her nose has never looked so pointy. 'I don't know of anyone who comes home at that hour of the night, every night of the week. Not to mind working through the weekend.'

When Norma's gone off to bed, Nuala says, 'I've a few clothes you might like. I've left them in on the bed for you.' I go into the box room and there's four or five navy tops on the bed, and the top with the woollen roses on it too. I wouldn't be caught dead in any of the tops. Nuala must think I'm in a bad way if she's giving me her old things.

I leave it a full fortnight before returning to Bean & Gone. I barely manage it, with all the anticipation, but I know it's the right thing to do. You can't have a fella thinking he has you too easily. You can't have a fella knowing you've been counting down the hours, sneaking glances out of windows to catch sight of him coming and going from work. I'm half afraid I'll land down and Luc will be holding another girl's hand at one of the circular tables, but instead I find him hunched over and turning the key in the lock on the shutter. 'Oh. Am I too late?'

He turns and rises to his feet. 'Hey,' he says, smiling. 'The dishwasher's broken. We had to close early.'

'I'll call in another time, sure. You probably want to head home.'

'How about we hang out for a while.' He throws his head. 'Come on.'

Myself and Luc meander along the silent street together, the streetlights pooling on mercury puddles. It's hard putting one foot in front of the other with all the adrenaline coursing through me. He stops in front of a pub. 'You want to have a drink?'

I smile at him. 'I could do with a drink alright.' I'm glad to be going in for the drink. The drink might consolidate the thousand million feelings I'm experiencing and make some kind of sense of them. We go inside the warm burgundy pub and find a table, and Luc goes up to the bar. When he's back with the drinks, I tell him, 'I've the photographs with me.'

He rubs his hands together and pulls his chair in closer to the table. 'Let's see.' I take out the sturdy envelope with my best photographs inside. Over several minutes, Luc looks through them carefully. 'You ever thought about exhibiting?'

'Oh, stop. They aren't that good.'

'I'll talk to Marco. His dad manages an exhibition space in Paris. Why don't you give me your number and I'll give it to him.' I write my number out on a beermat and he puts it in the inside pocket of his leather jacket. I know the talk of the exhibition space is only a ruse for getting my number, and that's fine by me. 'You know, Katie, you and me have a lot in common,' he says, looking me intently in the eyes. 'You're a dreamer. I'm a dreamer too.' This couldn't be going any better. It's all unfolding in the best way.

'I suppose we are. Dreamers.' Like with like. 'It's hard-going, though. Wouldn't you agree?'

'Absolutely. And not everybody gets it. The creative spirit. It can be hard to find your place in the world,' he says, supping on his beer. 'A lot of people are jealous. People who know they're nothing special. People with nothing to offer.'

'There's a lot of hoping and wishing. It can be very tiring, following your dream.'

'Hey. It's more tiring if you don't. You don't want to have any regrets.' It's great having someone to talk to like this. Someone who understands. It's like a meeting of minds. He sets down his beer on the table. 'I'm gonna go have a cigarette. You smoke?'

I haven't tried smoking before. I hope I can get it on the first go. 'I'll have one alright.'

Outside on the street, a tribe of tourists wearing Viking hats and capes rumbles along the cobblestones bellowing the lyrics to 'Wonderwall'. Luc rolls cigarette papers with his fingers, dabbing with his tongue. 'It's really tough to roll cigarettes here. The wind blows the tobacco everywhere. And every time I buy new papers, they turn to mush in my pocket from the rain. It's the worst.' I watch him draw the first drag, cigarette pinched between thumb and forefinger, and now he's looking into the distance, into the future, like there's something painful in his past. Or perhaps I'm only imagining it.

'How are yourself and Nuala getting on?'

Luc rubs his forehead. 'Ah, shit.' He runs the tip of his tongue over his upper lip. 'Do we have to talk about that? It's a little heavy.'

'We can talk about something else if you want.'

'I mean, we've gone out a couple of times. And Nuala's good for the soul. She's trusting and sweet. But.' He breathes out. Bristles. 'You're gonna hate me.'

'I won't hate you.' Holy God. What's coming next?

He hesitates. Looks down at his shoes and then back up at me. 'That night at Club Dynasty. I had no place to stay. I didn't have enough cash for a hotel or a hostel or anything. I was pretty fucked.' He only stayed with Nuala to sleep in a bed. Jesus.

'Why have you kept seeing her on the Friday nights?'

'I share a room with Marco. He has a girl over on Friday so I think I should have some fun too. I'm a shit, huh. A big French shit.'

'Do you think you're going to want a relationship with her?'

'A relationship? *Pfft.* It won't come to that.' It's himself and myself that are dreamers. Like with like. 'I just hope she's not in too deep.'

'I understand. I get it. As soon as you're close with someone, they make things uncomfortable. They hold you to a standard that you can't meet. They expect things from you that you're not willing to give.' I think I'm saying the right things. I feel that I'm being honest and speaking from the heart, and coming out with feelings I've harboured myself.

'Yeah.' He eyes me curiously. 'Yeah. I think it's something like that. People expecting too much from each other.' We stand close and we kiss. The white fire consumes me. I feel as though I won't eat for at least a week, won't sleep for two.

'It's been great hanging out,' he says, pulling out of the kiss. 'I'm pretty tired. We call it a night?'

'I was about to say the same thing.' I would have stayed out all night with him. I would have had ten glasses of wine and smoked forty cigarettes if it meant staying out all night with him.

Luc accompanies me to a taxi rank, and I return to the apartment high on wine and rapture. This'd be some story to tell Evelyn. This is like something Evelyn would do, and Evelyn'd get away with it. I wonder if, in some way, I'm living vicariously through Evelyn, or if, somehow, Evelyn's living vicariously through me.

Nuala turns from the television where herself and Norma are watching *Big Brother*. 'Where've you been?'

'Work,' I tell her.

Norma peers over at me and purses her lips. 'You look like you're on drugs.'

I go into the box room and lay face down on the cool pillow. *This is what it feels like. This is how I've been waiting to feel.* Not only that, but Luc's the sort of person with a dream too. It's the most attractive thing about him. He gets it. And he gets me.

'We're gonna rule this campaign, Mervin. I've got it so fucking inte-grated,' Edwina says, bobbing up and down on the exercise ball. *Scuff, scuff, scuff.* 'Mm-hm. I've always got room for another client. I was getting bored.' She ends the call, looks over at me and says, 'It's time for you to take on more responsibility.' The new client is in New York, she says, and they're five hours behind, and she tells me to expect late evening calls. The developers working on the campaign are based in India, and they're six hours ahead, and she tells me to expect early morning calls. 'Let's see if you can hit the ground running,' she says before cracking open a pineapple-flavoured energy drink.

'I'm sorry this is happening to you,' says Neil, and I don't decline the joint. I'm into the smoking now in a big way. We have smoking breaks on the hour every hour. 'Edwina's sort of out of control.'

'She has me working around the clock. Is it even legal? A person could die from a lack of sleep.' I could fall asleep now and drop off the side of the roof terrace and slam into the pavement below, and I don't think that'd even work to rouse me.

'It's the culture,' he says. 'And Mervin likes it this way. You know, maybe you should cut your losses.'

Nuala and Norma are on high alert: there's a hot-water bottle in the bed every night when I get home, and my pyjamas laid out on the radiator. I sleep, at most, for five hours per night, before hauling myself into the agency at cock crow for conference calls with the web developers. I develop conjunctivitis in both eyes, chomp on caffeine pills and live off Chinese food delivered to my desk. Neil runs out to Bean & Gone at intervals to pick up coffee and pastries, and I rack up fifty-seven missed calls from Mammy and Daddy. Mammy texts: *What sort of a life are you living up there? We never hear from you.*

I go and sit on the toilet and stare at the poster tacked to the back of it: a kitten hanging onto a washing line with the words 'Hang in there' at the end of the poster. I don't know how much longer I can hang in there for.

I haven't heard from Luc in eleven days. I'm up to high doh, wondering have I misread the signs or said the wrong thing. Maybe I'd be better off with a fella from down home.

Nuala taps on the thin door of the box room. I wouldn't mind but I'm pure strung out with exhaustion. I was up all night working on a pitch for an organic tampon brand, and all day I've been seeing abnormal flashes in my peripheral vision. I call for her to come in and she sits on the end of the bed and tells me tearfully that Luc has ended things. She invited him over for chilli con carne, and he came over and ate it, and he even had a second plate, and then he ended things. 'The bastard. If he'd had the manners to call me and tell me before I went to the supermarket, I wouldn't have spent all that money on the chilli con carne.' I wonder what can it mean, Luc ending things with Nuala. It's been a fortnight now since we went to the pub together, when I kissed him and gave him my number on a beermat. 'I told him I had a dream about him,' she says. 'It might have scared him off.'

'You can't go telling a person you had a dream about them. There's no predicting how they'll react.'

'I know that now. I'd never again do that.' She gestures for a hug. Tears stained with mascara seep onto my pyjama top.

'Yourself and Luc aren't right for one another,' I say firmly. 'He isn't a straightforward person.'

She comes out of the hug and looks at me with glistening wet eyes. 'Do you think so?'

'You want someone who's easy to figure out when you're in a relationship. Any kind of relationship.'

'You're right,' she sighs. 'It's just I thought I'd at least be engaged by now. That was always the plan. I thought I'd meet a nice fella in college. I thought I'd be married by twenty-five.'

'You can't plan your life like that, Nuala. There are too many unknown factors.'

'You're right,' she repeats, tracing a pattern on the duvet with her finger, and then she says, 'I'm surprised you haven't met anyone nice yourself. It doesn't make sense. You're so pretty and interesting. I thought even Luc had a thing for you at one point,' she says, and I try to appear taken aback. I've had the sense, on occasion, that there's something Nuala sees in me that she'd like for herself. 'If you don't mind me saying, Katie, you can be a bit distant. It's like you take too long to get to know people. You're guarded. I think people feel they're not worthy of your friendship. People get frustrated with that and they move off.'

I don't like this. 'I don't think that's true, Nuala. I've a lot of people in my life.'

'You've been up in Dublin for several years, Katie, and you're still only friends with myself and Norma. And you've never had a boyfriend. Do you not think that's unusual?'

'I've loads more friends than yourself and Norma. Loads more. You've just never met them.'

'Forget I said anything.' She hops up off the bed and makes for the door. 'Never mind me. I'm not thinking straight. I'm upset.'

'Whatever, Nuala.' *Dickhead.* Who does she think she is, coming in here and making out that I'm slow to make friends. I just haven't met the right people up in Dublin.

I suppose it was inevitable. I fall asleep on the bus and end up travelling a loop of the city and back out to the bus depot in Donnybrook. 'You've missed your stop, love,' the bus driver shouts out of his cabin.

It feels as though I've been wakened by way of electric shock. 'Holy God. Can you take me back into town?'

'I'm finished me shift. You'll have to ask God to phone you a taxi.'

Jesus. Saint Jude. I'm two hours late for work. I scramble up the steps of the office building, skid across the waxed lobby floor and slam on the elevator buttons. I'm only dropping my coat over the back of the chair when Mervin's door swings open. 'You might grace us with your presence, Katie.' *Fuck*. The pale-faced account executives whip their heads round like ostriches as I undertake the walk of shame into Mervin's office. Edwina's seated next to him with her arms folded and wearing a silk turban on her head.

'I'm sorry I'm late. I fell asleep on the bus. It'll never happen again.'

'We wanted to talk with you,' Mervin says in a serious tone. 'Edwina tells me you're struggling.'

I'm caught on the hop. Caught for words. 'I wouldn't say I'm s-struggling. I've been getting used to everything. There's a lot to it. There's a lot to do.'

'You missed an important conference call with Anika and Rohan this morning,' says Edwina, and the turban slips down her forehead.

'When a person complains about having a lot to do, it sends up a red flag. It tells me the person doesn't manage their time. It tells me they're not working smart.' Mervin gives an insincere smile. 'If you'll indulge me for a moment. I have a little story I like to share in these situations. Back when I started out in the industry, I got a call from an old friend. Pete. Pete was heading up an airline. HighTail Airlines. They've since gone out of business.'

'Pete died.'

'He…yes,' blusters Mervin. 'Pete died. The point I'm trying to make is that sometimes things don't work out and you look back and it's really a blessing in disguise.'

'It's fine,' I mumble, rising from the chair. I know what's coming next, but I don't care any more. My heart hasn't been in it. I was only fooling myself. It was worlds away from the dream.

I return to my desk and take up my handbag and coat, still warm. 'You're off,' Neil says, weaving a scalp massager with prongs over his head.

'I am. I'm off.'

'It's a pity. You only had a month left on the probation. You almost managed it.'

'I'll see you, Neil. Good luck.'

I walk out onto the clamorous street. It's all over. All of it. There's a strange relief to be had in failure. I shakily purchase a box of cigarettes and a lighter from a newsagent's and sit down on a concrete bench. I wonder what'll I do now. Where'll I go every day. I don't know who to phone, so I phone Nuala. 'I was let go,' I tell her.

'How did you manage that?' she says, gasping. 'Where are you? I'll come and meet you.'

I stay put on the bench and light up a cigarette. I put it in between my lips and it falls out. It isn't long before I spot Nuala zig-zagging through the crowd in a navy business suit, looking concerned, her curls whirling in the wind. 'You'll get something else,' she says. 'Plenty of people get let go.'

'Mm.'

'Tell you what you'll do when you get home. Why don't you have a nice hot bubble bath, get into your pyjamas, and later on yourself and myself can watch something silly.'

'Mm.'

'Did you know when I was seventeen I lost my summer job in a nursing home. I tripped over a commode and it fell over and ruined a carpet.'

'Jesus.'

Nuala says she'll ask her father if I can stay on in the apartment for a month or two without paying any rent while I'm waiting to get a new job. I tell her I wouldn't feel right about it, but thanks all the same. I don't want to be beholden to anyone. I don't want the tension skyrocketing with Norma. 'I'll get you another job,' she says. 'Don't worry about a thing. It'll all be sorted yet.'

'What kind of a job?'

She scrunches up her face. 'Would you be open to doing door-to-door sales?'

'I thought you were doing media recruitment.'

'They took it off me. I was better at the door-to-door sales.'

I've another idea altogether, and I've made up my mind about it. I'm going back to Glenbruff. Maybe a person shouldn't venture too far away from where they're from. Maybe it only leads to a sense of fragmentation, as though you've left half of yourself behind.

Norma takes delight in warning people. She warns that it'll be hard to return to Dublin if I leave it too long. 'I'm only telling you for your own good.' She knows someone who went to Australia for six months, and when the person returned, they didn't know if they were coming or going.

'Glenbruff is hardly comparable to Australia,' I say. In any case, I can't see myself coming back up to Dublin. It's run its course.

'We'll miss you,' says Nuala in a sad voice. She's standing at the door of the box room, looking in at me with her hands on her hips. 'It'll be strange having another girl in your place. I've several girls interested in the room already.' I hadn't thought about someone else staying in the box room. Someone else on the couch and going on the nights out. 'Promise us you'll come and visit.'

'Of course I'll visit.' I'm surprised to feel a bit sad leaving Nuala.

'Would you not just fly off somewhere and see how it goes? London or Sydney or anywhere at all,' she says, looking all forlorn.

'I can't afford it, Nuala. I've no money,' I say, heaving open the zip around a suitcase.

'I'll give you money.'

I smile and shake my head. 'No. Don't be daft.'

I spend all day Saturday crushing my clothes and shoes into two suitcases. I give Nuala and Norma my toiletries as I don't want them leaking into the clothes. I haven't much left after that, except for the camera, still in perfect working order. I wrap it up in bubble wrap and tuck it between the layers.

At five o'clock, a text lands into my phone: *Hey. It's Luc. Marco borrowed my leather jacket and took it to France. He came back last night and I found your number. Are you free later? Bisous.*

It's now or never, I'm thinking.

Sometimes you walk into a place and you know you're going to have a good time. You know you're about to act out, like something's been brewing inside of you and you're about to go off like a rocket. This is the only night that ever mattered, and you belong to this night, and you're going to give it everything you've got. This is a night that will change you forever.

People are watching myself and Luc and wishing they were having half as much fun. We've been dancing for two hours straight at Electric Jake's Basement. Thrashing, flailing and raising dust. Luc's shouting in my ear. He says he's going to Rio, and he's going to hit up all the big music festivals. 'It's like one day I'm gonna die and I wanna feel like I really lived while I had the chance.' His papa is very strict, and keeps threatening to cut him off financially, but he gave Luc the money after he promised to go to law school on his return. I tell Luc the advertising job hasn't worked out, and I'm leaving Dublin, and I doubt I'll be coming back. 'I don't know why you took the job. You want to work in films. You've got to make it happen,' he shouts.

'What about you? You're going to law school. It doesn't seem right.' I put my head on his warm chest and wrap my arms around him.

'Come to Rio with me. Leave it all behind.'

'I can't. There's stuff I have to get back to. People I have to see.'

'What stuff? What people? Come to Rio and forget about it. Every night could be like this.'

I raise my head. 'Let's go back to the apartment.'

'I'm not doing that.' He laughs. 'Are you kidding?'

'Why not.'

'You know why not. You're crazy.'

Myself and Luc bundle into a taxi at three in the morning, wielding kebabs. 'I don't know if this is a good idea,' he says, smiling and wincing all at once.

'I've had kebabs from that place before. They were grand.'

'No. Not the kebabs. What if we get caught?' The taxi driver looks up into his rear-view mirror.

'We won't get caught.' I don't feel in the least bit apprehensive. Nuala's got nothing to do with what's happening between myself and Luc. The likes of Nuala doesn't end up with the likes of Luc, and if she was ever to find out about it, she's the kind of person who'd forgive a thing like that. She's soft. 'We'll get up early. Before anyone's awake.' It's a fine idea.

'This is fucked up. I thought you and Nuala were sort of alike. But you know what, you're pretty dark actually.'

I wake up cold. Luc's taken up all of the duvet. I tiptoe out of the bedroom to fill a glass of water, and Nuala's sitting at the kitchen table wearing the pilled dressing gown with a plate of scrambled eggs before her. I freeze. 'Did you bring someone home?' she says teasingly. 'Aren't you the bold girl.'

Suddenly, Norma's screaming blue murder out in the hallway. Nuala grabs a hold of her butter knife, jumps up and runs out to her. I look through the open doorway to see Luc standing there, dishevelled, and with his hand on the latch of the front door. He's wide-eyed, tousle-haired and poised to sneak out. Nuala hurls the butter knife at him, misses, and it bounces off the back of the door. Luc leaps, yelping, and yanks the door shut behind him.

Nuala and Norma turn about to me, agog. 'How c-could you?' stammers Nuala. 'We thought you were nice.' I suppose she thought we were better friends than that.

'Get your shit and get out of here,' rails Norma. 'You're a disgrace. And don't ever come near us again.' It's a good thing I'm already packed.

I breathe a long sigh of relief as the train pulls out of Heuston Station. It's late in the afternoon, the carriage is warm, and amber sunbeams pour in on top of me. 'I'm only home to explore my options,' I imagine myself saying to people in Glenbruff. 'I don't know yet what my plans are, but sure that's part of the fun of it.' Will I call up to Evelyn's house, or pick up the phone, or what'll I do? Would it be mad if I wrote her a letter? Will I be downplaying the job in the agency, or talking myself up? It'll all depend.

On the approach to Glenbruff, I gather up my things, sling a backpack over my shoulders and make my way down the aisle of the train. I've two big suitcases to haul out of the luggage hold. Dylan Hartigan spots me huffing with the cases and helps me place them down on the station platform. He flashes the catalogue smile, but there's nothing but deadness behind the eyes.

'Hello, Dylan.'

'Hello, stranger.'

'How's the golf?'

'Never better. I'm after turning semi-pro.' It's only later I recall that he never used my name, and likely hasn't remembered me at all.

3
Glenbruff

Daddy collects me from the train station. 'I thought you were permanent in that place,' he says gruffly, and only barely looking at me. Daddy's had an aversion to unemployment since the quarry closed up in the eighties and he lost his job. There were no jobs again until Amperloc opened several years after.

'I was on a short contract.' It's not right to lie about the job, but telling the truth would create too much alarm and fuss.

'Have you some sort of a plan?' he says. Can a person not have a minute to themselves without being asked what they're going to do next! Can a person not enjoy the present moment.

'Of course I've a plan, Daddy,' I tell him, but the truth is that I've no plan in mind, only to sink into old ways of being.

As soon as I'm landed in the door, I go down to my bedroom and put on old clothes: tracksuit bottoms with the knees standing out in them, a hoodie with a comforting scent that's seen the inside of a drier one too many times, and well-worn running shoes. I rifle through the drawers and come across mixtapes I haven't listened to in years, and I throw them in the tape deck of the dusty stereo. I dance around in the gap between the bed and the wardrobe, and I unzip a suitcase and take out a few things to fulfil the homecoming. Books. Slippers. The pyjamas still stained with Nuala's mascara tears. It's then I notice something awry. There's an indentation in the clothes where the camera is supposed to be. Someone must have gone into the luggage hold on the train and whipped it out. I'm rigid with disbelief. What can it mean, the camera gone? What can it mean, the camera being taken? It feels like a cosmic incident, a sort of portent contrived by unknown entities.

Daddy's voice is raised above in the kitchen, and Robert's too. Daddy's asking *what exactly* is the nature of Robert's friendship with Desmond Duignan. 'Has that man no friends his own age?' Robert has maintained a good relationship with Desmond Duignan over the years. He's on first-name terms with him, and calls him Des. Robert looks up to Des as a sort of role model, with the effect of distancing himself from Mammy and Daddy. Robert and Des go for pints together in Donovan's and they go off fishing in the River Suck for the full day.

I creep up along the corridor, up close to the kitchen door, and have a listen in. 'Myself and Des find one another interesting. He's a highly intelligent person. He has life experience. He's been kidnapped by the FARC, and been involved in secret talks in all sorts of war-torn countries.'

'Bunk,' Daddy says. 'That man wants the adoration of young people. He'll tell you anything you want to hear. He's too fond of you, and no wife or a hint of a woman about him.'

'Jesus, Dad. Did it ever cross your mind that we might have an intellectual connection? A shared philosophy, like.'

'You should be going around with people your own age.'

'I've no interest in going around with people my own age. I've nothing in common with people my own age. Lookit. Myself and Des have plans. He's going to help me with my career. He has a network in the States.' Robert's completed his engineering degree but he's had difficulty securing a job as a bridge engineer. Mammy tells me he's been sleepwalking and losing weight, and he's even broken his accordion in a rage. She says Daddy hauled him out of the house by his collar and roared at him to pull himself together.

'Think very carefully about that man's motives. Don't let the career dream blind you.' Daddy's talking to the wall, but still and all, it is a bit unorthodox, Robert going around the place with his old teacher. You'd have to wonder if there's more to it. Even Mammy's saying that man is only a fraud and a fantasist. Why did he go around driving cheap cars if he had all his money made on the stock market?

The handball alley is more than two hundred years old. It's made up of three walls: a high back wall and two wings either side that taper to the ground. There are big boughs of horse chestnut trees hanging over the wings. I go around the sides of the handball alley, picking clumps of velvet moss out of the crevices and smelling them.

Robert's belting a tennis ball against the high wall and catching it. The handball alley resounds with echoes of the tennis ball clapping off the wall, and the clap of it landing back in his hand. *Poc!*

After a bit, he relaxes in himself. The hunched shoulders broaden out, and his face softens. He stifles a laugh. 'I've a story for you. I don't know what you'll make of it.' Robert tells me he took Maeve Lynch over to the cinema in Adragule to see *The Notebook.* He says he collected her up at the house, and she was dolled up to the nines, and as soon as she sat into the car, he knew he'd made a mistake. There was something about her that made him tense up. He says his mind was screaming. He says she was laughing at the wrong times during the film, and crying at the wrong times, and when the lights came up afterwards, there was blood all around Maeve's mouth and on her chin and spattered on her top. She was after getting her lip caught in her braces, but she was oblivious to it. Robert was disgusted. He took a tissue out of his pocket and handed it to her, and she spat on the tissue and tried to wipe all the blood off herself. She was shaking and bawling, and he'd to take her straight home, and the lip was bleeding all the way there. He says he's been avoiding her ever since. 'That's the women of Glenbruff for you. Awkward as fuck.' He resumes the belting of the ball, and after a time he says, 'Aidan was in Glenbruff this morning. I mentioned you were home. He was wondering if you'll be going to the bonfire.'

Oh. It must be five years since I laid eyes on Aidan Morley. The Stephen's Night party when he made a holy show of himself. 'What bonfire is that?'

'Summer solstice bonfire. Kenneth's organising it. It'll probably be shite.'

'I wonder will Evelyn be going,' I muse aloud, and I've a shudder down my spine that I can't discern as being either fear or excitement. It could well be a mix of the two.

Kenneth is going around with a bucket collecting the entry fee. It's five euros to stand in the field with the bonfire. 'What are we getting for our money, Kenneth?' people are asking.

'A free bonfire,' he says.

There's a yellow cast to the sky, and the atmosphere rumbles with indecipherable sounds. Small children roll down the gentle slope of field, and there are dogs racing around at high speed, chasing hares, yapping and yowling. The locals stand in clusters, talking about the stretch in the evening. It's half past nine and you could thread the eye of a needle in the twilight. Kenneth is tending to the bonfire now, lobbing firewood at it haphazardly and broken bits of pallets. Sparks leap from the flames and fritter away into the sky. There's something alive in the bonfire; if I look at it with one eye closed, I can see fiery demons whirling around inside it.

Evelyn steps between myself and the fire, appearing in silhouette. 'Would you look who it is.' She's standing with her feet planted out, clad in Doc Marten boots reaching midway up her calves, and her fists are jammed in the pockets of her denim jacket.

'Hi.' I'm prickling with electricity, like there's a network of bare wires under my skin instead of veins and arteries.

'What are you doing down here?' she snaps, looking cross, her pout crinkling with displeasure.

'I was laid off.' It's what I've decided to tell people. It's the handiest way out of it. I don't want a 'Poor Katie' story doing the rounds. *Katie couldn't hold on to the job. Katie wasn't able for it. Katie wasn't cut out for it and had to come home.*

'Laid off from what?'

'I was working in an advertising agency. I was coming up with ideas for advertising campaigns and liaising with clients and making the plans to implement…the plans.' I can feel my throat beginning to close over.

'*Liaiiiising,*' she says, drawing out the word before making a snorting noise in the space behind her nose.

'We did a campaign for a fortified porridge. We had a woman parasailing off the top of an office block. We did buses and billboards. You might have seen it.' This is only a warm-up, I'm telling myself. It takes time to reignite a friendship. It's not something that'll happen overnight. You have to invest in it: time, energy and fawning.

'I'm not sure if you've noticed but we don't have buses or billboards in Glenbruff.' She flicks her long hair over her shoulder. 'What happened anyway?'

'I was laid off,' I repeat. 'They might have extended the contract only we lost one of our big accounts. It's a common enough thing to happen in the industry. It's all swings and roundabouts.'

Evelyn looks at me with great intensity, and then she says, 'I just have a problem with advertising on, like, a fundamental level. It's like all you're doing is hijacking people's brains. It's not a noble creative pursuit. Not like film or drawing or other kinds of art.' I had thought she would think it was cool. I had thought she would think it was daring. I thought she'd be impressed, or envious even.

'I don't know. I think advertising is important. And it's a career.'

'Do you not think the concept of having a career is dangerous. People getting caught up with having to have a career and they end up limiting themselves, and limiting their potential to try other things.

It's actually sad how many people feel the need to have a *career*,' she says, pulling her hand out of her denim pocket and making quotation marks with her fingers. It occurs to me that it wouldn't matter what I'd been doing in Dublin but she'd find a way to denounce it or demean it.

'I don't know.' I shrug my shoulders. 'Maybe. Probably. What about you. Are you still doing the art?'

Peadar's approaching us now, swaggering across the grass in a Radiohead T-shirt. He has a cigarette propped over his left ear and his fringe is falling in his eyes.

'Peadar. Are you well?'

'Oh, I'm in great form,' he says confidently, dropping a tanned arm over Evelyn's shoulder. The arm has a streak of motor oil on it. 'I've everything figured out. The meaning of life.'

'I'm just telling Katie that I'm giving up on the art. There's no point making art if no one ever sees it.'

'Here we go,' he gripes, making a fed-up face. 'What about doing it for yourself and not other people?'

'People make art because they want the attention. They're always thinking about who's going to see it. What you're saying is a cop-out.' She pushes his dirty arm off her shoulder.

'What about Van Gogh,' argues Peadar. 'Painted over nine hundred paintings and sold only the one while he was alive, but Vincent just carried on with it. The painting was a bodily function, like shitting and eating. That's real artistry. Not caring who's looking but doing it for the sake of it.'

'All that talent and nobody acknowledged him his entire life,' she says, raising her voice. 'He just wandered around in fields and on the road, thinking he didn't matter. Thinking he's a nobody. Then as soon as he's dead, some Japanese wanker buys one of his paintings for millions. I'll tell ye now, I'm not taking that chance.'

She's right, I suppose. It hurts to live your life like that. But imagine thinking so highly of yourself that you'd equate yourself to

Van Gogh, one of the most important painters who's ever lived. Is she for real?

'You know,' she goes on, 'the only way to become really successful in music or acting or anything at all is to die. At least then you've a bit of mystery to you and people are left wanting more.'

'You give up too easily,' Peadar says, and Evelyn takes to sulking, and it gets me thinking that she's all talk and no show and always has been.

Peadar says he was up in Dublin for a while and he didn't like it and came home again. 'I couldn't settle. I don't know what it was. It's not for everyone. I wouldn't be mad gone on city livin'.' He got back into the trucking on his return to Glenbruff and he's on the road two weeks out of four. When he's not on the road he does a bit of singing in Donovan's Bar. He asks me to call in on Friday night as he's keen to sing to a decent-sized crowd, and I say I'd only be delighted. It's nice being asked places now that I'm home.

Kenneth beckons Peadar over to him. He wants to roll an old tractor tyre into the bonfire but hasn't the strength on his own. 'Yourself and Peadar are still together,' I say to Evelyn as we're observing Peadar straining at the side of the tyre.

'Yeah,' she says. 'We're not a couple though. Like, we're not exclusive or anything. It's like an open relationship but there's no one else involved.' She turns to me, tilts her heart-shaped face and narrows her hazel eyes. 'How come we haven't heard from you in so long?'

'Oh. You know yourself. I just got caught up with work and the social side of things. It's hectic up in Dublin.'

The hazel eyes bore into me. 'You were gone so long we nearly forgot about you,' she says, and my heart begins hammering. 'You can't just come back here and try to be one of us again. It doesn't work that way. You didn't even come out to see us at Christmas time. We thought you didn't give a damn about us.'

I cough nervously, my airways clenching. 'I've always felt that we've one of those kinds of friendships that no matter how long it's been we can still get together and it's like we only saw one another yesterday.' The sentiment comes out all daft and hokey, and I'm hit with a wave of searing embarrassment.

'You were needed down here,' she says, and there's the catch of hurt in her voice. There's great reassurance in the catch of hurt.

'How d'you mean?'

'Don't give me that. You must have heard the stories.'

'I never heard any stories. I'm out of the loop. Honest to God.'

'Dad hired Stacey Nugent for his office. He left us and went off with her. They're living in an apartment over in Adragule. Over the medical centre.'

'I can't believe it.' Stacey Nugent is the same age as myself and Evelyn. She must be twenty years younger than Dan Cassidy. He's some rotter, but haven't I always known it.

'I thought it was Peadar she was after when she came working for us. I suppose I was wrong.' She sets her jaw. 'Anyway. I made the most of it. Dad gave me a blank cheque and I bought heaps of new equipment.' What sort of equipment, I'm wondering, but now isn't the time for asking.

'I'm awful sorry, Evelyn. I was trying to make a go of it up there. I'm sorry.' I hope she'll accept the apology now we've addressed the resentment. 'It's good to have the chat with you and sort things out. Wipe the slate.' The words stay floating between us, throb excruciatingly. 'Where's Maeve? Is she around here someplace? Will she be coming down?'

'She's on holidays with Amanda. They're over in Tenerife. If we've any luck they won't come back.'

For all of Aidan's enquiring about me, there isn't sight nor sound of him all evening. Feck him anyway. What about him. Myself and Evelyn sit in the grass facing the unwieldy bonfire, the sparks whisking around it, and we've no inclination to say very much at all. We've the sort of friendship where you don't need to be always engaged in talk. We can sit together companionably, lifted through the other's presence.

'That's some stretch in the evening,' I say after an unknowable amount of time. I can almost see molecules in the air with the naked eye. The components of memory.

'*Ehhh*, it's the summer solstice,' she jeers. 'And I thought you were college educated.'

I can't think of one good reason not to resume the friendship. Life's like a film with Evelyn in it.

'Evelyn said you were coming. I thought she was pulling my leg,' Maeve says gaily. She's dressed all in white: linen trousers, a crochet top, a necklace made out of seashells and bleached pieces of coral. 'How long are you staying around for, Katie?'

'I'm not sure yet. Just the summer, I'd say.' A summer in Glenbruff is a shapeless, endless thing. You'd forget what day of the week it is. 'How'd you get on in Tenerife?' Maeve went with Amanda and John to Tenerife. It was her first ever holiday abroad. She purchased lots of gaudy accessories on the trip, and has a blue fabric starfish fixed to the side of her head. It's a bit much. It's daft-looking.

'Oh, it was pure luxury. The whole thing,' Maeve coos. 'We'd the whole place to ourselves. A five-bedroom villa. Amanda said we could use it anytime we want. And the beach is only a five-minute walk.'

Evelyn arrives in wearing her old velvet choker and the black dress with spaghetti straps. 'Move your big hole, Maeve. Shove up there and make room.' She forces her way in alongside us in the nook and the handbags are toppling to the ground. Maeve's caught now with an armrest in the ribs. 'Take that poxy yoke off your head.' Maeve fumbles with the blue starfish and removes it with a jerk, tearing strands of hair from her scalp. 'Well. Tell us. How's your fancy mammy? How'd you get on?'

Maeve smiles serenely. 'We got along perfectly. I am so like her in so many ways. We've the same taste in clothes and food. Wine as well. It's mad, girls.' She's still walking on air after the holiday, and the words are babbling out of her. 'It was roasting hot from dawn to dusk. We had cocktails every day. We had cocktails with our breakfast. Tenerife is like paradise on earth. And the beach was nearly a mile long. If you'd have seen it.'

'Jesus, Maeve. It's only Tenerife. I've been there a million times and so has everyone else,' says Evelyn. I've never been to Tenerife but I don't say it.

Maeve's euphoria fades. She places a glass of fizzy orange and vodka to her lips and gulps down two or three mouthfuls, and then she says, 'Amanda's coming down to Glenbruff to see me. Herself and John. They're coming next week. They'll be meeting Mary and Tom.' Evelyn scowls, and Maeve says, 'I'm not going over it again. That was years and years ago. People make mistakes. Anyway,' she continues, 'let ye be the first to know. I'm changing my name to Roxanne.'

'*Roxanne*,' Evelyn snorts. 'Are you fucking joking me? Are you having me on?'

'Roxanne Dowling is the name I was given when I was born. It's my actual name,' Maeve says defiantly.

'Don't fucking change it. Roxanne is a prostitute's name.'

'It's only a song about one,' I pipe up, attempting to keep the chat on an even keel, and Evelyn rolls her eyes.

'I'll do what I want.' I suppose Maeve doesn't want to be Maeve Lynch any more, and that's understandable.

Peadar lands into the bar wearing a sheepskin coat, leather waist-coat and thin fabric tie. Everyone's taking notice of him. He has that kind of way about him, that kind of look about him. He'd catch anyone's eye. He strolls over to the corner and sits up on a high stool. He adjusts the mic stand, and takes a minute or so to tune his guitar, and then he moves his mouth in close to the mic. 'One-tchew-one-tchew.' The conversation in the bar quietens. All eyes are on Peadar, transfixed by the handsome face *chiaroscuro* under soft spotlights, the tragic cheekbones emphasised. A textured, sensual voice flows out of him. He sings 'People Are Strange' like he's channelling a ghost, and the tantalising sound rolls over us all.

'Myself and Peadar are very close,' Evelyn whispers, as though she's in a sort of reverie through looking at him and listening to him. 'We're kindred spirits.' Perhaps it's the drink talking and the resulting rise in sentimentality, but not long after, she says the same kind of thing about Maeve while Maeve is away powdering her nose. 'Myself and Maeve are very close. She's been through an awful lot.' Evelyn's remarks are interesting, I think. They indicate a sense of ownership over people. The marking of territory. I imagine her saying the same kind of thing about me. *Myself and Katie are very close. We're practically sisters.* I have a swell of pleasure at the thought of it.

She wants to go out for a cigarette and Maeve has to mind the seats. We head out the back door and sit ourselves down at a weatherworn picnic table with a big, dirty umbrella above it. The wood of the picnic table is soft and yielding. I take out a box of my own cigarettes. 'Oh. You're a real smoker now,' she says, and she sounds to be happy about it. 'What brought that on?'

'I took it up at the agency. I had a friend who smoked.' I'd say Evelyn isn't the least bit interested in hearing about the agency, or anyone in it, and I promptly switch to her preferred topic of conversation. 'Isn't Peadar very talented.'

'Oh, he is,' she gushes. 'He has it in him to be hugely successful. You wouldn't believe the plans we have together.' She takes a good long drag of her cigarette. 'He's even written a song about me.'

'Has he. A song.'

'It's called "Caution to the Wind",' she says, exhaling, and I watch the plume of smoke flooding into the air before her. 'There's something special about Peadar. Pure raw talent. I'd say there's every chance he's Jim Morrison reincarnated.' With the lit cigarette still in hand, she takes up her long dark hair and makes a big bun on top of her head, and then she lets the hair drop down and shakes it out around herself. It's hard to say what is her best feature. The puffy little mouth or the slinky hair slipping over her shoulders or the intelligent-looking eyes.

'What do you make of Amanda Dowling?'

She tuts. 'That's a shit show due any minute.' She looks up through a hole in the umbrella and squints. 'The thing about Maeve is that she always wanted to be somebody else. She was never happy in her own skin. Mary and Tom were always telling her she was a lovely girl and she never believed it. She stopped listening. She was always a bit lost until the letters started coming, and then she became like a new person. Talking differently, wearing different clothes. She even went on a few dates.' Evelyn's always been the one to fill me in on what's really going on with people. It's the indication we're picking up where we left off. 'Amanda's a piece of work, Katie. She's a liability. She could ruin Maeve yet.'

'Why d'you say that?'

'She was hooked on heroin by the time she was fifteen, and when she had Maeve, she barely fed her. The neighbours didn't even know there was a child in the house because Maeve never cried. She was two and a half when she was taken off Amanda and her head was rolling with lice. You remember the bald patch.' I nod. I remember. 'The infestation of lice was so severe that the hair stopped growing. It was wicked.'

'That's awful. I'd no idea.'

'That's why Maeve is as odd as she is. That's why I give her the attention and tolerate her and go around with her. Mam told me the whole lot when I was young and swore me to secrecy.' Poor Maeve has reason to be odd. She has reason to become a crackpot, but still and all, she's done well for herself. You'd nearly admire her. 'I've been giving out to her non-stop. She has herself convinced that this is some sort of happy-ever-after tale, like herself and Amanda are going to be the best of pals, but I've a bad feeling about the whole thing.'

'I suppose we'll have to wait and see. There's nothing we can do only wait and see.'

She sniffs. 'I'll be moving on soon, Katie. I'll be moving on from Glenbruff and Maeve'll be left behind. I've to do my own thing. I've to live my own life, and I can't be watching out for Maeve any more.'

What's this now? 'What are you planning to do? Where will you be going?'

'I'm just waiting on a few things to fall into place but it'll be a big move. A big change. That's all I can say.' Might I be going with her? Would I be welcome?

We hear the rapturous applause for Peadar inside in the bar, and we return to the nook, where Maeve's sitting with a cross face and the blue starfish reattached to her head. 'I've been minding the seats for ages. I was about to head for home.'

'We were only gone two minutes. Keep your knickers on, Maeve.'

Peadar comes down to the nook to us and crushes in alongside us. The set was well received and there are drinks arriving down to the table for him. 'Good man.' 'You're a credit to us.' 'Next stop Nashville.' A drink lands down from Dan Cassidy and Stacey Nugent, who're perched up at the bar and the two of them half cut.

'I have to say you're very impressive with the singing,' I tell him. 'I enjoyed listening to you.'

'I do a lot of Jim Morrison covers. He's a big influence. I've been reading up a lot on him.'

'What is it about him that appeals to you?'

'Well.' He leans forward. 'Did you know that when he was a child, he was with his family driving through the California desert and they came across an accident and there were dead Indians lying on the road. Morrison said he was possessed by their spirits. I had a similar experience to that. The night of Mam's wake.'

'What was it? What did you see?' I press him. Maeve looks perturbed and shrinks back.

'Ah. I'll tell you again.' He rests his back against the padded seat, looking satisfied in himself. 'You'll think I'm losing it.'

'He finds it hard to talk about,' adds Evelyn.

Aidan strolls in unexpectedly and I have a big rush in the chest. 'I heard you were around. I said I'd better stall in and say hello,' he says. His face is plump and healthy-looking, his skin clean and smooth. His eyes are shining bright, and the white teeth are gleaming. I can tell by looking at him that he's put himself back together again. The dark blond hair is cut in a conventional style, and he's wearing a casual shirt with jeans and loafers.

'Wow. It's great to see you, Aidan.' There was always an energy going between us, a warm and exhilarating chemistry, and a certain way we had of talking to one another, and a certain way we had of looking at one another. There were always the shy glances. There was always the shy spark.

'What's brought you back to Glenbruff?'

'I was made redundant.'

'Shite,' he says, and he looks to be sympathetic. There's something about having known a person all your life. You tend to care for them. You tend to want the best for them.

'I'll figure something out. I'm just taking some time away. Life can get so crazy that you forget what you really want to be doing. You get swept up.' I flash a smile and he reciprocates. His smile is mesmerising.

'Are you around for long, Katie?'

'Til I figure something out.'

'Give something a go, and if it doesn't work, you can try something else.'

'That's it. The only way to move forward is to try something. Keep an open mind.'

'You're still interested in the photography?'

'I am, yeah.'

'I've been taking a few shots myself. Football matches and that. You must call up to the house one of the days and have a look. See what you make of them.' I wonder does he mean it, to call up to the house, or is that just one of those things people say but don't expect you to take them up on it. He looks down at his watch. 'You'll have to excuse me. I've to be up early for training. But it was good seeing you, Katie. It's good to have you home.'

'Of course.' I'm frustrated. 'Safe home. See you.' All I've ever had from Aidan were moments that came to nothing, near misses that only ever led to disappointment. The whole thing makes me suspicious of God. You'd wonder why he's always presenting me with things I'd love to have, but he never lets me have them. Is it all a big joke to him, people's actual lives and feelings? It'd have you thinking there's no one in charge, and there's no such thing as fate, and it's only ourselves responsible for our own lives.

The rest of the night drifts by in a smatter of talk and reconnections, and eventually, we're all up dancing. Kenneth is hunched over a music deck, bouncing his head up and down in time with the beat, a headphone as big as a doughnut pressed to one ear. There's no doubt but that he'll be driving out the regulars with the thumping club tunes. It was Kenneth's father, Finbar, who bought Donovan's a few months ago as he always fancied the idea of running a pub, but he wasn't up to it in the end with losing the foot to diabetes.

Evelyn, Maeve and myself all walk home together, and Peadar too, the guitar case high up on his back, the birdsong commencing and the horizon's edge shading into pale blue. I make a joke about the sign in front of Nancy's Café informing customers that they're selling 'latties' and 'crossaunts', and we laugh uproariously, but I remind myself that I'm not to be too snide about Glenbruff. It's their home, and it's my origin.

'It's a crying shame Angelo's is closed,' bemoans Peadar. 'You'd be hankering after a bag of chips late at night. You'd be dreaming of chips.'

'Has Pascal shut up shop?'

'He has. A few years now. He's gone over to Vegas to play poker professionally.'

'You're obsessed with chips, Peadar,' says Evelyn, walking along in her socks and clutching her high-heeled boots in her hand. 'It's all you fucking eat. You're malnourished-looking.'

'It's the frontman look,' he says, plucking the sheepskin collar.

'Go on and tell me what you saw, Peadar. I'm intrigued,' I say. 'The night of Louise's wake.'

Peadar looks to Evelyn and then to me, building up the anticipation. He stops on the road and we all look at him. 'It happened like this. I was running towards the humpback bridge when I saw the ghost of a monk. He was hovering a few feet off the ground with a black hole for a face. Next thing I was thrown back on the road. It was like being flung out of a catapult. I was never so afraid in my life.' He shakes his head slowly. 'I'll never, ever forget it. Long as I live.'

I shiver. 'That's some story. I'd have been traumatised.'

'It's because they built Amperloc on the grounds of an ancient monastery,' Evelyn explains. 'It's sacred ground. The spirits of the monks aren't happy about it.'

'Jesus. I never knew that.' We reach the front gate of my house and I wave them off. 'Goodnight. Watch out for the monks.' Evelyn and Peadar approach the brow of the hill, and Maeve trots behind them in the camel-coloured coat, and they slip over the top and away.

It's hard to fall asleep with Peadar's singing voice still sounding in my ears, and thinking of Maeve who's headed towards some sort of disaster, and wondering if the time will ever be right for myself and Aidan, and if it really matters at all, because wherever Evelyn's going, I intend to go too.

Robert's fuming, pelting the balding tennis ball off the wall in the handball alley with a fearsome force. 'They've brought Des in for questioning. He's up in the station in Adragule.'

'Why? How come?'

'Apparently Maureen Cooney found a letter up in her loft inside the lining of an old suitcase. She says it's a strange thing for a teacher to write such a personal letter to a child.' It was Evelyn said Desmond Duignan should have been spoken to by the guards, strung up by the toes and interrogated. Evelyn's sharp, I'm thinking. She knows things. 'The guards have decided it's evidence of grooming. It's the maddest shit I've ever heard.'

'What was in the letter?'

'Nothing,' he spits. 'The letters were only intended as encouragement. He used to write letters to all of us. I had several myself over the years. We all got them. It wasn't that Pamela was singled out.'

'I suppose it's difficult to say if we haven't read the letter ourselves.' There must be something peculiar in the letter if they've gone so far as to bring Des in for questioning.

'Maureen told the cops about the tape Des brought from the States when Pamela expressed an interest in dancing. But we all got things like that from him. You remember the book about bridges I had when I was young. It was Des who sent off for it for me.'

'It must be a misunderstanding, so.'

'A man tries to do his best and look what happens. It's the same story every place nowadays. Good men being vilified all over. He could lose the job over it.'

'Still. If you haven't read the letter yourself...' I say, my voice faltering.

He throws me a contemptuous look. His black eyes are smarting. 'What am I after telling you.'

'Alright. You know him better than I do.'

'I know him better than anyone.' Is Robert in some sort of denial? Has Des gotten into his head and taken it over? 'Now don't go saying this to Mam or Dad, but myself and Des are moving in together. As soon as the guards let him out. He needs good people around him. He needs a friend.'

Mammy pays a visit to Mary Lynch. Mary says Tom is out on the farm and he won't come in. 'He won't talk about it,' says Mary. 'He's too upset.' Mary confides in Mammy that Maeve hasn't two pennies to rub together in spite of the good job. She cannot understand it. She says that Maeve was in the kitchen a few days ago, and a black crow flew down the chimney and startled her, and it was a harbinger of doom. Something bad was on the way. They were only waiting for the misfortune to take place. It could be a death or an accident or a fire. They'd have to wait and find out. One way or another, it'd be a bad shock.

'Aidan wants you to call up,' Robert says, gutting a snouted pike fish over the kitchen sink, his hands awash with blood. Des has been released without charge after Robert stormed down to the garda station with a stack of letters he had under the mattress, and himself and Des spent the morning at Lough Easkey.

'What's that?' I turn down the volume on the one o'clock news.

'Aidan Morley,' he says, lopping off a head and tail. 'He was down at the lake with his camera. He says Terry and Peadar are heading out for the afternoon to buy Peadar a motorbike and he wants you to call up to the home place.'

My stomach is clenching in waves. 'When?' This'd better be the real thing. This'd better be it.

'He'll be up there now, I'd say. He'll be back by now. He's eager to see you.'

I'm walking along the road under the canopy of trees. I'm taking my time, taking it all in and savouring it. The leaves are glowing luminous in the sunlight. Petrol-blue dragonflies zip and roll in the warm air. My heartbeat accelerates to see the familiar bungalow up ahead and Aidan inside and our fates about to collide.

He carries in a plate of custard creams, or 'teacher biscuits' as myself and Evelyn used to call them, and an overflowing cup of tea that slops out on one side. 'I spent three hundred quid on the camera lens. It's the one all the big sports photographers use. That's what they told me in the shop,' he says, sitting in close to me on the couch, and I could faint with the longing. He proceeds to show me his photographs of sliding tackles, jubilant spectators and the gurning faces of young players in a slideshow set to a soundtrack by U2. 'That was a beaut of a day,' he says, frisking his dry hands together. 'We hammered Saint Malachy's. Annihilated them.'

'That's a good shot there,' I say, pointing at the screen.

'You think so,' he says eagerly. 'You think it's good.'

'You could enter it into a competition and see how you get on.'

'You might bring me good luck.' I can feel the wishing in the air, but no one makes the move. It won't be me who makes the move.

After several minutes of small talk and wholesome banter, I come to realise that Aidan hasn't asked me a thing about Dublin at all. I'd say he thinks I haven't changed a bit. I'd say he thinks I've no good stories, or else he's not interested in hearing them.

'How d'you find the teaching?' I ask him, tiring of the football photography and talk of Saint Malachy's Parish. It's like the Crips and the Bloods at this stage.

'I love it. It suits me.'

'Isn't that great. I'm happy for you,' I say, supping on the bland tea. Aidan forgot the two sugars I asked for. All of an instant, I'm recalling the crystal pins falling out of my hair and hitting off the dance floor at the Debs' Ball.

'I was lucky to get the job at all.' His expression hardens. 'It was stupid of me to have given the interview to the papers. Pure stupid, looking back on it. It did more harm than good.' He closes down the screen of the laptop. *Harrumph.*

'You're entitled to tell your side of the story.' I rest the cup of tea on my knee. 'I thought you did well.'

'When I went looking for a teaching post I could tell they'd looked me up online. They'd let on they were hiring from within the existing staff and the ad was only a legal obligation, but I'd see the same

post being advertised for weeks and months afterwards. Tyre-kickin'
bastards.'

'That must have been rough,' I say, careful not to toss the teacup
as I reach for a custard cream.

'Peadar told me to keep going, to keep sending in the job applications. He's always saying I'll be exonerated.'

'I suppose you heard about Desmond Duignan.'

'I did. There was nothing to it apparently. He was out again last
night. Didn't I meet himself and Robert at the lake earlier on.'

'Mm.'

'D'you know what, I'd sell my soul to know what happened Pamela.'

'You would?'

His shoulders drop forward. 'You don't know what it's like. No one
does. I've been over it and over it in my head. The most likely scenario
is a drunk driver knocking her down and hiding the evidence. But…'
He grimaces. 'I know I shouldn't dwell on it. I know I've to move
past it.'

'Did you ever try searching for her? By yourself.'

'Oh, I did. At the beginning. I even took out Tom Lynch's metal
detector up and around the bog to see if I'd find some small scrap of
evidence, but I never found anything and it made me feel worse. I
had to put a stop to it.'

'Do you ever see the Cooneys around the place? Whatever happened to them?'

'They moved away years ago. The investigation was going nowhere
and the mother gave up hope.' He begins rubbing his palms down the
fronts of his trouser legs. 'Can I trust you not to mention something
to Evelyn? I know ye are good friends.' His eyes are fixed upon me.

'Of course. You can trust me.' What's this now.

'The Cassidys' trucks are always coming and going from Glenbruff.
Can't you imagine a scenario where Pamela is coming along the road
and a truck pulls in alongside her and she's taken away in it. Up towards

Adragule and the motorway only twenty minutes beyond. It'd be easy conceal someone in a truck and take them away to God knows where.' There are beads of sweat forming on his forehead. 'That's what I think happened her, and there's more than myself thinks it. Peadar thinks there might be something to it as well, but you know he can't say it. Not with Evelyn and the job. He won't even discuss it.'

'Could such a thing happen in Glenbruff? Is the place that bad? Are the people that bad?' Could there be something to it? Would there be any way of finding out if the trucks were searched?

'There've been rumours about Dan Cassidy for years. Drug trafficking. Human trafficking. And he's well in with the guards and judges. People are afraid of him.' He swallows. 'I think I'll go mad if I don't get answers, Katie. It's like a parasite inside me, eating away at me.' He pauses. 'Will you have more tea?'

'No, thanks. I'll be off now in a minute.'

He coughs into a closed fist. 'We should go out ourselves sometime with the camera,' he says, a stilted pitch to his voice. 'Go off for the afternoon up to Lough Easkey. I've plenty of time now with the kids off for the summer.'

'Alright. We'll go one of the days.'

He lingers on the doorstep as I make my way out to the road. It seems my passion for Aidan has been like a flare going off, full of colour and light, but falling from the sky and coming to nothing.

Geraghty's Newsagent's has a tier of faded boxes of washing powder in the front window, and black bananas hanging from butcher hooks on the ceiling inside. An open-topped freezer in the centre aisle is making a protracted groaning sound like there's someone dying inside it.

Kenneth's father Finbar sits behind the counter on an old stool with a cracked leather seat and asks me forty questions. 'Who are you?' 'Where do you live?' 'Who's your father?' 'What does he do?' There's nothing worse than telling a person your business and them telling you nothing in return.

'Kenneth is running Donovan's now. He'll enjoy that, won't he.'

'I don't know where you heard that,' says Finbar, like I'm some class of eedgit.

'He told me himself. Wasn't I in there the other night.'

'You're dreaming. Kenneth doesn't run a pub.'

'He does. He told me himself. He told me he's taken over the pub.'

Finbar throws the box of cigarettes out onto the counter. 'You heard wrong.' God Almighty. It's like the twilight zone around here.

I'm up at the top of the town and passing the church gates when Mickey Cassidy bounds out on the path before me. 'It's only me,' he declares. 'It's Mickey.' The look of him is unsettling: the pinched child's face and the big red mouth slicked with wet. The white-blond hair sticking out all over his head, and not only that, but he's reeking of petrol. Robert says he has a job laying patio tiles. I don't know how you could trust him to count to ten, never mind laying a patio.

'Mickey.' I press my hand to my chest. 'You frightened the life out of me. What are you playing at?'

'I saw you and thought I'd give you a fright.'

'Well. It worked. I'll see you.' I make the move to head off along the path and Mickey blocks me.

'I've news,' he says.

'What?' I snap at him.

'Evelyn's going to a film festival.'

'What do you mean?'

'Herself and Peadar are going to America. To a film festival.'

'What would they be going to a film festival for?' A film festival. In *America?*

'They made a film and they sent it off and it's going to be in a film festival in a place called New Mexico. They just got word today.' Hold on now. They made a film. I can hardly breathe with the shock. How has all of this taken place without me, and not one word said to me about it. 'Come on and I'll walk you out home.'

'Go away, Mickey,' I cry out, and my eyes prick with tears.

'I only want a chat.'

'I want to be on my own.' Mickey's following me along the path. 'I said I want to be on my own.'

'It's sad being on your own. If I keep talking to you, you won't have the chance to feel sad. You can listen to me instead.'

'Would you ever just fuck off.' I've never before been cruel to Mickey Cassidy but today's different. Today's the day my whole life came crashing down around me, and I've never felt more alone or useless. It's supposed to be me and Evelyn, not Evelyn and Peadar. It's supposed to be me and Evelyn doing these kinds of things together.

Evelyn's floating around in the community centre, looking like a heavenly creature. The place is packed out with people all jostling to talk with herself and Peadar. She's walking through a big crowd of locals, and they're all pressing in around her, pulling at her and praising her. A golden future awaits Evelyn and Peadar, and golden praise wherever they go. It'll all take off for them now. Maeve lands in and says she's sorry she's late, she was working, but she's as happy as anyone for the two film-makers. The seating is laid out in a horse-shoe shape, and by the time it's eight o'clock, there isn't a free seat in the house.

Flora and Phenomena is an hour long. I suppose you'd class it an art-house documentary. It's a meditation on old Ireland left to rot and the stories being lost as a consequence. Small places like Glenbruff are vulnerable to having the life drawn out of them; the farming is dying out, the young people are leaving, the graveyards are full and no one's building houses.

There's a time-lapse in the old cottage. The five armchairs standing empty. Birds flying in and out of it, snow drifting down through the gaping hole and a grey figure on the stairs. Great sheets of paisley wallpaper rolling off the walls. A scalloped orange fungus attached to a stack of books, a gigantic tree root shifting the floor tiles in the kitchen. Windows laden with silt. The cutlery on the countertop crusted arsenic green. The clock in the hallway stopped at half past three and the glass dome holding droplets within it. Paper-like curtains with jagged holes. Footage from the Vaudeville nightclub. The old casing of the neon sign. The fragile swaying poppies. The sunken floor like a green lagoon. The sole of a shoe set in lino. The shell of the famine workhouse and swirling vapours atop the bog. A Morris Minor absorbed into a tree. The Neolithic tomb. The hawthorn. The torched manor. Ghost children playing in the handball alley.

I always felt that the pictures and images in Glenbruff belonged to no one but myself, and I'm supposed to be the one capturing them, not anyone else. But who's going to give a damn about my photos of junk and broken windows now that Evelyn's gone and made a whole film. *Since when did Evelyn want to be making films!*

When the lights come up, people look to be spellbound by what they've seen and heard. There's a big clatter as people push back their seats and stand and give a solid, resounding applause that lasts for almost a full minute. I stand too and clap hard. I clap until my hands are burning. I've done all the right things, the things you're supposed to do, and told to do, but it's Evelyn who made the beautiful film. She went and did it without me.

Maeve leans in to my ear. 'Isn't it great for them?' she whispers.

'Mm. It's great for them.' It's a traitorous trick. It's sickening beyond belief.

'They're waiting to hear back from another competition. They're on a shortlist.'

'Are they now.'

Along comes Aidan, grasping Peadar in a headlock. 'Don't forget where you've come from,' he says, scrubbing Peadar's scalp with his knuckles. 'Don't be getting all high and mighty on us.'

Evelyn flits towards us in the red dress, her face flushed with exhilaration. 'I always knew something big would happen me. Didn't I always say it. I'd a feeling about it for years. Every decision I've ever made in my whole life has led to this.'

Peadar's looking dazed. 'We never thought anything would come of it. We never imagined it'd all work out as it did. Lo and behold, here we are now about to hit off for New Mexico.'

'I imagined it,' says Evelyn. 'I knew we had it in us. All we had to do was put our minds to it.' It's happened for Evelyn and it hasn't happened for me. Evelyn's someone and I'm no one. She's left me behind, as I always knew she would. 'You know, there's two kinds of people in this world. People who make things happen and people who don't.'

'Ye should have told me ye were making a film. I would have dropped everything,' I say, trying hard to sound casual about it, but there's the wobble of hysteria in my voice. 'Ye kept it very quiet.'

'Sure, you were off doing your own thing,' she says breezily. 'Come on out for a cigarette. I need some air. Everyone wants a piece of me.' I follow her out to the front of the community centre. We walk down to the far end of the boundary wall and she takes her cigarettes out of her bag.

The mature person gives credit where it's due. 'The film is incredible,' I say, knowing for certain that if I'd have kept in with Evelyn, I'd be going to New Mexico too. I don't know a thing about New Mexico, only that it's in America, where everything and anything is possible for the likes of Evelyn Cassidy.

'I'm fed up talking about it already and I haven't even gone to New Mexico yet,' she says, but it's only to avoid coming across as being too proud. She'll need to try harder than that.

'You'll have to get used to it. You're going to be asked loads of the same questions. You'll be asked the same questions over and over again. You'll have to write yourself a script. Will they give you the time off work?'

'Oh, I'm not going back to Amperloc now. Not a hope in hell. Myself and Peadar are going to hit off for London after the festival, see what the reception's like to the film and set ourselves up. We're going to start our own production company.' London. A production company. God, I'd love that. 'I won't be half glad to leave Glenbruff. There's so much I want to do in life. I see myself as a sort of human projector.'

'London. That's an exciting move.' I want to blurt out that I'll go to London with her, but I swallow the words. It's too soon to be saying things like that. It's best if Evelyn invites me to London herself. It's best to be wanted.

'Myself and Peadar have to get out of here or we'll never have our chance. We'll be making documentaries, probably. And one-of-a-kind feature films.'

'That's amazing. A production company. Amazing.' I know now that it's London I want, and Evelyn, and the production company. Any minute now she'll be asking me along too. Didn't we always say we'd go off and do great things.

'We're going to call ourselves "Au Contraire Films".'

'That's a good name. It's memorable. Congratulations anyway. When are ye off?'

'We're going to New Mexico in two weeks. We'll go on to London then after the wedding in September. Peadar is Terry's best man.' Terry's getting married again to a yoga instructor from Wales.

'Congratulations.'

'I heard you the first time.' A smirk crosses her face for a millisecond, and I know I've diminished myself. I'm only a spoofer, and Evelyn's the shining light. I'm not in the same league as her at all. There's more of Maeve in me than there is Evelyn. I can feel my personality draining away from me, seeping out through my shoes and into the ground.

I stay at home brooding for several days, reading the opening chapters of books and casting them aside, and smoking out the bedroom window. Evelyn has me confused, causing me to wonder if it was ever my dream at all. I had thought it was my dream, but she has possessed it, taken it over, occupied the dream and acquired it, as though it was never mine to begin with. The anguish is compounded with the guilt of fine summer days spent indoors.

Robert clatters on the door. 'Have you died on us?'

I stub out the cigarette and call out, 'No.'

'Mam's asking if she should phone Doctor Fitz.'

Mammy comes inside into the room and sits on the end of the bed. She has a good, long serious look at me. I feel uneasy and throw my eyes over at the wall. 'I don't like you being down here,' she says. 'I don't know what happened in Dublin but you can't be hanging around in Glenbruff. A ship wasn't built to stay in a harbour.'

'Mm.'

'What'll you do with yourself, Katie? Have you a plan?'

'I don't know what to do, Mammy. Things haven't been working out for me. I'm awful confused.' How is it Evelyn hasn't asked me to go to London with her?

'You're feeling sorry for yourself. The only cure is to go out and have fun, and make a new plan.'

'Mm.'

'Most people's problems come about through a lack of imagination. Haven't you plenty of imagination of all people. Wouldn't you be wise to start using it.'

The sun is glaring and white, and the clouds break and reform. The cool wind creates a pattern of shimmering knives on the lake's surface. White light permeates us, and bleaches the colour out of the place. 'Funny old weather,' I say, pushing my sunglasses up my nose. I've been waiting for the old romantic feelings to rise up in me, but there's nothing doing. It's like ordering something from a catalogue and forgetting all about it. Making do with something else. And by the time the order arrives, you've lost the desire for it.

'Funny old weather,' Aidan repeats, crushing a petrified dog turd under his loafer shoe. 'Unusual for the time of year.'

'What do you make of Peadar and Evelyn's film? They'll be over in New Mexico soon.'

'Arrah.' He throws his blond head. 'I wouldn't be into any of that pretentious shit.'

'Didn't they do well? Getting into a film festival. You must be proud of Peadar.'

'I'd love nothing more than for Peadar to see the light and be shot of Evelyn.'

'It's looking like the pair of them are on the up,' I say, and Aidan tsks with disdain.

'I don't know how he sticks her. I've never met anyone who believes their own hype as much as Evelyn Cassidy.' My heart is racing to be having the illicit conversation about Evelyn. There's something

226

delectable about it. 'Sure, it's her that's more interested in a relationship than him.' Hold on now.

'Why's he with her, so? He wrote her a song and everything.'

'Peadar'd get nothing done if it wasn't for Evelyn. She has him out playing music and singing and getting involved in film-making. She gives him confidence. She's convinced him to get out of the trucking too, and now he doesn't know whether to go full time with the singing or the films. *Daft.*'

'How did they manage it? The film. They must have been flat out working on it.'

'I'd say Dan bankrolled the whole thing. Sure, anyone can make a film if they've the money. You can do whatever you want if you've the money.' He's right. It's a painful truth, but people can do whatever they want if they've the money.

'You don't like her.'

'No,' he says bitterly. 'She has everything handed to her. A person like that doesn't develop any character.'

We meander about the lake and watch the ducks skittering across the water and into the rushes and reeds. Aidan squats down and takes a few photographs with his expensive camera and supersized lens, looking like a sort of wildlife paparazzo. I'm sore about my own camera having been stolen, and I feel that we're filling the time with banality until Aidan says what he's been building up to saying. He rises to his feet and scratches the back of his head. 'It's good to hang out. The two of us. Do you think you'll be going back to Dublin or staying closer to home?'

'I don't know, Aidan. I burned a few bridges up there. The job ended badly.' It's the first I've admitted it to anyone.

'Tough times are the making of a person,' he says, and then, 'If you're going to be around for a while, I'd like to see you again. We may as well.'

I take off the sunglasses. 'Of course you'll be seeing me. I'm around for the whole summer, amn't I.'

'I've always had a soft spot for you, Katie. I'd like us to have a rela-tionship.' The old Katie would have been high off a kiss from Aidan Morley, but this kiss feels sorrowful and inevitable. Aidan's lips are cold, and mine are reluctant. The kiss is nothing like how I imagined it'd be. It's nothing like Luc's kiss. I lower my head and break off the kiss prematurely.

'How come nothing happened between us when we were young?'

'I don't know. I suppose I hadn't the wherewithal to know what I wanted from you. And then I met Pamela and everything changed.'

'She was good fun. Wasn't she?'

'She was a cracker,' he says, sighing heavily. It's time he got over Pamela Cooney, I'm thinking. It's time he moved on, and told a new story. It's an awful waste of his looks and vitality. What's going to happen him if he doesn't have a new story for himself? For fear he'd take on the mantle of Johnny Grealish with the sad stories on repeat.

We head away from the lake then, and Aidan drives us back towards Glenbruff way below the speed limit. I wonder is he trying to extend the car journey by driving at a slow pace. The journey is verging on the unbearable. On the approach to Glenbruff, he pulls up close to a ditch overlooking a plot of land. 'What do you think of the view?' he says. 'Do you like it?'

'It's grand.' The view is only alright. It's nothing special. It looks like any sort of countryside place. 'What about it?'

'It's mine. I'm after buying it.'

'What did you buy it for?'

'For building on. I'm building a house. The year after next.'

'A house. What are you building a house for?'

'To live in,' he says, looking at me like I've two heads. 'What else would I be building it for.'

'Won't you be lonely in it?'

'Not at all. Sure, I'll get married at some stage and have a family and all that.'

'God. I never think that far ahead. I'm nowhere near building a house, or getting married. There's a lot I want to do first.'

'Maybe if you're not married by the age of thirty and I'm not married either we could have a pact.' There's simply nothing more detrimental to romance than neediness. It's like the turning off of a mains supply. It shuts the whole thing down. He follows up with elbowing me in the ribs. 'I'm only rising you,' he says, smiling weakly, but I don't think he's rising me at all. 'Will we meet up again tomorrow?'

Sure, what else am I doing, only biding my time. 'Alright.'

We drive past Amanda and John out jogging with their elbows jabbing the air. Amanda has a sweatband on her highlighted hair and a shiny Lycra tracksuit clings to her well-maintained body. It's hard to believe she was ever a heroin addict. John is a tanned, lean man with shaved legs and expensive-looking trainers, and the two of them look like the people on late-night shopping channels selling exercise equipment and power juicers.

I go out to Daddy in the yard and putter about beside him. 'Daddy. Is Amperloc built on top of a sacred monastery?'

'Hah.' Daddy's crouched down and filling the lawnmower with fuel.

'Was it built on sacred ground? Is there a ghost of a monk in Glenbruff?'

'Where did you come up with that?' he says, scrabbling around for the fuel cap on the ground. 'Amperloc was built on an old pig farm belonging to the Gormleys.'

'Oh. It was Evelyn said it.'

'That lady's full of rubbish.' Daddy doesn't like Evelyn's film made about Glenbruff. He says it's a foolish enterprise. He says the romanticisation of broken-down Ireland is only a distraction from the jobs that need doing. Modernisation. Infrastructure. He says he can't see how a film like that is any good to a place like Glenbruff or the people living in it. 'You're doing a line with Aidan Morley.'

'It's nothing serious,' I say, feeling defensive of Aidan in spite of the desperate overtures.

'Myself and your mother think you should go back up to Dublin for yourself and not be getting caught up in another's tragedy. If you carry on with him you'll have a hard life.' He's pulling on the cord of the lawnmower, huffing and puffing and having no luck in getting the motor going. He's never had much luck with motors.

'I'm not marrying him or anything.'

'Life has ways of catching you out. There's nothing for you down here. Nothing and no one,' he says, and he pushes the roaring lawn-mower out to the garden, lavender smoke billowing out of it.

Inside in Nancy's Café, myself and Aidan are looking out at the street and watching the people we've always known going about their business. I've ordered myself a hot chocolate. I've been craving hot chocolate for days. A teenage girl brings it to me in a tall, thick glass. I draw out the long-handled spoon from the glass and lick the back of it.

'Dad's planning his wedding.' He rolls up the sleeves of his checked shirt. His forearms are bulky and strong-looking. 'He wants to know who's bringing partners. Would you say you'll be around in September?'

I smile sweetly. 'I'd say so.' I hope to be moving to London in September. I hope to be flat-hunting in Clapham Junction, and soaking up the sights and sounds of the King's Road and Piccadilly Circus.

'You know, I haven't told Dad or Peadar about the two of us. I'd say they'll get a great kick out of it when I tell them I've ended up with Katie Devane from over the road.'

My laughter is hollow. 'I suppose they wouldn't expect it.'

'It's gas how things turn out in the end,' he says contentedly. *The end*. I hope to God this isn't the end, but it feels like it is.

We hear the sound of a motorbike ripping up the street and look out to see Peadar tearing along with no helmet on him. Aidan cranes his neck looking at him. 'He'll kill himself on that yoke before the summer's out.'

'What's the story with the new bike?'

'Dad got it for him. It's a present for being best man. I'm a bit pissed off about it but what can I do. I always got on better with Mam and he got on better with Dad.'

'What'll he do with it when he goes to London? Will he bring it with him?'

'He'll hardly bring it to London. I'll be surprised if he ends up in London at all. Only last week he was talking about the great money to be made in Australia, working down the mines.'

'You're joking. The mines. Would he change his mind that easy?'

'A person like Peadar likes to keep his options open. He's always been changeable that way. It's like he hasn't yet decided who he is.' It seems that Peadar is unknowable, even to himself, and in my eyes that makes a person dangerous. Aidan's voice drops down. 'I'll let you in on something if you'll keep it to yourself.'

'What is it?'

'Peadar's had Stacey Nugent on the side for years.'

'I thought Stacey Nugent was going with Dan Cassidy.'

'Peadar's playing with fire, but I suppose he likes it that way.' This is something Evelyn needs to know. There's a high chance it'd put a spanner in the works for herself and Peadar going to London. There's a high chance it'd take Peadar out of the picture altogether, and put me back in it. 'You know, he wasn't home at all the night Pamela went missing. He was down in the clubhouse fooling with Stacey. We'd to think fast when the guards called around looking for an alibi. Peadar spoke for me and I spoke for Peadar.' Aidan takes up his cup, glugs back his coffee and sets the cup back on the table. He takes my free hand in his. His grip is too hot and too firm, and he's rubbing my palm like he's trying to wear a hole in it.

I pull my hand back and shake it out. 'Ow.'

'Anything new with yourself?'

'I'm just getting ready for New Mexico. I'm after booking the flights. Only six days to go, Katie.' She yawns wide like a cat, stretches her slender arms way above her head, swinging them backwards and forwards with her fingers hooked together. 'It's the sort of festival that really kick-starts a film-maker's career. There'll be loads of like-minded people there. Producers. Cinematographers. Screenwriters. All sorts of cool people like that.'

'Did you ever write a screenplay?'

'Oh, I did, yeah. Several. I wrote one about a man who buys a second-hand coat and the original owner of the coat was a psychopath, and now the man who bought the second-hand coat is a psychopath too because of the ghost living in the coat.'

'I like that. That's original. I'd watch that.'

'Peadar's written a screenplay as well.'

'Has he.' She hasn't a bull's notion about Stacey Nugent and the goings-on over years and years, but I can't bring myself to break her heart. Not before she goes to New Mexico. I couldn't do that to her. It could turn her away from me altogether.

'It's about a painting that people keep stealing because of the way it makes them feel. The painting starts a war.'

'Oh.' I'm intrigued. 'What sort of painting is it?'

'We don't know yet. The concept is still in development.' She rolls up a tuna sandwich and stuffs it in her cupid's-bow mouth.

'Maybe everyone who looks at the painting sees something different in it,' I suggest.

'Maybe. Myself and Peadar spent four days on Doona Island last summer. We wrote the two screenplays in full. We lived off boiled frankfurters and tea and we decided to send our film out to festivals, and we decided we'd move to London as well. It was the actual best four days of my life.'

'Is that so.'

'Myself and Peadar are one another's muse. We can't live without each other. That's the way it is between us. It's very intense.'

'Will you have a scone there, Evelyn?' I say, keeping the smile wide. You can hear the smile in a person's voice. 'And you must take some cake home with you. I've enough for ten people. I'll wrap it up in tinfoil for you.' Afternoon tea is all the rage in Dublin with gangs of friends going to posh hotels together, nattering over cakes and sandwiches and drinking copious amounts of tea until they're reeling in the head.

'I'm really not that hungry,' she says languidly, and I'm annoyed with myself. I shouldn't have gone to all this trouble. She isn't an afternoon tea kind of person. I've made myself look desperate, going to so much effort to win her favour. Bending over backwards to make her feel special when she already feels special enough. 'Had you a boyfriend yourself up in Dublin?'

'Oh, I wouldn't call him a boyfriend. We only spent a short time together. It was more of a fling.'

'What was he like?'

'He was an illustrator. He was French. Unreal-looking. He was working in a coffee shop.'

'An illustrator working in a coffee shop,' she snorts. 'Where is he now?'

'He's gone over to a music festival in Rio, and then he's going back to France to become a lawyer or something.'

'It sounds like he hasn't got his shit together. Bouncing around from one thing to another. Did you love him?'

'No. But I was mad after him. I was high as a kite when I was with him.' I think of the last time I saw Luc and him dodging Nuala's cutlery at the apartment door. I never heard from him again after that.

Evelyn lets out a sigh. 'It's funny. Peadar says he doesn't see a future here in Glenbruff. He says he's only gasping to get out. And Daddy's very hard on him as well. You know what Daddy's like.' She toys with her hoop earring, swirling it through the pierced hole in her earlobe. 'But there's something up with him recently. Something's different with him.'

'What's different?'

'Every free minute he has he's gone off on the motorbike, going one place or another. I haven't seen him in days,' she confides, looking discomfited and shifting about in the chair.

'What do you make of it?'

'I'd be worried he won't come to London because of the bike. I know it sounds daft but the bike's all he's interested in.'

'Would you say he has cold feet? He said he doesn't like city living. He said it at the bonfire.'

'I had thought he was just making conversation, but maybe there was something in it. Maybe he does have cold feet.' She swallows anxiously.

'If he changed his mind about London, what would you do? Would you still go?' I'd be tempted now to unleash the truth about Peadar and Stacey. It's on the tip of my tongue, dancing there and poised to leap.

'I can't bring myself to even think of it, Katie. I can't be without him.' She rests her jaw on her fist.

'Mm.' I'd say the thoughts of me going over to London with her hasn't even entered her head. What if she goes over there without me and takes up all the opportunities and attention and praise until there's none left.

'I'm hoping the bike is only a phase. He's always going through one phase or another. He's always been like that.' The thought strikes me that if I don't get going to London with Evelyn, I might have to think about letting go of her. 'What's your story, anyway? What have you been up to? I haven't seen you since the screening.'

'Oh, I haven't been up to much.'

'That's not what I heard. I heard you've been going around with Aidan.'

'We've been hanging out a small bit. Going for walks. Taking photographs at the lake and that sort of thing. It's casual.'

'Have you kissed him?'

'I have,' I admit.

'I knew it.' She slaps her hand off her thigh. 'Isn't he the sly dog.'

'How do you mean, *the sly dog?*'

'You hardly had your suitcase in the door but he was after you.' She pulls at another sandwich, rolls it up and stuffs it in her mouth, grinning all the while as her teeth gnash up and down.

'What do you mean?' I have to wait for her to finish chewing, wait for her to swallow the gluey sandwich. 'Come out with it, would you.'

'No one else will go out with him, Katie. And it's not for the lack of him trying. He's had a crack at every girl in Glenbruff and no luck. You're the fall-back option.' My heart drops like a cold stone. 'You'd a thing for him for years and he didn't bother with you. It suits him now to take up with you.' God. She's right. Of course she's right. Didn't I know it in my gut. Only for Evelyn I wouldn't have put my finger on it. 'Did he tell you he gave up the drink?'

'No. Why'd he give up the drink?' How could I have missed it? Isn't he always making tea and taking me out for coffee, not to mention taking photos of ducks with his preposterous-looking camera.

'He was hauled out of Donovan's for smashing things. He ripped the picture frames off the walls and broke them. He ran his arm along the counter and knocked all the drinks off it. Only for Kenneth having the place now he wouldn't be let back in.' She abruptly rises out of the chair and the chair legs screech along the tiles. 'Anyways, Katie. It was good seeing you but I've things for doing.'

'Oh. Right. Will you bring some of the cake with you?'

'No. I hate cake. I thought you knew that. I've always been more of a savoury person,' she says, and lets herself out the back door.

I pile the leftover afternoon tea onto a tray and lash a sheet of tinfoil over it, and moments later, Robert saunters in and peeps under the tinfoil. 'Is this for public consumption?'

'Evelyn wasn't hungry,' I reply absently, thinking hard about Aidan and how I'm only the fall-back girl. It seems I can have nothing for myself.

'Are you cold?'

'No,' I say tersely. 'I'm grand.' Don Henley is playing on the radio: 'Boys of Summer'.

'Here. Have my jumper.' Aidan peels off his jumper and places it around my shoulders. 'There you are now,' he says, and I grit my teeth. This is toe-curling stuff. 'Have you ever thought of nursing, Katie? You'd make a grand nurse, so you would. You've a lovely way about you.' He doesn't know me at all. He never bothered to get to know me. He has some idea in his head about who I am and it's the wrong idea.

'I'd have no interest in nursing, Aidan. None whatsoever.' I light up a cigarette in the silver car. It's old now, with moss growing in the seams of the windows, and the upholstery stinks of stale apple cores.

'Would you be smoking all the time these days,' he says, looking over at me with a disapproving expression. 'Would you be smoking every day?'

'Sometimes. It depends. When I've a lot on my mind.'

'I have to say, I don't like it when girls smoke. It's unfeminine.' He wrinkles his nose. 'I'd prefer it if you didn't.'

That's it now. I can't let it go any further. I have to put a stop to the whole thing.

'I'm starting to think that we mightn't be right for one another. I'm starting to think it's best if we stay friends.' It's slipped out, but Jesus, it had to be said. 'I'm sorry.' I am a bit, but it's his doing. I sneak a brief glance over at him, and see that his jaw is hard and grinding over and back beneath the skin. I have a sharp pang of pity for him. I've never before ended things with a person. I never imagined I'd be ending things with Aidan.

The time begins to slow, begins to churn. A half a minute gone. The silence is desperate.

'We would've been great,' he murmurs eventually. 'We would've been perfect. You're the last person I thought would let me down.'

'I'm sorry.' I'm worrying over what to do with the hot cigarette butt between my fingers. There's no suitable place to put it. 'It's a pity it didn't work out between us. But we'll always be good friends.'

All of a sudden, he raises clenched fists and crashes them down hard off the loose plastic dash. I yelp, and the miniature Virgin Mary hops over on her painted head and topples to the floor. 'Friends? I'm not your fucking friend. Are you trying to wind me up?' He jolts out of the driver seat, pushes his face close to mine and roars, 'Let's be fucking clear about this. You're ruining fucking everything. Do you hear me.' Droplets of warm spit are flying at me. He's pointing in my face. 'I've done all the right fucking things. I've been a gentleman to you.'

I squeeze my eyes tightly and mash myself up against the door. 'You h-have. You've been a gentleman. I never said you weren't. You've been lovely.'

'I suppose you think you're too good for me now. Is that it?' The roar out of him. My ears are ringing.

'No. That's not it.'

'You're another one who won't give me a fucking chance. Another closed-minded bitch. I don't know what's your fucking problem.'

We're parked up close to the Vaudeville. There isn't a sinner about. If anything happens me, no one will hear me scream. He could do anything he wants to me and no one would ever know. He retreats back in his seat, panting, and I pull hard on the door handle to no avail.

'Lookit. I'm sorry. I'm sorry, okay.' He clenches the steering wheel, collecting himself. I scrabble at the handle, frantic. I'm caught. Trapped. 'Will you stop fussing. Will you fucking relax. You're making me nervous.'

'I'll faint. Open the door or I'll faint.' He hesitates before leaning across me, grunting and forcing the door handle. I dart out of the car. *Go!*

'Hey. *Hey!* Get back in the car. Get back here,' he bellows. I'm running, and whimpering out of fear, and now the car is rolling alongside me. 'Get in. Come on to fuck.'

I keep running. The projectile tears are shooting out of my eyes. He throws his hand up and the silver Toyota accelerates away up the road in a cloud of dust.

I pelt like mad in the direction of home, my throat and lungs burning with the effort, and then, like some kind of godsend, I spot Tom Lynch coming along in the tractor. I flag him down, and he gives me a lift then in the tractor cab, and as if I haven't been through enough already, Tom is raving on and on about Maeve. 'The poor girl is very low. Will ye mind her? Will ye call in to see her?' I'm too rattled to even listen to him, and I'm fit to burst by the time I get home. I run into the house and don't speak to anyone, and I have a long shower to dull the tremors.

Aidan's unhinged. I had some idea in my head about who he was, and it was the wrong idea. He had me well fooled with the slacks and loafers. The custard creams. You'd have to wonder if Pamela ever tried breaking up with him. You'd have to wonder if he did away with her himself. He must have done away with her, he surely did away with her, and me only a whitewash, a part of the façade. Just a nice girl to have on his arm for going to weddings with. To think it could have been me if I'd got what I wanted. To think that Pamela took my place.

Two days later, and I'm only just steady enough to go up and tell Evelyn what happened at the Vaudeville, but there's something even more pressing going on for her by the looks of it. 'What's the matter?' I say, rushing at her. 'Had you bad news?' It's four in the afternoon and Evelyn's in her dressing gown with coffee stains down the front of it and make-up round the collar. There's a roll of toilet paper crammed into one of the pockets and a trail of paper hanging out of it.

She slumps onto the bottom step of the stairs and buries her face in her hands. 'Peadar says he won't come to London.'

I sit down next to her on the step. 'What? How come, Evelyn? How come? What's he said?'

She looks up, bleary-eyed. 'He says he likes the singing in Donovan's – and going around on the bike – and the bit of trucking – *hic* – and he's made his mind up not to go. He says he's happy as he is – and why would he be changing things when he has everything going his way.'

'I thought it was all planned out. I thought he was on board. Why did he go around making the film with you if he didn't want to pursue the film-making? What sort of carry-on is that.'

'It was me pulling him along the whole time, dragging him round the place. He only took credit for it,' she says bitterly.

'What about the four days on Doona? What about the screenplay he came up with?'

'It was a shite idea for a screenplay. A painting that starts a war. Have you ever heard anything as daft.' I had thought it had potential. 'What am I to do now? I've been trying to get a hold of him and he's not answering. And New Mexico only a few days away. I'm trying to pack for it and I can't think straight. It's a pure disaster.'

'I'll help you. Come on and we'll go up to the room and I'll help you. We'll have you packed in no time.' I wrap my arm round her waist and heave her up the stairs and into her bedroom, where there's an eye-watering mound of clothing covering her bed and countless shoes strewn all over the floor.

She drapes herself over a beanbag and begins shuddering and weeping into the chenille-fabric covering. 'What'll I do, Katie? I'm stuck. I've my heart set on London.' She's in a bad way, as bad as the time she didn't get into the art college. 'I'll die if I've to stay in Glenbruff. I'll just die.' I'd say she might be sick on herself if she doesn't let up with the crying. I might have to call for Doctor Fitz if there's no let up to it soon.

I crouch down next to her, smoothing her hair. 'Is there any hope at all he'll go?'

'There's no hope. He hasn't an ounce of ambition when it comes down to it. It's like trying to get blood out of a turnip.' I picture Peadar driving along in the big truck, altogether in his element, belting out songs and beating out the rhythm on the steering wheel. What need has Peadar for film-making and going to London with nothing at all to prove to anyone.

'You'll be stronger without him, Evelyn. You just wait. You'll come into your own.'

'All the plans we had. Films and music and all kinds of travel and projects.'

'You'll do all those things yet. Haven't you your whole life ahead of you. There's no fear of you not getting to do all the things you want to do.'

She raises herself upright and scrabbles the dark hair away from her face with her thin fingers. 'Do you know what, Katie?'

'What?'

'I'm going to start the production company with or without Peadar. I don't need him. I thought I did but I don't. It was always myself who had the vision.'

'Good girl yourself, Evelyn. That's the spirit.' She's difficult, and conceited, but she's pure magic. It delights me to delight her. I'd say we're great friends because we've no sisters between us. I've always thought that girls with sisters don't need friends in the same way that girls without sisters do.

'Hold on a minute. Why don't *you* come to London?' She's finally said it. She's finally come out with it. 'I don't know how I didn't think of it before. Sure, what else would you have for doing.' *Halle-fucking-lujah*. I'm euphoric. My whole brain is buzzing. Myself and Evelyn over in London, meeting everyone worth meeting, making films and art and a name for ourselves.

'Do you know, I wouldn't mind going to London with you. I wouldn't mind it a bit. I'd say it'd go great for us.' Everything has aligned in a particular way to have brought this about. I could leap into the air and float way up into space.

'Good,' she says resolutely. 'That's it, so.'

'That's it decided.' The dream is underway. I had thought the day would never come.

'You won't be troubled leaving Aidan,' she says, snickering.

'I won't be one bit troubled.' There's no use getting into the long story now. Aidan's irrelevant, and Peadar too.

'I don't know what you were thinking. You must have been lonely. You must have been missing the French lad from the coffee shop.'

'There'll be plenty more French lads in London. And Australian lads, and American lads. We can take our pick, Evelyn.'

'I've always felt like an American on the inside. Maybe an American lad would suit me. I'm finished with Irish lads, that's for certain.'

I laugh, and begin pulling up items of clothing from the mound, holding them out before me. I sniff the armpits of the clothes to see if they need washing, and it's quickly apparent that everything needs washing. 'What's the weather forecast for New Mexico?'

'I don't know. It'll be hot anyway. Don't forget to pack my gladiator sandals. They're under the bed.'

I go down on my hands and knees searching for the gladiator sandals. I'm crouched down, the blood rushing to my head. I see there are old canvases and paintbrushes and stumps of pencils under the bed. Remnants of the art career that never was. 'Will you be alright going to the film festival on your own?' I call out. I wonder how much would it cost to change the name on Peadar's plane ticket.

'I'll be well able for it.'

I lob the sandals into a suitcase, and a pair of flip-flops too. I pull out a yellow sundress from the mound and shake it out and Evelyn rises up off the beanbag. She takes hold of the sundress from me and scans it with distaste. 'I hate all my clothes,' she says. 'I might dump the whole lot. Put them all out in the field in a pile and set fire to them.'

'Could I go through them first? I might find a few things for myself.'

She throws me a funny look, screwing up her eyes. 'No. That'd be weird. You going around in my old clothes, like you were trying to be me.'

'Alright.'

'It's just I have a distinctive style. I don't like people wearing the same kinds of things as me.'

'Alright. They're your clothes. You can do what you like with them.'

'Oh my God,' she says, suddenly pressing her fingertips to her temples.

'What?'

'I'm having a déjà vu.' She perches on a free corner of bedspread and blows out her cheeks. 'It's taking me over.'

'It's alright. It's normal. It's a sort of illusion. It's electrical impulses misfiring in your brain.'

'No, it's not,' she says, gawping at me like I've said something moronic. 'Déjà vu is a sign that you're on the right path. It means it's the right thing, the two of us going to London. It's all predetermined.'
It's predetermined. It's fate. Everything has aligned in a particular way to have brought this about. I'll be on the up from here on out.

'What do you think'll happen Maeve, Evelyn? What'll happen her when we leave Glenbruff?'

'Who cares. We're not bringing her anyway. She'd drive us soft.'

'I know. She's deficient or something.'

'She'd bring us bad luck. She's cursed.'

'Still and all. We'd better call over and tell her.' I bite my lower lip. 'Break the news.' I've a feeling she'll take the news badly, but there's no room for Maeve in the dream. She's no good to us in the long run.

'Jesus. Do we have to?'

'Come on. We'll go up to her now and get it over with.'

〜

Myself and Evelyn traipse in the small gate, up the path glittering with mica stones, and stand in under the hood of the porch. There's no doorbell, only a wire hanging out of a hole. I rap on the door and Mary Lynch opens it straight away. She has a red face, like her blood pressure is sky high, and she clasps her hard red hands together. 'Aren't ye good girls calling in. I knew ye'd come.' She's wearing dense tan-coloured tights, a lilac housecoat and shoes with Velcro snaps. You wouldn't know what age she is, and you wouldn't see any resemblance between herself and her sister Alma.

Mary fusses over us, filling up the kettle and asking if we want a piece of cake. 'We're grand, Mary. Ah no. We're grand.' She goes rooting around in the press and takes out an aluminium box with porter cake inside it. We're handed two wedges of the cake in grease-stained paper doilies. 'Thanks very much, Mary.' I put the piece of the cake inside in my pocket. It's as hard as a rock. It could be decades old. A relic.

'Maeve is down in her room. Let ye go on ahead. I'm only holding ye up.'

Maeve has a simple room with magnolia walls. She has a single bed, a tallboy wardrobe and a dressing table. She has a Glenbruff football jersey hung over the headboard, and a novena to Saint Jude stuck with a thumb tack on top of it. There's a pot of moisturiser on the dressing table, a hairbrush with a nest of wild hair caught in the bristles and three pairs of shoes lined up at the end of the bed. A daddy-long-legs scampers along the window sill next to a gilt-framed 'Footprints in the Sand'.

Maeve's sitting on the neatly made bed. She's puffy in the face, like someone who's slept hanging upside down from a tree. She has burst blood vessels around her eyes from crying, and a facial expression like she's trying to solve the world's most perplexing brainteaser. 'I don't know what's the point of anything,' she says, and the big wet eyes slowly roll round to us. 'Is life worth living at all?'

Amanda's stopped taking her calls, she tells us. She's said that Maeve's phoning her too frequently. She can't talk to her every day, and she's up to her eyes with the sailing, going to events and managing her investment portfolio. 'You'd think she'd be falling all over herself trying to make up for the lost time.'

'You're expecting too much, Maeve,' I say. 'Don't you think she's had a hard life herself, putting you up for adoption and coming off the drugs.'

'What drugs? What are you on about?' Maeve mightn't have been told about the drugs. 'I gave Amanda and John all my savings to invest in a block of apartments and now I've nothing left and the apartments can't be sold. I gave them everything. A deposit for a house. More than that, and I gave it all away to them and now they won't talk to me.'

'Did you sign something? Is there paperwork or anything?'

'No. I thought I was helping them out. I thought I'd get twice the money back. They came down to Glenbruff and said they'd make me a director of the company if I transferred the money, but they didn't, and now they're pretending I don't exist.'

'Go to the guards, Maeve,' I urge her. 'Get a solicitor.'

'I can't do that. She's my actual mother.'

'You fool, Maeve,' Evelyn says sternly, folding her arms. I'd say she's fit to be done with Maeve altogether, and who could blame her.

'I know. I know I am. I can't help it, girls. I am who I am.'

'Some eedgit is who you are.'

'All I've ever wanted is what everyone else has. Why is it never me?'

'Jesus,' Evelyn huffs. 'You'd think you were the only person who's ever suffered. Who's ever had a bad thing happen them. I'm after ending things with Peadar and you don't see me feeling sorry for myself.'

'Oh.' Maeve looks sheepish. 'What happened?'

'He's let me down badly. I'll never forgive him.'

'I'm sorry to hear that. I didn't know. How would I have known?'

'Well, you know now. Anyway. Myself and Katie have come to tell you that the two of us are moving to London.'

Maeve's mouth drops open. She clutches the side of the mattress and her knuckles flush white. 'What about me? I'll be here on my own, girls. I'll have no one.'

'What about Mags Moynihan,' Evelyn says, indifferent. 'Aren't ye good pals?'

'I hate Mags Moynihan. I've nothing in common with Mags Moynihan.' Mags Moynihan runs everywhere instead of walking. She smells things. Door handles. Trees. Her own hands. 'Why can't I go to London too?'

'You're not like us, Maeve,' I tell her gently. 'We're different to you. We're artists and you're not.'

'So what. The three of us are friends and that's all that matters,' she cries, rising to her feet. 'Ye won't go to London without me. I won't let ye.'

'Why would you want to go somewhere you're not wanted.' Evelyn makes for the door. 'I'm off. I'm bored of you. You're boring.'

'You're not going to London without me. I won't allow it. I'll put a stop to it.'

I follow Evelyn out to the front of the house, feeling somewhat disturbed. 'What's she on about, not letting us go to London?' I say, pulling the front door closed behind us. 'What can she mean?'

'Never mind her. She's mental.'

I stall at the small gate. 'Maybe she could move to London but live far away from us. Maybe she could come and visit us once a week on a Sunday.'

'No. Absolutely not.'

'What if she does something stupid, Evelyn? What if she swallows tablets and kills herself?'

'You've no idea how happy that'd make me.'

Evelyn's gone to New Mexico. She's gone two full days. I wonder how is she getting on. It can't be all it's cracked up to be, going to a film festival. Everyone wearing black and taking themselves seriously, and carrying on like the film festival is the centre of the universe and nothing else going on in the world matters at all. Of course I'd love to be there too, and taking myself seriously, but I've London to think of now. It'll be a whole new life in London. It's what I've wanted, and I don't have long to wait.

I take my hefty old college laptop and bring it into Nancy's Café and set myself up at a table way in at the back. I've a story in my head about a girl who doesn't have a name but I can worry about that later. This is a girl with an ordinary life, a lonely life, and one day she passes a bookshop she's never noticed before, and she's drawn to a book on a shelf inside. It happens that she has just enough money to buy the book and take it home with her. The book is enchanting, with lively characters, and the girl can hear their voices in her head. Funny enough, some days afterwards she meets one of the characters from the book, and she can't quite believe it but this character befriends her, and some days after that, the same thing happens again. The girl's been so lonely her entire life that this is the best thing that's ever happened to her, all of these new-found friends materialising out of a book. When she returns to the bookshop to make further enquiries, she finds that it's just an old building shuttered up and scheduled for demolition.

I'm all stirred up and energised with writing the screenplay, so much so that I forget all about Evelyn in New Mexico. I don't know what time it is when I raise my head and the place is emptied out and a teenage girl is mopping round the table legs and over my shoes.

I pack up my things and come out the door when I observe Aidan standing over the road. He's swaying back and forth, and pissed out of his head. He shoves his hands in his pockets and rummages about in them, and there are papers and coins and cash falling out on the path. He staggers onto the road and an oncoming driver brakes to a halt and blares their horn at him. 'Mam,' he shouts, waving sloppily at me, his eyes glassy and bloodshot. 'Mam. When are you coming home?' I turn about quickly and walk at a brisk pace. 'Mam. Mam. Come back.'

'You gave poor Aidan the heave-ho,' Robert says at home while I'm clattering around with the printer and trying to get it to work.

'Where'd you hear that?'

'He was chewing my ear off in Donovan's last night. He was chewing everyone's ear off. He was found asleep in the old phone box this morning.'

I shiver, feeling repulsed. 'Will you do me a favour and tell Aidan nothing about me and what I'm doing. I want to steer clear of him. I don't want to see him.'

'He wants to see you. He was sure of that. He wants to make it up to you.'

'Will you keep him away from me, Robert. I want nothing at all to do with him.'

'Everyone wants to work with me, girls. They're saying I'm an original.' She's wearing mirrored aviator sunglasses from the duty free and I can't see her eyes, only my own bobble head. 'There was a panel discussion about guerrilla film-making and it ran over time because everyone was asking me questions. There was an actual queue at the microphone. I had them eating out of the palm of my hand.'

'Aren't you great,' I murmur, looking down to see the access-all-areas neon wristband she's wearing. How is it that Evelyn makes me feel superior and insignificant all at the same time.

'We got free tickets to a pool party on a rooftop and it didn't finish up until eight in the morning. I was in bits after it. I even did two whole lines of cocaine. Hands down I'd do it again.'

'Cocaine,' says Maeve, sucking in. She's scuttling along the road beside us like a crab on the ocean floor. 'You're gone wild, Evelyn. You're like a real celebrity.' I haven't been to America even the once, and now Evelyn's been to a real pool party on a rooftop and snorted cocaine. It's far from cocaine and pool parties we were reared.

'It was everything I thought it'd be and more. I made a hundred new friends. I'd the kinds of conversations I've wanted to have my entire life.'

'What kinds of conversations?' I ask her, and she ignores the question. *Dickhead.*

'It's, like, you go through life knowing that you're different, and you're on a whole different level to everyone else, but I actually met people on my own wavelength in New Mexico. They actually exist.'

'Is that so,' I say flatly, making no effort to sound enthusiastic. I'm beginning to wonder about how it's going to go in London. There'll be no point in me going to London if it's to be all about Evelyn. It can't be all about Evelyn all the time. Can it?

'So what have you been up to?' she says to me. 'It must have been quiet for you.'

'I wrote a screenplay. I had an idea and I just stuck with it and wrote it over a full day.'

She yanks up the sunglasses and embeds them in the thick dark hair. 'A screenplay,' she says in a suspicious tone. 'What's it about?' Maeve looks to Evelyn and then to me.

'It's about a girl with no friends who's reading a book –'

'A girl with no friends reading a book. Sounds like a laugh a minute,' she snorts, looking purposely at Maeve, and Maeve laughs on cue.

'Hold on until I finish,' I say in a hard voice, flaming with irritation. I could whip the sunglasses off her head and stamp on them. 'She's reading a book with really interesting characters, and then she starts dreaming about them, and then the characters start showing up in her actual life and become her actual friends. It's magic realism.'

'Or boring and shite,' Evelyn snorts, and Maeve throws her head back with laughing. I can see her teeth have begun separating after having the braces taken off.

'What are you being like that for?'

'I'm joking. Jesus. Give me a read of this screenplay anyway. See if it's any use.'

'Have you been on to Peadar since?' I hope Peadar hasn't been *plamásing* Evelyn, telling her what she wants to hear and foiling our plan. I hope he hasn't been sending her the long, winding text messages laden with cajoling language. I hope he hasn't written her another song.

'Peadar. Peadar's great. He has an agent now. He wasn't even searching for an agent, but he was approached in the green room at the festival and signed on the spot because he has the look they've been looking for. He has three meetings lined up. Over in London.'

'Oh. Peadar went with you in the end, did he,' I say coolly, masking the burgeoning fury. I suppose he's coming with us now, is that it. Is that the latest. You'd think she'd have consulted with me about Peadar coming to London. How will we end up making any films at all with one relationship crisis happening after another. 'It's back on with Peadar, is it. After all the trouble.' It's supposed to be me and Evelyn, not Evelyn and Peadar. It's supposed to be me and Evelyn going to London and no one else along with us.

'It is. I sent Daddy over to him and he put him straight.' It's all I can do to hold my tongue. 'He has a screen test booked for a film. It's a biopic about a troubled musician who died in a romantic way.'

'What's this talk of London again,' Maeve says crossly, her barrel body taut, her arms stiff beside her. 'I said I don't want ye to go and ye're still going on about it.'

Evelyn titters, but I have the sense that something's passing between herself and Maeve, a sort of telepathic dispatch, and Evelyn shudders from her legs up through her torso. 'I'm moving on from Glenbruff, Maeve. Whether you like it or not. I have to move on.'

'We'll see,' says Maeve under her breath. It seems that Evelyn's right, and Maeve's actually mental, but it's something new to me to witness Maeve standing up to Evelyn, let alone to see Evelyn rattled by it. It's almost like she's afraid of her.

I go up to Evelyn's house with the screenplay and roll it up and shove it in the letterbox. I can hear bare feet slapping along the tiles and the sound of pages being gathered up. I can see the flash of peach-coloured dressing gown in the swirled glass panel by the door.

Robert has work now in Amperloc, helping Daddy. He went up to see Des a few days ago to talk about the new living arrangements, but there was no one there and the house was up for sale. People are saying Des has resigned from the job following on from the letters controversy. They're saying he's fled to a commune in the States and he'll never again come back.

THIEF CHARGED AT ADRAGULE
DISTRICT COURT

A thief was arrested at Glenbruff train station following suspicious behaviour on the Friday evening service from Dublin Heuston.

Nine separate thefts of personal belongings had been reported over a six-week period on the same train service, Detective Garda Dermot Kilgariff testified yesterday at Adragule District Court.

Gardaí investigating the thefts were on standby at the station to arrest the suspect, Dylan Hartigan (23) of Saint Malachy's Road, Glenbruff, upon the arrival of the train.

'He came out onto the platform holding a golf bag. We asked him to open up the bag and he refused. He dropped it on the ground and began running. He was apprehended by Garda Noel Healy, who got the cuffs on him,' Detective Kilgariff said.

When the golf bag was searched, Hartigan was found to have concealed two wallets, a quantity of jewellery and €300 in cash, all of which was determined to have been stolen. Hartigan later handed over additional items including laptops, cameras and mobile phones. Gardaí are making efforts to reunite the items with their owners.

Defence barrister Lisa Durkan said the accused had been under a great deal of stress and financial hardship, having recently retired from a stint at professional golfing that had not proved to be lucrative. She asked that this be taken into consideration during sentencing.

Judge Gerard Madigan handed down a twelve-month suspended sentence and ordered Hartigan to complete forty hours of community service.

Evelyn phones me early on Saturday morning. Maeve wants to get new curtains for her bedroom, and she doesn't feel like driving, and Evelyn's provisional license has expired. Will I take them up to the fabric shop in Adragule?

'Maeve's got very bossy. She was never like that before,' I say. She's been acting up since we told her we're going to London. I've even noticed her wearing some of Evelyn's clothes. Nice clothes. A blazer with jewelled shoulders and the yellow sundress.

'Half the reason I'm going to London is getting away from Maeve. She has me damned. She's like a child, Katie. She has a child's mind. I'm fed up of her. I'm starting to really hate her,' she complains before hanging up the call.

We're in the car on the way to Adragule. Evelyn's holding a cigarette in her right hand. She rolls down the passenger window and rests her left hand against the outside of the car. I see her shoulders are speckled with dainty freckles from the New Mexican desert. Her turquoise feather earrings whip about in the rushing air and tendrils of her dark hair flap out behind her. I'm thinking I'll need a new look in London or I'm going to be pushed into the background. I'm thinking I'll need a new haircut and better clothes, but it probably won't be enough. It'll never be enough. 'How come Peadar didn't take ye to get the curtains?'

'I can't get him. He's gone on the bike. Step on the gas, chicken, will you.' She flicks cigarette ash onto the car floor and positions her feet up on the dashboard.

'If we were to end up in a crash, your knees would smash into your eyeballs and burst them. You'd be blinded for life.'

'Fuck's sake.' She lowers the feet in a huff. 'You're an awful nervous driver. You're uptight.'

'I need to stop and go to the toilet,' Maeve calls loudly from the back seat.

'Can you at least wait until we get to Adragule?' We're barely on the road ten minutes.

'I'd three cups of tea before I left the house. I've to go now, Katie. I'm bursting.'

'Jesus Christ.'

There isn't a pub or petrol station in sight, or anywhere else with a toilet, so I pull in for Maeve to urinate behind a hedge. Myself and Evelyn are smoking in the car at the side of the road, waiting for her with the hazards on. *Chk-chk-chk-chk-chk-chk.* Evelyn takes her phone out and begins fooling with it. The phone bleats like she's playing one of those downloaded games. I notice she has black nail polish with an iridescent sheen, like a beetle's back. 'So. Had you a chance to read the screenplay?'

'Mm. I'd a look at it alright.'

'Well. What did you think?'

'It's in the wrong font.'

'The wrong font.' Is that all she has to say about it?

She inhales through clamped teeth with her lips curled back. 'It needs a lot of work if I'm being honest. It's kind of unrealistic.'

'It's supposed to be unrealistic,' I say, stinging. 'It's magic realism. It's a flight of the imagination.'

'I don't like your lead character either. She's got too many issues and she's also really self-absorbed.' A thick band of dread tightens round my chest. Is this what it's going to be like in London, Evelyn dictating what's good and what isn't. My ideas living and dying with Evelyn's say so. If only it was as easy as reading a book to conjure up friends for yourself.

'I thought we could consider it for Au Contraire Films. That's what I wrote it for. I thought we could work on it in London.'

'Actually, myself and Peadar met a producer in New Mexico and he loves the whole concept of *The Psychopath's Overcoat*. He wants to start principal photography in November, so we're going to be pretty busy as it is.' She looks up from her phone. 'Actually, Katie, it might be better if you just do your own thing.'

'Do my own thing. What do you mean, *do my own thing?*'

'It's just that myself and Peadar have a creative connection that's really working for us. Having a third person could disrupt the flow.'

The shock is nuclear. A white-hot implosion, instantly devastating. 'You're asking me not go to London. Is that it?'

She's looking right at me, callously nonchalant. 'You can't even afford it, sure. Where would you get the money? It's expensive over there and you're always broke.'

'I would have found the money. I would have got it from somewhere.'

'It just seems like if you came to London it'd be like you're riding my coattails or something. I mean, I'm the one who did all the work. I'm the one who made a film in the first place.' I can't feel my arms or legs and it's as though my head is taking off, swelling up like a balloon, and it's going to pop and I'm going to die. 'The film-making is sort of my thing anyway. It's not like you've any experience.'

'We always said we'd go away together and do great things. Whatever happened to that?'

'Sure, that was years ago,' she scoffs. 'Why don't you figure things out by yourself, Katie, instead of looking at me all the time and what I'm doing. Do you want me to wipe your arse for you as well.'

'Why would you say that? What are you saying that for?' I want to hurt her badly. Sew up a voodoo doll and set fire to it. 'Peadar's going to drop you like a hot snot when you get to London. He couldn't care less about you. He's going around with Stacey Nugent, taking her out on the bike every night of the week and everyone in the whole town knows about it.' I've said it now. I've come out and said it and there's no going back.

Evelyn laughs. The laugh sounds like it's caught behind her nose. It's a derisive, contemptuous laugh. Hard and mean. 'Peadar says you're in love with me. He thinks it's hilarious, you traipsing after me to London. He says you're a lovesick lesbian weirdo. He's been saying it for years, and he's right.' It sounds like something she's rehearsed, or prepared. 'You're in love with me, Katie. Admit it, would you. You're obsessed with me.' My heart's about to sputter to a stop. This is it. This is how friendship ends. Not only that, but the dream is over. I should have stayed above in Dublin with Nuala and Norma. I should have applied for the teaching, even.

'No, no, *no*.' Maeve's slipped into the back seat without either of us noticing. 'All this talk of London has to stop *right now*. Will no one think about me for a minute? Does no one care about me at all?'

'Oh my fucking God, Maeve.'

'Shut the fuck up, Maeve.' I attempt to turn over the car engine but there's nothing doing. The car is broken down. Piece of fucking shit. 'We'll have to hitch a lift back to Glenbruff. Everyone out.'

'Are you joking me? I'm not hitching a fucking lift. I'm calling Peadar to come and get me.' Evelyn takes up her phone and dials Peadar's number, but he doesn't answer. She tries again and he still doesn't answer. I can see the neon wristband is grubby and frayed round her wrist.

'Everyone out, I said. I'm locking up.' This is the actual worst day of my life.

We're walking along in the hard shoulder. I'm out in front. Maeve's behind me, and Evelyn's several feet behind her, and her high-heeled boots go *gadum-gadum-gadum* on the road. My head's melted. I want to go back and undo everything. Undo the friendships and choices I've made, because Evelyn's had a hand in everything, and look at how I've ended up. I've nothing now. No London. No films. No art. I'll never do anything worthwhile. I'll never be someone. It's Evelyn who's set for life. It's Evelyn who gets what she wants. I could pluck up a rock now out of a stone wall and knock her out with it. Bash in her brains and finish her.

Maeve's whistling softly between the peg teeth. 'I could kill her, Maeve,' I mutter, blinking back hot tears. 'I could murder her. How have you stuck it out down here with her?'

'Oh, I've often wanted her dead, but I'd have had no one if I'd done that.'

Minutes pass that feel like hours. There are no cars coming and we can't hitch a lift. 'Evelyn,' starts Maeve. 'You can't leave us behind and go to London. We're supposed to be friends. We're supposed to go places together. That's what friends do.'

'Get a fucking clue, Maeve,' barks Evelyn. 'No one wants you in London. You're an embarrassment. You're a mental case.'

Maeve spins about. 'I am not a mental case,' she bellows. 'You think you're God's gift, but you're stuck-up. You think you're Cleopatra or something, but you're not.' Go on, Maeve. Give her a piece of your mind. Do it for the both of us.

Evelyn rears up, her face contorting. 'Do you know what. You're no good to anyone. No one at all wants you. You're a waste of space. You should never have even been born.'

I come to a standstill on the road. 'You can't say that,' I admonish. 'You've crossed a line there, Evelyn.'

'And you. Why don't you just go away, Katie. Why did you come home at all? What more do you want from me? I'm sick of looking at you.'

'We're the only friends you have,' cries Maeve. 'You'll be sorry yet with the way you've treated us.'

'Friends. Some friends. I'm only sorry I ever met ye.' Evelyn flounces away up the road – *gadum-gadum-gadum* – and it isn't long before we lose sight of her altogether.

Myself and Maeve sit ourselves down on a stone wall. 'Do you think she meant it?' says Maeve. Her face is white and crumpled, like an old paper plate. Her eyes are big and round and look as though they might fall out. 'Everything she said about us. Do you think she really meant it?'

'Whether she meant it or not, she said it, and that's bad enough.' A lovesick lesbian weirdo. After all we've meant to one another, that's what she thinks of me. I turn my shoes together until the soles are touching.

Maeve shakes her head from side to side. 'She hasn't a friend in the world now. Not one friend.'

'Are you finished with her?' I know myself that I'm finished with Evelyn. I know now where I stand, and there's no more confusion.

'I am. I'm finished with her for good. She doesn't deserve friends like us.'

'You couldn't be more right. You did well to stand up to her.' It's as though a heavy storm has broken, and there's cool clarity in the aftermath of it.

'What will you do now, Katie?'

'I don't know what I'll do. I'll have to come up with something.'

'You could stay down here. You might get to like it.'

'No, Maeve. No offence.'

'Do you know, I've a feeling I'll be gone soon myself. I've been thinking about it long enough. It's been time for something new for a long time now.' We slip off the wall and commence the journey home. 'Will we go for a drink in Donovan's later? Myself and yourself.'

'Alright. Why not.'

As we approach the outskirts of Glenbruff, a dumper truck roars past us on the road. 'Did you hear they're filling in the quarry,' she calls to me above the din.

'Are they? How come?'

'There's animals falling in and breaking their backs.'

Maeve is taking her time with the drinks. She's up flirting with Kenneth at the bar, giggling on her tippy toes and leaning over the mahogany counter.

'Free drinks,' she says cheerfully, planting down two vodka tonics in front of us.

'Free? Good woman yourself.' I take a nice cool sip. 'Mm.'

'He's a nice lad really. It's a shame he's so bad in bed,' she says, and I almost choke on the drink. 'Did I tell you I've a work conference coming up? Over in Florida.'

'No. You never mentioned it.'

'There's a fella in the Florida office called Salvador. We've been getting to know one another over the phone. He's a manager on the supply chain end of things as well.'

'Will you meet up with him at the conference?'

'I will. We're going on to Disney World the day the conference is over. It was myself who suggested it.'

'Do you know what. You're full of surprises.' Maeve's company has me feeling emboldened.

'My life is only just starting, really,' she says, looking over at me earnestly. 'That's the good thing about it. I might even be able to get a transfer if I play my cards right.'

'God. That's great. Will you still change your name to Roxanne?'

'I don't know. I'm in two minds.'

Peadar lands in, and there's no sign of Evelyn with him, and Stacey Nugent is nuzzling at him and swinging out of him. 'How is it that Evelyn lets Peadar away with his carry-on?'

'Oh, I think she enjoys it. It keeps her going. The drama of it. It's like fuel.'

'I always thought she'd come to Dublin but she never did.'

'Sometimes staying at home in your own place is more interesting to a person than moving away.' It has me thinking that Maeve is smarter than she looks. She draws on the long necklace around her neck and yanks the pendant out from beneath the fabric of her blouse. She drops the pendant down between her fingers and idly swings it about before her. It's the ballet slipper pendant belonging to Pamela Cooney. 'I got a new chain for it. Do you like it?'

I can feel my blood running cold. 'Do you not feel strange wearing it?'

'No. I thought if she was ever found alive I could give it back to her. There was no use leaving it in the shed.'

'You must tell me now. How did you come across it? Tell the truth, Maeve.'

She chews on her crinkled lip. 'I found it in the car, Katie. The silver car. Myself and Evelyn and Aidan and Peadar drove out to the famine workhouse to go ghost hunting. I was sitting behind the passenger seat and I looked down and saw it under the seat. I just picked it up and took it.' A girl's necklace broken in Aidan's car. It's like something that'd happen during a struggle.

'How is it you never told anyone?'

'I did. I told Evelyn. I told her only recently. I saw a blood spot too. Evelyn said to say nothing for fear the lads would get in trouble.'

'A blood spot.'

'It isn't there any more. Still, I should go to the guards over it. I should have gone long ago.'

'It could happen to another girl and you'll feel badly.' It could have happened me, sure. It almost happened me, only Pamela took my place. How lucky I've been and didn't know it. 'You know what. We're the lucky ones, Maeve.' It's hitting me hard how lucky we are.

'The lucky ones,' she says softly. 'I've never thought of myself as being lucky.'

'We didn't get caught up with fellas or events at home. We'll be getting away and doing our own thing. That's why we're the lucky ones,' I tell her, as she trails a forefinger along the condensation on the side of her vodka tonic. Maeve's come together now, at long last. You can sense it. The talismanic pendant concealed in the folds of her blouse. The blue starfish hairclip. The blazer with jewelled shoulders. Perhaps the black hole inside her wasn't empty at all, but whirling with the promise of metamorphosis. 'Did ye happen to see a ghost at the famine workhouse?'

'I didn't see anything. But Evelyn did, according to herself. A woman in rags with black gums came flying at her, according to herself,' she says, smiling the peg-toothed smile, and I have to laugh. She has Evelyn down pat.

It's a Sunday afternoon in September. Evelyn's wearing her mirrored sunglasses and sitting up in bed with the curtains drawn. 'What are you doing here?' she says listlessly, and staring into space.

'I was sent for.' Alma Cassidy phoned Mammy especially, and I went up immediately, for all the good it'll do. Doctor Fitz has been and gone before me.

'I'm going to London in the morning. You can come if you want.'

'What? No.' The place is like a bomb hit it. I can't see how she'll find her way out of it to go anywhere in the morning. The doors of the wardrobe are flung open and not a thing hanging up inside it. The beanbag has a hole and there's a stream of polystyrene filling gushing out of it.

'Now's your chance, Katie.'

'You must be joking.' The pages of my screenplay are strewn about the floor with footprints and filth all over them. 'Go and shite.'

'Myself and Peadar have ended things. He won't be coming with us if that's what you're concerned with.'

'This again. I suppose Peadar cancelled on you.'

'He didn't cancel on me. He got the part in the biopic film. He's to play a fella called Wiley Stevens.'

'Wiley Stevens. I've never even heard of him.'

'He was a folk singer in the seventies.' She lights a cigarette from the box on the nightstand and places it between her dry lips. 'His girlfriend stabbed him in the neck with a broken beer bottle for sleeping with groupies.' She takes a long and joyless drag off the cigarette. 'We always said we wouldn't hold one another back. We had that agreement.'

'Sure, that mightn't go ahead at all. Don't you know what he's like.'

'He's sold the bike. That means he's all set.' She sniffs. 'You're certain you won't come?'

'I won't. As you said yourself, it's better if I do my own thing.'

There's a long silence. She's smoking hard now and contemplating. 'I'm sorry, alright. Is that what you want to me to say?' I turn my face and run my tongue along my teeth. 'Don't be like that. God. It's like you hate me or something.'

'What's so special about him?'

The little nostrils are flaring in and out and there's smoke wafting out of them. 'He loves me. He'd do anything for me. Anything I ask of him and he'd do it.' I'd say she's only saying it in order to believe it.

'Will you go with him to the filming?' I have my hands on my hips and I'm standing over the bed like a matron.

'No.'

'Why not?'

'I don't know. I'd be a distraction.'

'Is that what he told you. He's a bastard.' There's a mystifying relationship if ever there was one. 'Would you not go on your own over to London? Haven't you plenty for doing with *The Psychopath's Overcoat?* Casting and scheduling and all of that business.'

She takes off the sunglasses and throws them carelessly on the cluttered nightstand. 'I'll tell you something if you promise to tell no one.'

'What?'

'There's no producer for *The Psychopath's Overcoat.* I made it up.'

'You lied.' What else has she lied about? The cocaine and the rooftop pool party? The hundred new friends and the 'Caution to the Wind' love song?

'People were expecting big things from me. I was expecting big things from myself. I got carried away.' I titter, and she glares at me. 'I said it to make myself feel better. I said it because I wanted to believe it. I'm no good at coping with disappointment.' She hoicks herself up in the bed and I can hear joints clicking beneath the duvet. 'Everyone thinks I've it easy. But no one knows what it's like to be me. No one understands what it's like for me at all. I've anxiety, you know.'

'Is that what you call it.'

'I get terrible headaches. Doctor Fitz said it was stress but I think it's more serious. I'd say I'll have to go in for tests.'

'Well, you'd better not go to London, so. If you think it's serious. You'd better stay at home and keep your sunglasses on you and stay in bed.'

She scowls. 'It's not just headaches. It's shakes as well.' She presses her thin forearms down hard over the duvet. They're thinner than I ever remember. 'I could be seriously ill and you don't even care,' she says accusingly.

'Would you don't be so ridiculous. You must get out of that bed and get moving. Come on. Get up.' God, she's exhausting. It's like she's trying to suck me up with a straw until there's nothing left.

'I'm not getting up,' she snaps. I'm annoyed now, and I reach out and take a hold of her elbow and pull hard in an effort to heave her out of bed. We're laughing at one another, and raging with one another, and I feel like screaming because she's so outrageous. 'Leave it, Katie. I'm staying where I am. I mean it now,' she protests, yanking her arm away and rubbing it.

'Get out of that bed before you die in it. This is pure stupid behaviour.' Have the lies only worked to steal her confidence? That's one of the dangers of telling lies.

'I'll get up when I'm ready to get up.'

'You're not going to London at all, are you. You've no suitcase out or anything. There's not one sign of you going to London.' There are invisible ropes tying her into the bed. Invisible chains connecting her to Peadar, and Glenbruff too. Are the ropes and chains real, or are they imaginary? Isn't it peculiar how some people never break free of the invisible ropes and chains.

'I don't want to go by myself. And I'm sick. I wouldn't be able for it.'

'What's this all about? You were always so ambitious. What's happened you?' The girl who galvanised the manic ambition is seeming spent and fatigued. The girl who was always taking me places and giving me ideas is in decline. What'll become of her, with the white fire extinguishing inside her? Was *Flora and Phenomena* only a swansong?

'What's happened *me*? As if you've ever done anything worth talking about. When will you realise that you haven't an ounce of brilliance inside of you, and no matter how much time you spend trying to absorb it from me by osmosis, it's never going to happen. It's never going to happen for you, Katie, so just give up.' She takes up the sunglasses and hurriedly props them back on herself.

I have a cold, hard lump in my throat that I can't swallow down. It's like my voice box has turned to glass and I can hardly get words out. 'That isn't the way friends are supposed to speak to one another.'

'Jesus,' she rails. 'Are you thick or something. We aren't friends. We're different people. We've nothing in common.'

I make for the door. 'That's it. I can't cope with you. I'm finished with you. Good luck.'

She summons a great roar from inside of herself. 'Fuck off, so. Get out. I don't want you here anyway. I never asked for you to come up here annoying me. Get out.'

I hurry down the stairs with tears falling from my eyes. I can hear her howling with sorrow above in the bed because Peadar doesn't love her, and because I'm leaving her again, and because the dream she so often spoke about was only a sham. Perhaps she only ever did and said things to seem cool.

Dan Cassidy is pulled up in the driveway with a suitcase tied to the top of his car and a trailer loaded up with odd bits of furniture. It looks as though he's moving back in. Alma is resting on the driver door and talking to him through the rolled-down window. Daddy says Dan is under investigation for evading tax and he'll likely end up in prison before too long. It strikes me for the first time the way Dan resembles Peadar, and carries on in a not dissimilar fashion.

I keep on walking, and light up a cigarette for myself. I'll give up the cigarettes in due course, but not yet. Not until I've set sail. Not until I prove myself to myself, and not Evelyn Cassidy. Already it's seeming that there's more room for me in the world.

~

The sky is streaked with otherworldly greys and greens, and small birds bounce across the road like wound-up teeth on feet. I come upon Mickey Cassidy standing still in a ditch and looking out over the fields. There are glaring blue and white lights above the quarry and the sounds of men shouting. 'What's going on?'

'There's someone in there,' he says, pointing across. 'Inside in the quarry.'

'How do you mean, *there's someone in there?*'

'Human remains,' he says, and his face is as white as a skull against the enveloping darkness.

—

The season is beginning to turn. Leaves are drying and curling and dropping from the trees. Mammy's old friend Hillary has returned to Glenbruff to research her family tree and the good room is full of laughter. You can hear the peals all over the house.

Hillary Bowman has a resonant voice that rings like crystal. She has black hair and blue eyes and wears blue mascara. She has silver hoops in her ears and an artsy printed scarf floats around her neck. She works as a theatre manager, which is the sort of job that doesn't really exist in Ireland. 'Honey. It's so good to meet you,' she says, smiling up at me. 'You look so like your mom. Isn't that something?' She's gone full Yank since she left Glenbruff. 'Home for the summer, huh?'

'Yeah. I don't think I'll be sticking around for too long more. I've big plans.'

Hillary blinks. 'What sort of plans, sweetie?' she says, still smiling.

I inhale hard, and come right out with it. 'I'm mad to work in films, Hillary. I'm going to spend the next few weeks making phone calls and sending emails and I won't stop until I get work. I'm very determined.' I'm bursting to be me in a big way. Like never before. I'll go mad if I can't be myself and do the things I've always wanted.

'Wow.' Hillary laughs politely. She turns to Mammy. 'My brother-in-law works in the industry. Jeff. He's a producer and director. We hardly ever see the guy.'

274

I don't hesitate. 'Does he need any help? All I want is a start.'

Hillary Bowman touches the printed scarf with her fingertips. 'Um, I could ask him, I guess.'

Mammy's eyes are wide and hopeful. 'Will you do that? Could you ask him today?'

'I guess so.' Hillary thinks for a moment. 'You know, we have a basement conversion we're not using right now. You're welcome to stay if you'd like to come to New York. Why don't I go ahead and talk to Jeff. See if we can figure something out.'

Hillary comes to the house the day after and says I'm to touch base with Jeff. He could really use some help. His assistant skipped out to take another job and he needs someone right away. Someone smart. Someone with a good eye. Someone who can start next week.

It has me thinking that maybe I'm good enough on my own. Maybe I was always good enough on my own. And maybe the hard road is the easy road after all.

—

Daddy's giving me a lift to the train station. He's humming contentedly as we spin through the town. He knows I won't be in a hurry back. He knows I'm going to make a real go of things in New York. Mammy has money kept aside from cleaning the church, and she's paid for the flight, and Mammy and Daddy together have given me a few bob to keep me going.

Once I'm on the train, settled into my seat and looking out over the fields and meadows, I feel the return of the white ball of fire, the burning in the heart and the lightness in the limbs, and I know for certain it's the dream I want more than anything. The dream was always insatiable. It was always bigger than Evelyn. It was there to begin with, and I used attribute it to Evelyn, but I know now that it was there all along.

But she'll always be the voice in my head and the flames at my feet. She'll always be the ghost in the cottage and the burned-out nightclub, the whisper in the canopy of trees that chills the spine and excites the brain.

Suddenly, the reflection of a face in the glass.

Heart-shaped with intelligent eyes.

The flicker of a phantom passenger.

Acknowledgements

My deepest gratitude goes to my husband Seán for his eternal optimism and unwavering belief in me. Thank you for helping to create an atmosphere in which I could write freely and happily.

My parents Matt and Noreen have encouraged me always and inspired my love of storytelling. Thank you both from the bottom of my heart.

Dorothea, your infectious determination has been invaluable. You made a big difference.

Marianne, you are a force to be reckoned with, and I'm truly grateful to have you as my agent.

Thanks to Alison for your keen editorial insight early on, and to Gerard for your generous legal support.

A final word of appreciation goes to Juliet and the team at Oneworld Publications who took a chance on me and my strange book. It means so much.

Frances Macken is from Claremorris, Co. Mayo. She completed a BA in Film and Television Production at the National Film School, Dún Laoghaire Institute of Art, Design and Technology. She has a Masters in Creative Writing from the University of Oxford and is the author of several short stories. *You Have to Make Your Own Fun Around Here* is her debut novel. She lives in Dublin with her husband and daughter.